RULING AMBI
The Story of Perkin

Robert Hunt

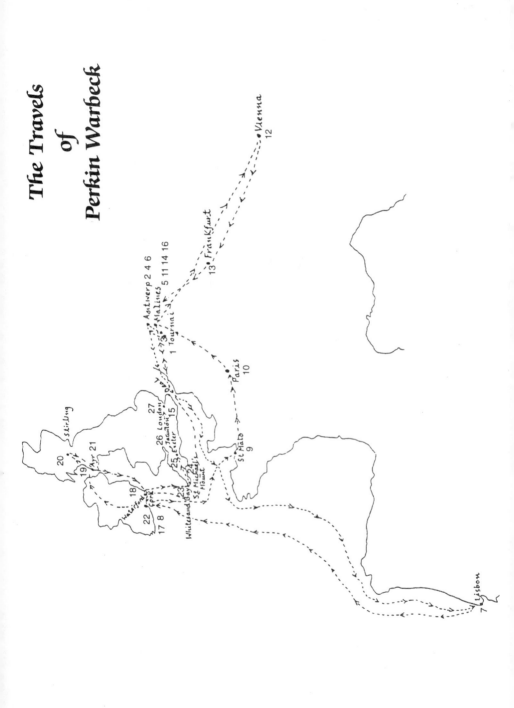

The Travels
of
Perkin Warbeck

Antwerp 2 4 6
Malines
5 11 14 16
1 Tournai
13 • Frankfurt
Paris
10
• Vienna
12

Stirling
20
19
Ayr 21
18
Waterford
22
17 8
Whitsand Bay
St Michael's
Mount
23
24
25
Exeter
Taunton
26 London
27
15
St Malo
9
Lisbon
7

RULING AMBITION
The Story of Perkin Warbeck

A NOVEL BY
ROBERT HUME

GEE & SON,
DENBIGH, NORTH WALES

ISBN 0 7074 0336 7

First Impression June 2000

Published and Printed by
GEE & SON,
DENBIGH, NORTH WALES

The House of York (part)

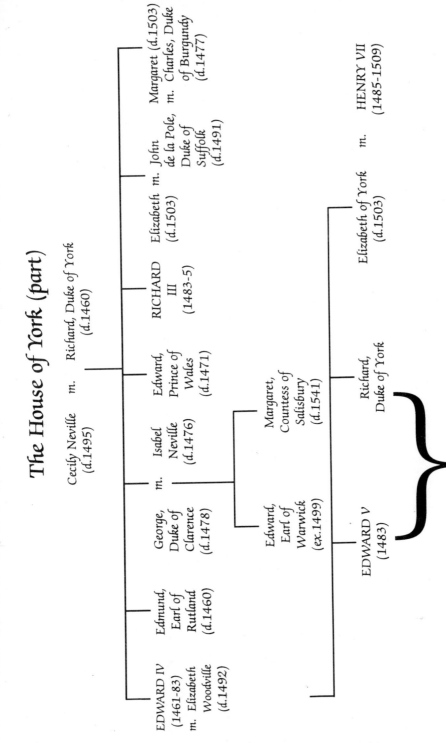

Cecily Neville (d.1495) m. Richard, Duke of York (d.1460)

EDWARD IV (1461-83) m. Elizabeth Woodville (d.1492)

Edmund, Earl of Rutland (d.1460)

George, Duke of Clarence (d.1478) m. Isabel Neville (d.1476)

Edward, Prince of Wales (d.1471)

RICHARD III (1483-5)

Elizabeth (d.1503) m. John de la Pole, Duke of Suffolk (d.1491)

Margaret (d.1503) m. Charles, Duke of Burgundy (d.1477)

Edward, Earl of Warwick (ex.1499)

Margaret, Countess of Salisbury (d.1541)

EDWARD V (1483)

Richard, Duke of York

Elizabeth of York (d.1503) m. HENRY VII (1485-1509)

The Princes in the Tower

Chapter 1

Grasping my thin woollen blanket - my only protection from the night cold - I began to rub the sleep from my eyes. The thud of footsteps and muffled conversation outside as the guards changed their shift had awoken me with a start. My forehead throbbed, my bones ached; I had had very little sleep. Whether or not day had broken I could not be sure, as only the faintest trace of light filtered into my cell deep within the dark confines of the Tower of London.

Slowly, I cast my still blurry eyes up the slimy damp wall to the rough-hewn ceiling where a narrow vent let in the merest hint of fresh air. But it did little to help alleviate the sickening stench in my cell. Nor did the sparse coverage of straw do anything to ease my aching bones, and my back felt sore and bruised. As I moved, the chains that bound me bit into my ankles.

Keys rattled. A ring of keys crashed to the ground. The sound of muffled curses as they were picked up again. Then the rough voice of Jonas, my gaoler, reverberated down the passageway. 'Rogues!' he snapped. 'Wake up!'

Groans could be heard from cells nearby mine.

From further down the passage came a moan: 'Leave a man to his sleep!'

Another jangle of keys, but this time closer. Threats shouted at the prisoners, coarse laughter, then doors slammed shut. The thump of heavy feet retreating down the passage. After that only an eerie silence.

I tugged at my blanket, pulling it up another inch or so, until its frayed edges brushed against the thickening stubble on my chin. We were in the last week of November now, it was bitterly cold, and I was unable to stop myself shivering. How many other prisoners before me had spent time here, I wondered? And what had been their fates? I knew them only by the curious marks they had left on the wall behind me that was covered with inscriptions from floor to ceiling. Here, their painstakingly carved initials were sometimes accompanied by a date, at other times by a carefully chiselled epitaph. Many testimonies were in English. A few were in Latin - priests must have made these, for who else knew Latin? For many, these often melancholy and now partly obliterated words would have been their final marks in this world. One carving, inscribed more deeply and intricately than the others, kept catching my eye: 'He that Endureth to the End shall be Saved.' Whenever I read those words they helped give me a little courage.

'Come on! Wake up!' Jonas's rasping voice was closer now. My cell door was unlocked, the bolts shot back, and light flooded in from his flaming torch. As my eyes adjusted, Jonas came into view, his unkempt figure and filthy clothes a familiar sight. He stood in the doorway, sneering, his left hand buried in the pocket of his cloak.

'Well, how fares my lord this morning then? Is he ready for breakfast? What would his lordship like? A platter of pheasant?'

With an evil laugh, he reached into a pocket deep inside his cloak and tossed over a hard chunk of bread that skimmed the trestle and fell to the floor with a strange splintering sound, as though it was a chip of wood. Then he turned and swaggered off, slamming the door shut again behind him. I heard the key turning in the lock, sealing me off from human contact; for, as much as I loathed the man, Jonas's presence was better than nothing.

A moth fluttered around in front of my face. I tried to brush it aside but missed. This hell hole! Vile and stinking, smothering life itself. Who knew what ghastly tortures were being inflicted even at this very moment on prisoners trapped behind its thick stone walls; their screams, like those of thousands before them, going unheard by the world outside? I shuddered to think of all the instruments I had been told about, that would reduce the most strong-willed of men into making a confession: hand presses and needle-sharp flesh gougers; a deep black pit swarming with rats; a great wooden rack which could stretch its victims until they were a foot longer; and then, at the last, the scaffold itself.

Close to my cell in the depths of the Beauchamp Tower a sombre avenue of bare trees stretches all the way to Tower Green. On the very day I was brought here I was led in chains along its course, past the scaffold where so many men have been made to cross the white stones and blood-stained planks, to lay their head on the gruesome block.

I tried to straighten myself, but several sharp pieces of grit sticking into my back made me wince. Propping myself up on an elbow, I began to brood about the day ahead. But I could bear it only for a moment, and I forced myself to think instead about happier times. After all, mine had been a life full of adventure and excitement – travelling from city to city, meeting some of the most important rulers in the world, being accepted as their equal. Oh for a return to those days! But only distant memories now are the sweet perfumes of palace rose gardens and the smooth texture of expensive silks against my skin; and gone forever are the magnificent banquets, glowing tapestries and dazzling jewels of the courts of Europe.

What a contrast they make to the foul air and mouldering walls of the Tower; these rusty iron chains that bind my ankles to the wall; the simple earthenware water pitcher and chunk of stale bread that lie on the wooden trestle beside me. And the greatest contrast of all - the silence and gloom.

You fool, Perkin! At one time your future had seemed so bright and assured. But no longer. You were carried away by greed and dreams of power. If only you had drawn back, resisted the temptation to get involved in these senseless plots and conspiracies that could only bring you down.

★   ★   ★

Again I tried turning my thoughts to happier times in Flanders, growing up at home in the bustling town of Tournai. I remember coming home one day with my mother and father, after visiting some cousins in a nearby village. I could see all the church spires rising above the town wall, almost as far as the roof of the sky itself; our horse trotting through a gateway, and on past the tall merchants' houses with their solid oak doors and gabled roofs.

The image of my dear mother's face floats before me, now, as I write these words - her loving smile, her complexion clear and smooth as a lily, her hair the colour of honey - for, if honey could be spun, that was how I imagined it would be. Those peaceful, carefree days, spent by her side at home, listening to little stories and passages from the Bible. I used to help by passing her needles and bodkins as she worked away at her embroidery. My hand would sometimes brush against the materials she worked with - silks, satins and velvets. Their texture had such a soft and reassuring feel against my skin, and their perfume I recall so vividly that they might lie beside me now.

In those early years, before my brother and sisters were born, I would go with my mother each week to market. We would take our time - looking in on the grimy blacksmiths, hammering in their sheds; at carpenters sawing in their workshops. On, into the busy quarter of the town, my mother's hand ever present on my shoulder, guiding me through little groups of apprentices, some playing football, others wrestling there, in the middle of the street. At last we would reach the square and the crowded market place, filled with little stalls. On Saints' Days we would come here to watch the local country folk dancing, we would clap to the tooting of the piper and laugh when the dancers took a wrong turn.

One sultry summer's evening, we made our way through the narrow cobbled streets to the town centre where a miracle play was to be performed. A large wagon had stopped where the street was just wide enough for an audience to gather around. We had arrived, breathless, just as the play was about to begin and the actors were scrambling aboard the wagon. My eyes rested on the black curtain at the back where someone had painted a beast, hideous and snarling - its jaws wide open, revealing teeth dripping with blood. From the jaws belched forth orange fire, the fire of hell. One of the actors, the tallest, was dressed from head to foot in white. The other three, all devils, were wrapped in black cloaks and hoods, their ears pointed, their red tongues forked. As I watched, they began to sidle up to the man in white. One rested a hand on his shoulder, and started talking to him as if they were great friends. Suddenly, the devils turned and started tormenting him. One produced a pitchfork from behind his back and prodded him while the others stretched their black cloaks across in front of him, hiding his face completely. Then, as the audience looked on in horror, he seemed to disappear before our very eyes into the beast's mouth and was consumed in flames.

The show I found both frightening and strangely fascinating. I saw all the actors afterwards - ordinary men, the kind of men my mother and I might pass any day in the streets of Tournai; but how different they were behind the masks. How terrifying they had become, as they teased and trapped their victim, much as a spider might catch a fly in its web. My face felt drained and cold, and the inside of my mouth was dry.

'Don't be afraid, Peterkin! It's only a play,' said my mother gently, putting her arm around my waist, comforting me and explaining the meaning of the play, about good and evil, and temptation. At night I know she prayed that I should always lead a good and honest life, perhaps become a cloth merchant in Tournai or nearby Antwerp, marry a local girl and settle down to raise a family. If only I had followed her advice! As I gazed up at the walls of my cell that hemmed me in, I imagined the open spaces of the countryside around my childhood home.

My mother had always been close to me; and even now I felt her presence. My father, always a more distant figure, was very different - so serious, and burdened with cares and worries that had turned his hair grey before his time. I saw little of him as he was often away travelling on business, sometimes as far afield as London; though I was never really sure what his job involved for he never spoke about it in front of us. But I knew it was important because I saw his name, 'John Warbeck. Controller,' on many of the public notices in the town.

Many of my relations also had important jobs in Tournai. My mother's father, Peter de Faro, was one of the gatekeepers who kept records of people coming into and leaving the town. Entrusted with the keys, it was his responsibility to lock the gate at evening curfew and open it again at dawn. He lived close to his work in a little house, just two rooms - that was until his house burnt down and he moved in with us while it was being rebuilt. I grew very fond of him: he played toy soldiers with me (which my father never would), using shavings of wood from the carpenter's shop. While we lined up the soldiers ready for battle, he would tell stories about all the important people he had met over the years - the ministers, ambassadors, even a bishop who had passed through the gate.

One winter's morning when my mother was busy sewing, I was sitting outside in the yard, watching my grandfather chop wood for the great fire that blazed all day long in the kitchen. Suddenly there was a shout. 'Peter, run to fetch a cloth, there's a good fellow. I've cut my hand!' I raced into the kitchen as fast as my little legs

11

would carry me and took from the linen basket a large white handkerchief that I wound across his palm. It was not a serious cut, and the bandage soon stopped the flow of blood; but my grandfather made the episode serve as a warning. 'That taught me a lesson. I shall have to be more careful next time. Remember to take care when you're chopping wood, Peterkin! Just one slip and you could lose a finger!'

'Why are *you* doing it, grandfather? *Matthew* always chops the wood!'

My grandfather ignored my question. Instead he pointed to a small, bright red stain that had begun to show through the bandage. My grandfather saw me staring at it. 'Noble blood!' he said, looking very serious.

'What do you mean, grandfather?'

'Noble blood,' he spoke quietly, looking around. 'We are the de Faros. Descended from a very important family, a noble family, you know.'

I looked up from the bandage. 'Important family? Grandfather, do you mean rich merchants, like the men who live in those tall houses?'

My grandfather gave a little chuckle into his beard. 'Oh no, much more important than that! Come into the kitchen and I'll tell you more.'

We went inside. By now, the fire was lower than it should have been, certainly too low to reach the weighty cauldron of stew hanging beneath the chimney. Making light of his injury, my grandfather heaved a great log onto the fire. 'No, not merchants. Merchants make their money quickly. They're just upstarts. The de Faros are different. They are relatives of the kings. Hundreds of years ago they gave them advice about how to run the country.'

I was wide-eyed with interest. 'And today? Do they still help the kings?'

My grandfather gave a regretful smile. 'Oh no, young Peterkin! We are nothing now. My brother is but a tradesman. As for me, well you know all about my job. I am just a gatekeeper - responsible position, I suppose, in a small way, but I'm nobody outside of Tournai. If the de Faros are ever to become great again it's up to you, my lad!'

At that moment my mother called to me from the next room to fetch a special large bodkin from her sewing box high up in the attic. It was an errand that I had been sent on many times before, and I could not refuse my mother, although I would much rather have stayed and heard more of my grandfather's stories. I can only have been gone a short while, as I knew exactly where the big wooden box was. There I was, about half way down the ladder again, the bodkin pinched between my fingers, when I stopped suddenly. My hands grasped the rungs of the ladder tightly. From the kitchen I could hear raised voices, my mother shouting at my grandfather. The thick oak door was closed tight but did nothing to conceal a single word of my mother's.

'Putting mad ideas into the boy's head like that!' she cried.

'It's a story, Catherine, just a story,' answered my grandfather sheepishly.

'I don't know what you are thinking of! We have already made plans for Peter. John will see that he is apprenticed and learns a good trade. He's going to make an honest living as a cloth merchant!'

By now I was at the bottom of the ladder, afraid, hardly daring to breathe. My mother and grandfather had never argued like that all the while he had been staying with us, and I had never heard my mother in such a rage.

My grandfather sighed. 'Catherine. Don't you want him to have ambitions?'

'Of course I do, but realistic ones - ones he can achieve, not fantasies.'

I shall never forget the tone of their voices behind that door, with me all the while a silent witness to what my mother hoped I would achieve with my life, my grandfather's dreams for me.

*   *   *

I can remember other, more light-hearted stories from my childhood. When I was very young, I remember my mother telling me a bedtime story about my father when he was a young man, still jolly and bright, and how he got mixed up in a squabble with a neighbour over a cask of wine.

'It was summer, you see, and your father had been stupid enough to bet that it wouldn't rain for a week.'

'And did it?'

'Rain? It rained cats and dogs! So the neighbour came to collect his winnings, which was this wretched cask of wine. That's when

13

all the trouble began because your father claimed he didn't know anything about a bet.'

I gasped. 'Wasn't the neighbour cross?'

'I'd say he was. He was absolutely furious! He swore his head off at your father. Then your father punched him on the nose! Oh, there was a terrible brawl. It took three watchmen to break it up!'

I squeezed my mother's hand. 'Then what happened?'

'Your father and the neighbour were both arrested and locked up for the night. Served them right, I thought. Well, the next morning when they had cooled off a bit, they were brought before the mayor.'

My little mouth was wide open. 'What did the mayor say?'

'Well, he found it hard to know who was more to blame, so he punished both of them, just to be on the safe side. And do you know what the punishment was?'

'No, mother. Tell me!'

'They were both made to cook supper for the whole town council, and share out the cask of wine among everyone who came. And they weren't allowed to have a single drop of the wine themselves until they were right down to the nasty dregs. You should have seen your father's face!' she laughed.

We both laughed.

Chapter 2

I rested my head against the cold damp wall, closed my eyes and was drifting back in time; when my thoughts were interrupted by scurrying noises in the far corner of my cell - one of the rats in the Tower was on the prowl for crumbs. I was so used to them by now that I looked upon them as a friendly presence.

More memories. This time memories of my first visit to London when I was five or six years old, my father having been asked to supply carpets to the royal court. It must have been spring, as the floors of the house we stayed in, situated right in the heart of the city, had been sprinkled with white blossom, and its sweet fragrance kept making me sneeze. Behind the tiny windowpanes passed a constant stream of merchants and tradesmen, shouting out their wares from first light till the shadows of dusk. (What a contrast to my home town of Tournai where the shops and taverns backed onto lush green fields, and where you risked stepping into an open sewer as you crossed the street). I remember catching sight of some of the important buildings of London - London Bridge, crammed with little houses and shops, glimpsing Westminster palace, and seeing the stark outlines of the Tower at dusk. How happy and innocent I was then, sitting for hours daydreaming on the embankment, chatting tirelessly to my mother, throwing stones into the river.

Suddenly, these blissful memories were disturbed - this time by the approach of heavy footsteps. I knew by their sound that it was the surly Jonas. Why had he returned so soon? There was a thud as some kind of container was placed on the floor outside. The familiar rattle of keys, of a key being inserted into the lock and the bolts being shot back. As Jonas sidled in, wrapped in his warm cloak, the light from his blazing torch lit up my cell once more, revealing a water pitcher that he proceeded to bang down hard on the trestle. I could smell his breath - foul and pungent.

'Wine for my lord . . .?' he sneered. 'And how about a sweetmeat . . . Prince Richard?'

Another sneer, and then Jonas left, the cell door thudding behind him. His vulgar laugh faded into the distance as he tramped along the narrow passageway to his quarters.

Now, other images floated before my eyes. Mealtimes at home, my mother doting on me and spoiling me, bringing a bowl of broth to me in bed when I could not sleep. Another time - my father being out as usual - I watched my mother and a neighbour struggle up the steps to the front door with a great wine cask from the cellar. How I wanted to quaff back wine by the glass as my parents did, instead of drinking the pale watery substitute they poured for me, as if I were a baby.

Some years later, when I must have been about eight or nine, I remember sailing with my mother by barge up the river to the bustling city of Antwerp. It was a chilly autumn day with a stiff wind, and my mother had covered her long blonde hair with a shawl. We stayed with my cousin John Steinbeck, a quick-witted man who made a very good living as a merchant. He and his wife were generous people: in their forties and still childless, they took great interest in me, treating me like the son they had always wanted. My cousin also saw to my education, and each evening would give me an hour's lesson. He taught me well, and before I left I was able to read passages from the new printed Bible, write my signature, add up a column of figures and finally even check a tradesman's receipt.

A few years afterwards I returned to Antwerp, this time I was the companion of a merchant from Tournai, a friend of my parents. He was looking for someone to help display his goods by actually wearing them - thinking that he would sell more if his customers could see for themselves how well they looked on a tall young fellow.

I smiled as I recalled the day we met. 'My name's Berlo!' he said in a deep, cheerful voice that seemed to come from the bottom of his boots. 'I trade.'

So, for a while I helped him, parading costumes in front of his stall, which was famous in the market for its high quality silks. A regular customer was the Bishop of Cambrai, a very kind man, who in spite of his great rank spoke to me as if I were a friend. Although a priest, he obviously enjoyed living in style, and many a time I delivered cloth and silks to his grand palace, sat in his solar and talked with him about far away places he had visited. He even taught me how to play chess; and though I was slow to pick up the game, he never lost his patience, nor raised his voice.

I was enjoying my life, my first taste of independence, when I was suddenly struck down with a fever, and was unable to work for several months. During this while, I was looked after by Mr Berlo's servant, Jacob, until I was well again. My master was kindness itself; but after some days he came to see me and explained that he had to get someone else to fill my position because he was losing trade. At that moment I felt too ill to care what happened to my job. When eventually I recovered, the young man who had replaced me - a local fellow with a family to support - was doing so well that my master said he did not need to employ two men for the work, and suggested that I move to the nearby town of Middelburg where he could find me a job. I was sorry to leave him, though I was excited at the prospect of striking out on my own. But when I got to Middelburg I was disappointed, finding it small, provincial and dull after the bustling cosmopolitan air of Antwerp. I did not like my job of selling cloth, much preferring my work at Antwerp, dressing in fine clothes and chatting to the girls who stopped by Mr Berlo's stall. Matters came to a head when my master did not pay me what he promised. When I tried to reason with him he broke into a furious temper and boxed my ears. So I wrapped up my few things in a cloth, and at dawn one day, just as the gates opened, I slipped out of the house, knowing that my master was so fond of his sleep that he would not hear me going.

Now, at little more than fourteen years old - a still impressionable young man - I began the life of a wanderer. The fact that I was always on the move has led some people to envy my adventures; and, to be sure, my life has never been short of excitement. But looking back over the years now, I see more clearly the mistakes I made that have brought me here, to this cold dank cell.

Perhaps I made my earliest error of judgement soon after I arrived at Malines, one of the main cities of Flanders. I was looking at the wares in the market place one blazing-hot summer's day, with the sun beating down upon the hefty rolls of silk and velvet. Suddenly I heard this voice asking me how much the silk was. I turned, and found myself facing a man in his thirties, of noble birth, finely dressed and well spoken. It was clear that the nobleman had mistaken me for the stall owner. I quickly corrected the mistake.

'Stall holder or no,' he laughed, 'you have a wonderful knowledge of these fine fabrics. May I ask you where you acquired it?'

'From my master, Mr Berlo, in Antwerp, sir. Do you know him?'

It was clear from the nobleman's blank expression that he did not, but that did not matter. For a few moments he said nothing, then he raised his eyebrows. 'I attend upon the Duchess Margaret of Burgundy. She relies on me to supply her with fine materials for her wardrobe. I think she might be interested to meet you. Someone with experience, such as yourself, could be useful to her. And you would benefit greatly from the introduction.' Then he tilted his head back. 'If you like, I can try to arrange an audience for you with the Duchess.'

I was stunned, unable to believe what good fortune had come my way - and all by chance. I stammered out my grateful thanks and assured him that I would be honoured to meet the Duchess.

'Good,' he said. 'Where are you staying?'

'I have a room at the Blue Boar inn,' I replied.

'I will send a message to you there, to let you know when you should present yourself. Remember to take great care over your appearance and manners. First impressions always count with the Duchess.'

And with a nod of his head he was gone.

*   *   *

Two days later, there I was at the Duchess's court, a court that was the envy of Europe. From here, she ruled over the many extensive and wealthy lands she had inherited from her husband, Charles the Bold.

As I expected to be met by secretaries and ministers, it was all the more extraordinary that on my very first evening I was received by the Duchess, in person. A courtier with a haughty manner called out my name loudly across the antechamber where I had been waiting. I stepped forward. The nobleman told me to follow him. As I left the room, the other people waiting stared at me with considerable interest. I followed the courtier down a long corridor, at the end of which a door was opened and I was told to enter. The sun was pouring in through the leaded paned windows, the tapestries on the walls gleamed in the light - wonderful workmanship the like of which I had never seen before. As I waited in a state of nervous excitement, I was taking in everything, all of my surroundings.

Suddenly, at the other end of the room, a small door opened, and a lady entered, a lady of perhaps the same age as my own dear mother, but severe in manner and dressed in a grand style. She trod carefully, as if she was stepping on glass; and as she walked she made strange buffeting movements with her hands, as though brushing aside imaginary cobwebs. I felt myself being pushed forward by the courtier and I bowed as best I could. But even as I straightened myself I saw another lady behind the first. Now I realised my mistake, for this second lady was obviously the Duchess Margaret. She was tall and slim with an upright deportment and dressed elegantly in black velvet trimmed with gold lace. As she came forward, her lady in waiting stepped aside. The Duchess dismissed her with a wave of her hand, and then at last she spoke to me directly.

Her tone was solemn and she stared at me intently. 'You are Perkin Warbeck?'

'Yes, Your Majesty.'

'I have heard such good reports about you.'

I flushed bright red with embarrassment. 'Thank you, Your Majesty. But I owe it all to my masters. They've passed on to me all they know.'

The Duchess brushed aside my modesty with another wave. 'I am looking for a young man such as yourself, someone already with experience of fabrics and eager to learn more.'

She paused. I was trying my hardest to take in everything she was saying, but found it difficult to look directly at her face which was very long and serious; and her dark grey eyes seemed fierce. I focused instead on a simple gold chain that she wore around her neck.

'I need someone who can advise my tailors and seamstresses, someone who can represent the court abroad. I hear you have travelled abroad. Which places do you know?'

'Well . . .' I paused for thought, my eyes moving for a moment from her gold chain to focus on the corner of the marble fireplace,

19

where there was a motif depicting a chained falcon - the emblem of the House of York. 'I know Tournai where I was born, Antwerp, Middelburg . . . and, of course, London, Your Majesty'

The Duchess appeared to be taken aback. 'London? You have been to England? What did you think of it?'

'I enjoyed it very much. My whole family went. My father was there to supply the court with carpets.'

The Duchess nodded and appeared interested. Her voice became more intense, even urgent. 'Whose court do you mean - that of my dear brother Edward, or that of the new king, King Henry?'

'King Edward, Your Majesty.'

A gleam entered the Duchess's eyes. When she spoke again she did so in a whisper. 'Really!'

I was astonished. Why was she asking me all these questions? I could not understand her interest in my life. Was there more to this than I realised?

★   ★   ★

The days passed at the Duchess's court. I cannot say I grew to like her any better, but I did come to respect her. She was a well-educated and unusually determined woman with an air of authority about her that I admired. And she was certainly interested in me, although at that point I did not realise why.

At court I enjoyed nothing less than the lifestyle of a prince, banqueting off silver platters at high table and dancing with the daughters of leading noblemen. A whole suite of special apartments was set aside for me, and I was given my own servants, including a groom.

Then, one morning, the Duchess summoned me to her apartments. The groom took me along corridors panelled with polished wood. All traces of breakfast had been cleared away and there was a great deal of activity, with officials and secretaries darting in all directions. The groom strutted along - more like a peacock than a man - his pace slow to the point of being irritating.

Eventually we ascended a wide carpeted staircase and stopped outside the Duchess's quarters. The groom smoothed back his hair and adjusted his waistcoat before tapping lightly on the doors. There was a pause. A few moments later they were swung slowly open. Two maidservants within quickly curtseyed and left, while the peculiar groom made an exaggerated flick of his wrist and drew the doors closed behind us.

The Duchess was standing on the far side of the room in front of a great fireplace. She beckoned me to come over to her; and in the moments that followed I discovered for the first time the real reason for my presence at her court.

'The new king, King Henry, has deprived me of all the revenues which my late brother, King Edward, granted me,' she said bitterly. 'But you can help me. You can be of great assistance to me. I am determined that the House of York be returned to power in England.'

I was bewildered. How could I, a mere nobody, be part of her plan? What could she possibly have in mind for me? My bewilderment must have shown because she came closer, staring at me intently.

'Yes. You will do very well! I can see the likeness.'

I became even more confused. What likeness? Was the woman mad? But a few more words from the Duchess made everything horribly clear.

'You shall be trained to impersonate my brother's youngest son, Richard Duke of York, my own dear nephew. He has not been seen for several years past, and is believed by many to be dead - murdered at the hands of his wicked uncle, King Richard. But this is not so. As you shall prove, he is still very much alive.'

I was too stunned to say anything. She really must be living in a world of dreams!

The Duchess continued to look me up and down. 'You resemble him. You are tall and have his long blonde hair. Your manners are fair and you have the airs of a man of noble birth. Also, I have been told, you are quick to learn. You shall be taught to speak English and everything you need to know about your family - all the names of your household and servants in London when you were a little boy. I shall expect you to learn them all by heart.'

There was another long pause. My eyes were fixed on her. I felt bewitched by her. How could such a scheme possibly succeed? I would never be able to accomplish it, even if I wanted to. And yet, at the same time, I felt so excited at the prospect she had offered me. She had chosen *me* to defend the rights of her family. For the last few weeks I had been uncertain about the future, but the

Duchess's plan now offered me advancement and adventure - more than what I might hope for in my wildest dreams. Could I do it? My heart was thumping. My hands were tightly gripped together. Could I? Could I?

The Duchess interrupted my thoughts. 'Naturally, in return I shall expect a number of things from you. When you become King of England, you shall pay me all the revenues my brother promised me. You shall also grant me the manors of Hunsdon and Scarborough.'

Suddenly, I remembered my grandfather's prophecy about my family's noble blood, that it was up to me to advance its fortunes. This was a sign that I could not ignore. Fate was pointing me in the direction of glory and riches.

'Well boy? You have said nothing.' The Duchess's lips tightened and a steely note entered her voice.

I fell on one knee before her, overwhelmed with emotion. 'Your Majesty, you do me great honour. I only wish to serve you in whatever way I can. I pray that I will succeed in fulfilling your expectations.'

'Will you swear to this on the sacred bones of Saint Thomas of Canterbury?'

I bowed my head in agreement.

The bargain was sealed.

After this, the Duchess explained her plan to me. It would begin with me sailing to Lisbon in the company of her good friend Sir Edward Brampton and his wife. At a later stage she would welcome me at her court as her long lost nephew.

*   *   *

I boarded the ship for Lisbon under an assumed name. Although apprehensive at meeting my new companions, I soon found the Bramptons congenial company: they were much the same age as my own mother and father, and for some months they became my adopted parents.

The journey lasted several days, giving us plenty of time to talk. Sir Edward knew Portugal well: he was born there, and grew up in Lisbon, though his name in those days was Duarte Brandao.

Odd, I thought, wondering for a moment whether there was something doubtful about his past. But how could this kind faced

22

man who sat opposite me with his twinkling blue eyes have a past that he wanted to hide?

'So, how is it, Sir Edward, that you are now called Brampton?'

'Well, about twenty years ago I went to London to be baptised at a home for converted Jews. It is usual when a Jew is baptised for the king to act as godfather, which he did. So, to pay my respects to the King, I adopted his name - Edward.'

'Did he also make you a sir?' I asked, slightly disappointed by the innocence of the explanation.

'No, that came later. I was knighted for my services to King Richard. In fact, I was the very first Jewish convert to receive such an honour', he replied proudly. 'King Richard then appointed me Governor of the island of Guernsey.'

I was puzzled. 'But King Richard died at the Battle of Bosworth more than three years ago now . . .'

'Well, yes. It has been very difficult since then. My wife and I have been exiles at the Duchess Margaret's court. We are waiting for the day when the Yorkists shall be returned to power in England.'

It was now clear to me why the Bramptons had been chosen as my companions, for the Duchess knew she could count on their complete loyalty. And so, I hoped, could I.

*   *   *

After about three days, we laid anchor in the busy port of Lisbon, and went ashore to take up lodgings in the town. I knew that sooner or later I would receive instructions from the Duchess, ordering me to return to Malines again. But for the moment I was settled, and felt safe in the company of the Bramptons who I felt I could trust.

The couple put me into service with an elderly knight who managed a great estate in the countryside. I acted as his valet, which meant seeing that his clothes were always pressed, brushed and ready to wear. In truth, I can remember very little about him, apart from the fact that he only had one eye, having apparently lost the other in a duel he had fought over a woman. I *do* know that I was not with him long, a month or two at the most, for he was seriously injured in a riding accident, and died shortly afterwards.

As fortune had it, I was not idle for long, because soon after this the Bramptons introduced me to a man with the curious name of Pregent Meno, a dealer in luxury fabrics in Lisbon who had built up his business from scratch.

At that moment Meno was looking for a mannequin to model clothes in front of his wealthy customers. I fitted his needs perfectly, being taller than most men and slim. I had had experience already as a mannequin for Mr Berlo; and, what is more, had been trained in Burgundy to behave in a dignified way and mix with people of noble birth.

Before long, I became Meno's regular assistant, strolling up and down outside his stall; and his customers here certainly liked my manner well enough, for I heard them say things like:

'Look how well he wears that magnificent fur hat!'

'Such elegant boots. And look at those turned down cuffs!'

'He must be Italian!'

One day, a ruddy-faced gentleman came alongside on horseback.

'This lad of yours, Meno. He is of noble blood is he not?'

Noble blood indeed! I grinned as I thought back once again to the conversation with my grandfather in Tournai when I was little, the conversation which had caused such an argument between him and my mother.

This was such a quiet period of my life, under the protection of a caring employer. But it turned out to be the calm before the storm, for suddenly, my happiness was broken. Mr Meno received a despatch from the Duchess Margaret of Burgundy. I had to sail at once, not for Burgundy but for Ireland, where I would be given help from the Earl of Desmond and the Earl of Kildare, both sympathetic to the Yorkist cause.

Of course, I knew the Duchess would be recalling me sooner or later, but I had kept such thoughts firmly at the back of my mind. So, when the message arrived, it came as a shock - particularly as I was not to return to Malines after all, but travel to Ireland!

In Lisbon I had been settled and happy. The Bramptons had been very good to me - they were very good to everyone. But I had promised the Duchess, I had even sworn on some holy bones. And, after all, assuming her scheme was successful, there would be even greater and more prosperous times ahead for me.

Besides, the Bramptons would soon be leaving Lisbon themselves, for the help they had given some of King Henry's men had earned them a pardon, and they had been allowed to return to England.

Before they left, they helped me pack my things together - no longer just a bundle held together with rag, but now a little wooden chest, some fine clothes and some money.

★ ★ ★

It was a mild autumn day when we boarded the Portuguese merchant ship that was to take us to Cork. At the quayside we were joined by John Taylor of Rouen, a bald headed old man with a straggly grey beard. He was well known to the Bramptons as a loyal supporter of the House of York. Before we sailed, an old and very wrinkled priest from a local church arrived to bless the ship and mutter some prayers, begging God to protect us.

But soon after we had set sail the sky became overcast, and in spite of the priest's prayers the sea turned rough, there were squalls and we were all sick. In the high sea our ship was completely at the mercy of the wind that blew in great gusts all day, tearing into our sails and splitting our tiny fore sail into shreds. There were times when none of us expected to escape with our lives, and all we could do was say our prayers. I thought of my mother and father back home in Tournai - and the distress and grief that news of my death would cause them. When the storm worsened, the whole crew vowed to visit a shrine to the Virgin should we arrive safely at Cork, and some of them promised to fast on bread and water the day after we landed.

The journey to Ireland took three days, and I was greatly relieved when its rocky coastline emerged out of the early morning mist. And yet when we arrived at Cork there was no one there to greet us, no sign of the help the Duchess had promised me, not even any interest. So, while the crew fulfilled their pledge to pray at the nearest church, Taylor and some of the others went off to try and find the earls.

It was almost noon the next day when they arrived. They came their separate ways, and not surprisingly, for two more different men it would be hard to imagine: Kildare, the King's lord deputy in Ireland, tall and distinguished - rather out of place in this rough country; Desmond, much more like the native Irish - with thick lips and a swarthy skin.

Kildare stepped forward to greet me, his long grey hair falling across his face. 'At last, My lord of Warwick, Clarence's son', he said with a broad beam. 'Welcome to these safe shores!'

I was confused. Was he being serious? Warwick! Me? This was not the plan at all. I was not to impersonate Warwick. He was far too well known. 'I'm not the Earl of Warwick!' I blurted out.

There was a stunned silence. Kildare's cheeks reddened, he looked perplexed. Desmond coughed so as to stifle a laugh, then he pointed a fat finger at me. His uncouth voice cut through the stillness. 'Then, if you're not My Lord of Warwick, you must certainly be one of the late King Richard's sons.'

'Surely you recognise me?' I gasped.

Close to despair, I began to walk up and down in front of the Earl and his men, much as I had paraded before Meno's customers in the market at Lisbon. It sounds ridiculous as I tell it now, but it was all I could think of then. I caused something of a stir, as the Irish had never before seen the like of such clothes as I was wearing - such fine silk and beautiful colours. There I was, towering above them - well over six feet tall. And though marred since birth by a small cast in my left eye, I cut a reasonably handsome figure, so I thought. Certainly, I did all I could to hold myself well, and had done everything to cultivate my manners to the point where they were as good as those of a person of noble birth.

Eventually, one of Kildare's men fell to his knees. 'Oh! You must be of royal blood, sir! Your appearance would fit the description we have heard of the late King Edward. You must be his heir, sir, Prince Edward.'

'No, I am *not* Prince Edward,' I said as calmly as I could. 'I am his *brother*, Richard. Prince Edward, God rest his soul, was killed on the orders of our wicked uncle, King Richard. But the gentleman to whom I was entrusted was kind and showed mercy towards me. Sirs, I am depending on your support to help me regain my rightful throne.'

I waited. Would they accept my explanation? Everything depended on their reply. Kildare came forward and bowed. Then, in a low voice, he said: 'I beg your pardon, your Royal Highness, for not recognising you.'

Other nods of recognition followed, all from men I had never seen before in my life! Then Kildare rested an arm on my shoulder. Desmond even managed an ingratiating smile. At last they appeared to know who I was; but would they actually give me any support?

The two earls arranged that Taylor and I be given lodgings in the city. I was put up with John Waters, a successful merchant, who had a house backing onto the river. What an important part in my life he was to play over the next few years.

During the following weeks I met Kildare and Desmond in secret several times, in the upstairs rooms of Cork's many inns. I expected to spend the time discussing how they were going to help me gain the throne of England. But Kildare was reluctant to discuss the Duchess's plan, claiming that Henry's spies were everywhere, and that he was putting himself at great personal risk. So our meetings turned out to be unproductive and pointless.

In the lull that summer came reports of the deepening war between England and France. News, too, of how a Genoese sailor had finally secured the backing of the Spanish King and Queen to set sail for the Indies. Exciting adventures lay before him. But what was in store for me? I had been in Ireland now for almost a year, and there was no news from the Duchess of Burgundy. What about the riches and glory that she had tempted me with? Where were these? Would I have to return to my existence as a trader's mannequin, forsake the lifestyle I was growing accustomed to, where I was treated on equal terms with the most important of princes?

Suddenly, when my prospects seemed doubtful and my debts were mounting, a most extraordinary thing happened. Waters had already retired for the night and I was getting ready to go to bed myself, when there was a terrific banging on the street door directly below my room. Lamp in hand, I went down to see what all the commotion was about.

Two men in dark cloaks were on the step. They were not Irishmen, too well dressed. They had been making great haste from whatever port they had come from, as they were sweating profusely. Then they spoke. Their accent was unmistakably French.

One of them gave a little bow and handed over a small roll of paper. My heart started to race. What on earth could it be? I tried to keep calm. Slowly, I broke the seal and carefully unrolled the document. I read the contents, and was speechless. It was an invitation to attend the French court in Paris, signed by King Charles the Eighth himself.

I took a few moments composing my thoughts, and when I did so my words came out awkwardly. 'It is a great honour, to be sure. But why does your king wish to see me?'

One of the men frowned. 'The King has many matters he wishes to discuss with you. You will be treated as a most honoured guest.'

'When does he want to see me?' I asked, pointing to the document.

'Straight away. We must leave directly!' replied the more senior envoy, taken aback that I should ask.

I could say nothing, just swallowed hard.

'*Immediately*,' he repeatedly firmly.

Chapter 3

It can have been barely more than a week later when we reached the port of St Malo. From here I was taken to Paris in a shiny new black carriage, the like of which I had never seen before - such large wheels, and a little seat high up for the driver to perch himself on. I myself sat facing the way we were travelling on a seat upholstered in thick black leather; opposite me were slumped the two envoys, not very talkative - one of them, in fact, asleep for most of the journey!

The streets were full of beggars and men who had fought in the wars - some without limbs. Prostitutes leant over doors, calling out to every man they saw. A drunk staggered out of an inn as we passed, and was violently sick in the road directly ahead of us. We slowed to pass through the town gates, before quickly gathering speed again as we emerged into the open countryside.

The day was mild, and the canopy had been turned back; but when the air cooled at dusk we stopped for it to be drawn over our heads, making it so dark inside that I could not even see the outlines of my companions' faces. The road must have been full of ruts and pot holes as the carriage kept on jolting; and the two horses squealed as we all bumped up and down in our seats. On one particularly bad stretch of road, one of the envoys was actually thrown out of his seat onto me, and spent the rest of the journey apologising while his colleague slept on, oblivious, beside him.

At dawn we were nearing Paris. Across the low box hedges on either side of the road full-blown roses were just beginning to drop their petals. It was a very pleasant early autumn day, fanned by a light breeze; and the countryside had been a delight to travel through. Yellow-green and copper coloured leaves already lay in patches upon the ground, and on the distant hillsides I saw a great many little windmills - more, in fact, in one place than I have ever seen before. After skirting around some magnificent gardens, the road swerved and the carriage clattered through a gateway into the great city of Paris.

Once inside the high city walls we were greeted by a mass of gables, dormer windows and lofty church spires in every direction, as in my home town of Tournai but much more abundant. Through the centre of the city in quiet dignity flowed the River Seine, winding its way between a multitude of structures - grand buildings with towers that jostled for space with modest shops and market stalls. The coachman shouted down from his lofty perch to draw our attention to a great royal palace on the north bank. But the apologetic envoy was quick to correct the mistake, pointing out that the Kings of France only lived there in war-time, and that the present King preferred to live at Amboise in Touraine, more than a hundred miles away.

Although the streets were much narrower than I had expected for such an important city, they were bustling to the point of over-spilling with wealthy tradesmen and merchants. Yet I was surprised at the number of very poor people, too: dejected looking beggars sitting in rags by the side of the road, some venturing up to our carriage, their bony hands outstretched for money - so close that I could see the hideous blisters that scarred their palms.

'They'll be smallpox scars - the disease has always been the curse of this city,' explained the apologetic envoy.

'Used to be still worse in my father's day,' joined in his companion with a yawn.

'That's true,' said the other, nodding. So many were dying then that they couldn't dig graves fast enough and they had to leave them unburied, rotting in the street.'

I shuddered at the thought.

'The wolves ate many of the corpses!' chipped in his companion, stretching himself and giving another great yawn. 'It's only recently that the mayors have bothered to do anything to improve these foul streets.'

But improvements there had been, and the houses we passed were a curious mixture of old and new styles: soaring structures with overhanging jetties contrasting with the more classical designs, now all the rage.

'Just look at that place!' called down the coach driver, pointing to a splendid mansion set in acres of woodland.

'And you see that building over there, the one with the grand turret. The Bishop of Sens has just finished building it for himself. How the wealthy manage to live!'

But of all the buildings, it was the Châtelet that stands out in my memory. Situated on the bridge to the island of the Cité and Notre Dame, it was surrounded by a sprawling labyrinth of grim, winding lanes. On each side of its pointed gateway were two stocky towers that flanked a dark, menacing tunnel. The building was used as a fortress and a jail, so it had no windows, just a few arrow slits. How it reminds me of this wretched place I am in now - this dreary, depressing tower from where I can see nothing of the world outside, neither sun nor moon.

But let me return to my story. Here I was, just eighteen years old, riding in style through the largest city in Europe, heading for the royal palace where the King had been in residence since the beginning of the war with England. Furthermore, the envoys told me that I would have still other favours bestowed upon me, including the protection of a personal guard and the support of more than a hundred English exiles.

The coachman touched the reins lightly, and the vehicle that had shaken our bones for nearly two hundred miles came to an abrupt halt on the stony driveway outside the palace. A valet pulled open the gleaming coach door, and, with drums beating a steady rhythm in the background, a retinue of officers welcomed me down onto a mounting block.

Two guards led me towards the entranceway where we were met by one of the King's courtiers, a senior figure judging from his white hair and confident manner. 'The Duke of York. Welcome!' he boomed, giving a little bow, and at the same time revealing a large white handkerchief in his right hand. It seemed a comical sight; but that was presumably the way they did things here. 'I trust your journey has been a comfortable one.'

I wanted to say that it had been anything but comfortable! My legs felt stiff as there had been so little room inside the coach; but I said nothing, of course, for it would have been ungrateful. 'Very comfortable,' I lied. 'We had a calm sea crossing from Ireland, and the carriage that brought me here was . . . a great novelty.'

For a moment or two longer we continued to exchange pleasantries about the unusually clement weather and the state of the countryside. Then the minister raised his hand to signal it was time to get down to business. 'The King wishes to see you right away, Your Grace. Please come this way.'

He beckoned me into the Guards' Room, where I was immediately dazzled by thousands of gleaming weapons - swords, lances and axes - some in cases, others strung at precarious angles on the wall. From there I was led into various antechambers, all finely panelled in dark oak, past secretaries and maids who greeted me with a mêlée of bows and curtseys, as befitted an honoured guest from foreign parts.

Eventually we reached the waiting room to the King's special audience chamber where I was offered a seat. The minister crossed to the other side of the room, towards one final door, where he tapped out a special secret knock, put his ear to the panel and then entered.

My pulse began to race. I was still unsure exactly why the King had asked me to Paris. Could he offer me help to take the throne of England? What a blessing if he could! But, just like the Duchess, he would surely ask me for something in return.

While I waited, I imagined the sumptuous room that must lay behind that final closed door, that most private of all doors, a door that gave access to the chamber of the man who governed France, the most important and most feared country in Europe.

After a few moments, the minister returned. Puffing up his chest, as if he was addressing a crowd at a considerable distance down the corridor, he announced 'The King is ready for you!' Then, lowering his voice, he whispered 'Be prepared for his appearance! He doesn't like people staring at him.'

He ushered me in, and there I was, face to face with King Charles himself. Though forewarned, I never expected to see what I did. For, instead of a handsome and athletic young man, I saw a frail and sickly creature, very short and slightly built, his head big, and poised awkwardly on a small and very flabby neck, just as if it were a ball on a stone pillar, about to topple off! His lips were thick and coarse, his eyes bulged, and his enormous fleshy nose was more hooked than that of the meanest looking eagle. As for his hair, it looked as though it belonged more to one of the street beggars we had passed than to a king - all scraggy and unkempt; and the thin reddish wisps of hair partly covering his chin made him look feebler still. For a small man, his greatly protruding paunch and long, spindly legs were at best pathetic, if not downright repulsive: so that far from inspiring respect, he provoked instead a mixture of pity and contempt.

I knelt before him, trying my hardest not to reveal my inner thoughts. 'Thank you, Your Majesty for inviting me to your Court and granting me a guard of my own. It is a great honour.'

An awkward silence followed. At length the King raised his hands as if to say that no thanks were needed. Then he started to explain why he had invited me to Paris, clenching and unclenching his fists nervously as he did so. 'You know, y-y-y-yes. . . why y-y-y-you are here . . .?' He understood passably good English as far as I could gather, but his severe stutter made his words sound ridiculous. 'We have . . . how do you say it . . . a sh-sh-sh-shared business interest . . . and an enemy in c-c-c-common.'

I was anxious to get down to practicalities; but if our conversations were always going to be this slow, business of this nature seemed a very long way off. 'Your Majesty. On the way here, your envoys gave me reason to think that you might be able to help me in my cause, to help me capture the throne of England.'

'I think I c-c-c-can help you . . . s-s-s-sir, and there are m-m-m-many . . . others at Court who are anxious to ass-ss-ss-ssist you . . . too.'

I could not bear to look at him when he spoke - it made me feel too uncomfortable. And he was clearly ill at ease in my company. I wondered how he managed when he must forever be needing to talk to diplomats and foreign ambassadors as part of his daily duties.

However, before he had a chance to speak again, a bell sounded from somewhere in the distance, and he quickly interrupted me. A special banquet had been prepared to mark my arrival, and it was time that we both took our places at table. He motioned me to the door, and we walked side by side slowly down the wide carpeted staircase and into the great hall where a woman with beautiful long black hair and flashing eyes joined us. The King did his best to introduce her as his wife, Queen Anne.

Then we sat down, King Charles to my left, Queen Anne to my right. While the King fumbled with his wine goblet, the Queen talked to me. How knowledgeable she was about places and politics, and how witty was her conversation. What an agreeable and charming alternative it made to trying to speak to her peculiar-looking husband!

33

The tables were laden to overflowing with a very wide selection of succulent meats and game - including pigeon that I had never tasted before, and enjoyed. Afterwards there were fresh moist cheeses and locally grown apples and pears, all washed down by the finest red and white wines. As we ate, drank and talked, a band of minstrels played sweetly on the balcony over our heads, the sound of the lute so restful and calming.

The meal was finished, the scraps had been piled up in the kitchens for the city's poor, and the dogs were sleeping in front of the great log fire. As I left the table to take my place in the great hall adjoining, the dancing was already in full flow. What a wonderful tapestry of colour: the women in their long blue, red and green skirts, pinned up to display their delicate underskirts; the men in elegant white shirts, short tunics and tight-fitting striped stockings.

After the first dance, the duc d'Alencon and his charming wife introduced me to their beautiful young daughter, Marie. She made a well-rehearsed curtsey before looking up to reveal an alabaster-white complexion, deep brown eyes and long shimmering black hair. After a few moments she rose to her feet again: such a pretty face, such a lovely figure.

That evening we danced with each other again and again, and the brief intervals between the dances gave me a chance to get to know her better. Although only sixteen years old, she was worldly wise and had already heard something about me. 'How did you manage to escape from the Tower?' she whispered. 'We heard terrible rumours that you had been murdered.'

'Yes, my Uncle Richard intended that I should be killed with my brother, Edward. He is such a sick and twisted man, motivated only by greed.'

'So, how did you manage to avoid such a terrible fate yourself?' she persisted, her brown eyes shining like buttons.

'I escaped . . .'

She looked at me in astonishment. 'You escaped?'

My cheeks burned bright red at her interest; and I could not resist taking the lie a step further. 'You see, the man who was given the job of killing me was really a kind man, and, when he heard my story, he took pity on me, and made it easy for me to escape.'

Marie looked puzzled. She seemed to disbelieve that it could have been quite so easy, that I was just being over modest.

'And so I have roamed from place to place, from that day to this, until I arrived here, where I hope your King will agree to help me.'

*   *   *

As the days passed, I continued to be entertained, pampered even at court. I danced again with Marie, we talked in the comfort of the solar and walked in the privacy of the palace gardens. If the situation had been different I might have pursued her, but at that moment I was less interested in chasing pretty young girls than in quickly discovering what, if anything, the King could do to help me capture the throne of England.

But, as I waited in corridors and antechambers, I heard nothing about invading England: nearly all the talk was about preparing to attack Naples.

'I should like to know how we can afford these wars against Italy,' exclaimed a burly courtier who spent most of his waking hours in the corridor outside my room. 'I see no point in committing our soldiers in such a mad venture, sacrificing their lives. The King is obsessed by greed and glory - self-glory.'

'You're right, of course,' joined in another opposite him. 'But seeing that he really is set on his Italian campaigns, I only wish he would decide once and for all what his tactics are, and then stick to them.'

The face of the burly courtier showed only contempt. 'Quite so. You never know where you are with him. One moment he's agreeing with you, and then, before you know it, he's been swayed by someone else, usually by Guillaume, or more likely Étienne - that low-born good-for-nothing.'

'Precisely. The problem with the King is that he always agrees with whatever the last person tells him. It's pitiful to watch, he's so gullible!'

'He's too anxious to please people. Had he been a woman,' continued his companion, who from his mirthful expression was evidently about to crack a joke, 'his chastity wouldn't have lasted long!'

They both roared uncontrollably with laughter, and it was several minutes before they got a grip on themselves at all.

'Nor does he understand how war is fought these days. What

does he know about cannon and gunpowder? All he is used to is jousting and tilting at tournaments . . .'

'That's when he's not out wasting his time hunting or playing tennis . . .'

'*Trying* to play tennis!' the other jeered.

*   *   *

Until then I had had little opportunity to speak with the King, let alone plan the details of the venture he seemed agreeable to. Eventually, one evening, when the other guests had retired to bed, he led me into his private quarters and closed the doors tightly behind us.

There was a long pause while he groped aimlessly for a seat, leaving me standing isolated in the middle of the room, waiting for him to speak. But he said nothing. It seemed that I was expected to start the conversation!

Finding it awkward, as I have said, to look directly at the King, I pitched my gaze just behind where he was sitting, and began hesitantly at first, to describe the scheme that the Duchess Margaret had so carefully contrived during my short stay at her court in Malines. As I got into my stride I started to speak with more confidence. 'Your Majesty, I have been trained to impersonate Prince Richard.' I felt my cheeks glowing: I knew I had seized the King's attention. 'As you can see, I have been taught English, told all I need to know about the English court. Your Majesty, I seek your help, the help of Europe's most important prince. I need your support to launch an attack upon England.'

I paused. I had reached a critical moment. I had made my case, briefly and succinctly. Was he now prepared to back his words with action?

There was a much longer pause. His blank face betrayed nothing. What was he thinking? Surely, he *had* to be interested in a project directed against England, his old enemy. If not, why had he called me all this way to Paris? One glance at his library was enough to prove that he loved *reading* about exotic adventures. Well, here was an opportunity for him to be involved in a *real* adventure. But would the lure be sufficient to attract him away from his ambitions in Italy, to assist me - who he knew so little about - in a more speculative adventure?

At length, he beckoned to me, and pointed to a padded chair close to the hearth where a perilously balanced log was beginning to crackle and spit. Nervously, I awaited his decision. Darting flames from the fire sent shadows around the room. Slowly he leant towards me and cleared his throat, ready to speak. 'Henry is a . . . m-m-m-most wicked man . . . he has ill-treated his c-c-c-countrymen and f-f-f-failed to honour the p-p-p-promises he made to the . . . his s-s-s-sister.'

'Your Majesty! There can be no doubt, no doubt at all!' I interrupted. I bit my lip as I realised what poor etiquette it was to interrupt a king, even this poor specimen of one.

Unperturbed, he continued. 'I ass-ss-ure you I . . . will do everything in my power t-t-t-to ass-ss-st you and restore just laws.'

How relieved I was to hear these welcome words. Though he had not indicated yet exactly how he would assist me, that was surely a mere detail. What mattered was that he had pledged his support, and to have the backing of the most important prince in Europe gave me courage and strength.

In view of this, what happened no more than a week later shook my confidence all the more. For, suddenly, when everything seemed to be going so well, I received a message from the King, dismissing me from court! At first I was completely baffled; and it was not until a lot later when I learnt the reason for it – that he had just signed a peace treaty with England.

For the moment at least, King Charles was not obliged to send me to England; but I could never rule out the possibility that he might do so in the future. The prospect of this happening greatly unsettled me, and I realised I had no choice now other than to leave Paris completely. But where was I to go? Perhaps I ought to return to Tournai to see my mother and father? I had heard nothing from them since I had left Portugal. Were they both in good health?

Before leaving, I tried to see Marie again. I had such fond memories of the afternoons we had spent together, and I wanted to say a proper goodbye. But she refused to see me. I could only suppose that she was no longer interested in me since I had been banished from court society, and was now a mere nobody.

Having no other means of transport, I had no scruples about seizing one of the King's own horses. After all, the King had raised my expectations and given me false hopes. For my part, I had done everything he had asked - leaving Ireland directly and returning with his ministers, as he had requested. To my mind, the horse was at least some payment for my time and effort - all of which it now seemed had been in vain.

As I left Paris alone, with just a few possessions, bonfires were blazing in the streets to mark the peace with England. But *I* had no cause to celebrate. There was no place for me here any longer. After such great attentions I now felt utterly neglected, my hopes dashed to pieces.

Chapter 4

Far from being unused to travel, I had, of course, spent most of my childhood and the early part of my youth being taken from one place to another by my mother and her friends. To be sure, this was very different to the kind of nomadic existence I was forced to lead now; but there were advantages - freedom, constant excitement, the exhilaration of travelling on the open road. Besides, I still had an ally. So, without further thought, I set off to Malines, where I felt sure the Duchess of Burgundy would protect and assist me.

Several times during my journey north across the wheat fields of Picardy, my mind wandered back with affection to the time I had spent at her court, my chance introduction by the nobleman I had met in Antwerp market. Through want of money, I was forced to spend a night sleeping in the stables at a wayside inn. As I closed my eyes, I soon began to dream about the magnificent court I remembered then: the banquet tables groaning with food, the rich costumes of silk and satin. At the centre of everything was the Duchess herself. What an impressive woman - well-read, sophisticated, and with such great personal presence that her spirit was felt in every room of the palace. She had frightened me at times; but I was younger then, of course, and had less experience of life and of dealing with people. Even then, my fears had been mingled with admiration, for she was a truly extraordinary woman with such energy and faith in herself - a faith that had enabled her to survive when the death of her father, brother and uncle in battle had left her alone and vulnerable.

Exchanging my tired horse for a fresh one, I was anxious to complete my journey while the weather was still fit for travel. But winter was beginning to set in, driving the last leafy traces of autumn away. Only occasionally could the low sun be seen, its light weak and watery; and for the past few days dark grey clouds threatened to bring snow.

I had to make haste, for I could not afford to replace my horse again, nor stay anywhere overnight. But when my horse cast a shoe I was forced to stop at an inn. Although it was not yet dusk, I could see the light from the candles flickering inside. A stable boy replaced the shoe while I stood impatiently in the corner, odd looks being cast in my direction as I turned down the offer of drink and a seat by the fire.

After a while, a serving girl came over to me. Her long sandy hair fell over her face as she leaned towards me. Smiling in an alluring way, she asked whether she could get me anything.

'Don't bother with him, he's just a boy!' yelled a man from a nearby table.

'Yeah! Come over here! I'll give you a good time!' laughed his mate.

Whether the girl obliged them or not, I do not know, for that moment the stable boy shouted out that my horse was ready. As I left the inn, my mind was on completing the journey before the rains began.

A few miles later I began to smell a delicious aroma, possibly some sort of stew. I began to feel hungry, and, as I followed the smell, my mouth started to water. Soon I could hear sounds - dogs barking frantically, children playing games.

I came into a clearing. Men carrying bundles of hay on their shoulders steered an uncertain course between the goats and beer barrels strewn across the ground. Children were dashing about between the colourful wagons: I had come across a gypsy encampment.

As I stood there taking in the bustling scene, I heard a voice behind me, soft and low, speaking in an unfamiliar accent.

'Can I tell your future?'

I spun around on my heel and saw standing before me a stunning young gypsy girl with a shapely figure and flashing black eyes.

'I'm sorry, I have no money.'

She smiled enticingly. 'That does not matter. Come with me!'

She took my hand and led me across the clearing to her tent where we sat on thick rugs.

Alone with her, I breathed in her exotic perfume, her long black curly hair gleaming in the candlelight. As her small hands encircled mine, a thrill of excitement swept through me. Then she began studying my palm, tracing the lines with her fingers. My hand was trembling in hers. But she predicted only disaster ahead. I was dismayed: 'Are you sure? Can you not be mistaken?'

She tossed back her head. 'Rosita is never mistaken!'

With that, she removed a red rose, and threw back her hair so that it cascaded down one side, wild and free, exposing her soft swan-like neck. The corners of her mouth creased into a lovely smile, her soft pink lips parted, she arched her jet-black eyebrows.

'What is your name?' she asked.

I hesitated. What name should I give her? I decided on the truth. What was the point in lying? 'My name is Perkin.'

She looked at me and said 'I can save you, Perkin. Stay with me here. Your life will be happy if you stay. We can change the future if we want to, you know.'

I didn't know what to say. How could I turn my back on all my hopes and plans, even for the loveliness of Rosita. But then I looked into her eyes. They seemed blacker than ever. I looked down, at the soft curves of her breasts, at her slender waist.

Behind us, the wind was cracking relentlessly at the tent flap; but I was unable to look away from Rosita, for throughout my travels I had never met anyone as lovely and exciting as this. She leant across to me and began to caress my cheek with the back of her hand. I held her tightly in my arms, and together we went fast to sleep.

*　　*　　*

As the daylight began to creep inside the tent, I gradually awoke. At first I was confused by the unfamiliar surroundings. Then I heard the sound of soft breathing. I turned my head and saw Rosita lying beside me. Everything came flooding back. I remembered what she had told me, and the promise of what the future might hold for us together. But I could not turn my back on what I had now come to believe was my destiny. For a wild moment I wondered whether I could take her with me on my journey. But if I were successful, she would have no place at the English court. Besides, would she be willing to leave her people in the first place?

I looked at her again, and knew that I would have to go alone. Quietly, I dressed. She stirred but did not wake. Before I left, I bent down and gently kissed her shoulder. Her skin was smooth under my lips. For the last time I smelt her perfume. Before my resolve could weaken, I turned and left.

Many times since that day, I have imagined what my life would have been like if I had chosen to stay with Rosita.

Early in the evening I arrived in Malines, feeling exhausted, having no money left. The shutters of the shops were down; the air was still and quiet. The court lay off the main street, with two Yeomen Guards standing at its entrance, their swords crossed to prevent anyone passing. But after a few moments they recognised me from my earlier visit, and stepped aside to let me through, the huge bunches of keys which hung around their waists rattling as they moved.

I smirked as the same effeminate groom, torch in hand, led me pigeon-step along the familiar long, winding corridors, smoothing his hair back the whole time. On both sides were beautifully engraved panelled walls, adorned with gilt-framed paintings and fine bright tapestries; from some of the rooms of state we passed wafted the smell of freshly balmed and polished furniture. Every so often the groom would make little tutting noises if someone was in our way, or things were not to his satisfaction.

As we continued to weave our way along the corridors, eerie shadows were cast by the light of candles housed in iron brackets at regular intervals along the wall. Several hours had now passed since sunset, and the lengthy evening ritual of preparing to go to bed had begun. A bevy of pretty maids was turning down beds, scurrying in and out with silk night-gowns and elegant silver bowls full of rose water. On the bed posts, tapering candles were already flickering in the evening draught.

Our route took us through ever more private chambers, each entered through a recessed door, some draped with luxurious Flemish cloth, others surrounded by intricate carvings of wild animals and fruit. Even the antechambers leading into each room were elaborate, with beautiful tapestries hanging on the walls. I paused to marvel at one of these tapestries that showed a detail from a bloody hunting scene. I wondered whether the deer would be nimble enough to escape the pack of hounds baying in pursuit? From there I began to reflect whether I myself would be one of the hunters in life, or would be one of the hunted.

'Please sir, please come along,' said the groom anxiously, puckering up his lips.

Suddenly, I was startled by the barking of a small dog in the next room. For while I had been day-dreaming over the tapestry, the valet had been announcing my arrival to the Duchess and was now holding open wide the final door, the door to her inner sanctum.

As I stepped forward to enter, the little dog, a whippet, bounded across the room to greet me. I do not especially like dogs but thought that it would be rude if I did not give it some attention, this dog, Leon, the Duchess's new pet. So I put my hand down to tickle it under its chin and stroke its back, as I can remember my mother doing to stray and abandoned dogs in Tournai.

The Duchess herself was standing by a window, across which was drawn a curtain of thick red velvet. She seemed even taller than before, as she was now wearing an immense steeple head-dress. How slim she was for a woman who must surely have been in her late forties, her deportment was remarkably upright, and her elegant forget-me-not blue patterned dress made her seem very dignified.

Placing the little dog in a basket in the corner, she came across to greet me, her hands outstretched. 'Richard!' Then she embraced me with all the warmth and affection owing to a long-lost nephew. 'Just when I thought I might never see you again,' she said in a voice loud enough for any eaves-dropper at the door to hear.

That was my cue. I forced out the words: 'My dear aunt!' But my voice seemed much louder than I had intended, and oddly stilted.

'Oh, how good it is to see you again. My white rose - the white rose of England!' she added decisively, with a nod. 'You have arrived on the feast of St Nicholas. This is a very important sign ...' As she spoke, she gave me quick, darting looks with her grey eyes. Then, she whispered 'I'm very glad you left Paris when you did and came here. Are you ready for what lies ahead?'

I opened my mouth, expecting to say yes, but no sound emerged.

As we stood there, so close together that we could only be kin, I noticed behind her on a little table a copy of *The Lives of the Saints*. The Duchess was a very keen observer of all the saints' days in the Christian year, and the book had been left open at the title page, revealing her signature - bold and purposeful.

With her hands still resting on my shoulders, she eased me gently away from her, until I was at arms' length. 'Richard, you must be tired! You've had a long journey, and it's best that you now rest. I have put aside a house for you, and drafted in a special guard, thirty men in all. You'll recognise them immediately, as they're dressed in murrey and blue.'

I had turned ready to leave, when there was a light tap on the door, so quiet as to be almost imperceptible. Leon leaped out of his basket in the corner and rushed towards the door. It was a seamstress, carrying a new gown for the Duchess to inspect. Immediately she bent down to make a fuss of the dog. With that, the Duchess came forward, beamed at me and started embracing me all over again, repeating my title loudly. No doubt, as was intended, the waiting seamstress would be relaying the news about the Duchess's long lost nephew all around the court within the hour.

At last the maid left, curtseying as she did so, and soon afterwards I also left, to search out my house and the special guard dressed in blue and purple.

*   *   *

Little by little, I became more used to the frantic pace of life at Malines. A great many people lived at court, the Duchess possessing a huge retinue of servants, including five ladies in waiting who would always curtsey when they came into the room and address her as 'madame.' She also had several clergymen, some in the chapel, others in the almonry where they gave food, clothes and a bed for the night to the city's poor.

As we talked in her private suite of rooms, a corps of secretaries constantly came and went, bringing in draft orders for her to peruse, and taking despatches away to the far corners of her lands. The Duchess would always scrutinise correspondence with great care: she had a frightful temper, and usually demanded that amendments be made. I wondered whether these corrections were really necessary, or whether she was just showing who had the upper hand.

On one occasion, while I was waiting to see her I could not help overhearing the Duchess reprimanding a young seamstress. Having been taught embroidery herself in the home of a noblewoman, the Duchess always cast a very critical eye on the quality of others' work, and woe betide anyone who produced pieces that were not up to standard.

Each day I was introduced to new people, far too many to remember by name. For, besides all those who lived at court, an enormous number arrived daily - harried ambassadors, meticulous financiers, pompous theologians. Every morning physicians would visit the Duchess, and each month they would bleed her - a course of treatment she had undergone ever since her husband's death, whether she needed it or not. Then there were astrologers who came to give her advice about when it was best to arrange important meetings, go into battle, sign peace treaties to her best advantage. There were communications to respond to from messengers weary after a day and a night's ride. Not least, there were the endless petitions to deal with, and pensions and gifts to grant flatterers, and sometimes to those who actually deserved reward. All this other business occupied most of the Duchess's day, well into the evening, with the result that I saw very little of her.

About once a month there was a banquet, and sometimes the guests wore masks. On these occasions, sweet-scented rushes would be strewn across the floor at the far end of the grand hall, so that the less important guests could sit down without dirtying their clothes. But, as fortune had it, I would always be a guest of honour, and was served at high table in the company of princes and important ambassadors.

One night, early in July, the Duchess's stepson-in-law, the Archduke Maximilian of Austria, was placed next to me at dinner. I recognised him at once from his portrait in the corridor, for he had the typical Habsburg jaw and beaky nose. A particularly large number of courses was offered that night - prepared since dawn by an army of experienced cooks. There was a great assortment of meat and poultry, including pork and lamb (roasted whole on a spit), peacock, swans, geese and pheasant - all cooked to perfection in rich fruity sauces. Accompanying the meal were great goblets of wine from the endless supply of casks that were reputed to line the palace's cellars. As we ate, love songs were sung from a gallery above us by the Duchess's own minstrels; and after the banquet was over an acrobat amused us by performing cartwheels across the hall. Then a young juggler rushed on, threw skittles into the air and nimbly caught them again, much to the applause of all the guests.

During the meal the conversation turned to politics, the war between France and Italy, the troublesome Scots. Maximilian was quick to vent his own dislike of the English King, who he saw as a usurper, and listened with great interest as I discretely outlined the

Duchess's aims for me. The entertainment broke up our conversation for a while but afterwards we were able to resume it. For although the hour was late, it was still light outside, and we decided on a walk around the rose gardens. We walked arm in arm, as if we had known each other for many years rather than just a few hours. In the lamplight we could see the white roses in full bloom and fragrant, and it crossed my mind that here was I, another white rose, being carefully nurtured and cultivated.

Those who strolled around the gardens were themselves a colourful scene, with each noble rank wearing a robe of a different hue - violet, purple, black, red, tawny and cloth of gold - all tailored from rich, patterned fabrics, and generously edged with white fur. The young men, as I had noticed in France, wore short tunics, but with tall hats, perched rather precariously, on their long, flowing hair.

The ladies who we passed - some in small groups laughing merrily, others resting on the arms of courtiers - were all very fair, their skins made whiter by face powder. One of them, whose name was Beatrice, struck me as fairer than the rest, and had already caught my eye the previous day. But she was with her companion, not nearly so pretty; and I did not have the chance to speak to her alone. I wondered whether I would ever be able to do so.

Many of the ladies wore jewelled turbans, and a few, like the Duchess herself, wore steeple head-dresses with transparent veils, especially stiffened to give a dramatic effect. Every so often they paused to admire the mauve and yellow hearts-ease which bordered the rose beds, or to savour the perfume of the roses themselves. From time to time, when greeting a friend, they would gracefully hold up their fur-lined skirt to reveal a delicate white underskirt below.

As we walked, we talked further about the plans my aunt had devised, how I might get the blessing of other European princes, and obtain stronger support next time I went to Ireland. In truth, I became so engrossed in talking to Maximilian about my travels and my recent disappointments in Paris, that we came abruptly to the end of the gardens without either of us realising it.

'Watch out!' cried a young boy, as an arrow whistled only half a foot from my right ear. I flinched, lost my balance and fell.

When Maximilian helped me to my feet, I noticed several shooting targets set out just within the limits of the tall hedge lining the far end of the gardens. Here, a group of young noblemen were having archery practice. I chuckled to think that their parents were spending such a lot of money by sending them to court in the belief that they were finishing their education!

We watched for a while, amused, then turned back towards the palace, and continued talking. So well were we getting on that by the time we neared the palace again there was no doubt in my mind that Maximilian was genuinely interested in the Duchess's plans, and in all probability would do anything he could to assist me.

Soon there was better news for me still, as before the month was out Archduke Philip of the Netherlands, and the Kings of Denmark and Scotland had all recognised me as the rightful King of England. Whatever may have been their real motives for pledging their support for my cause (for I cannot believe that they were taken in by my imposture) their interest was a great source of encouragement and inspiration to me.

*   *   *

That same spring, many important men came across from England to offer me their assistance. The highest ranking of these was Sir Robert Clifford, at one time one of King Henry's own ministers. At first I trusted him completely; although he turned out to be no more than a spy working for King Henry, easily tempted by presents and a pardon into revealing the names of my supporters.

When I heard that even Sir William Stanley - the richest man in England - had agreed to go over to my side, I was particularly suspicious. Why should the very man who had made King Henry's victory possible at the Battle of Bosworth (and who he had promoted to Lord Chamberlain) suddenly desert him? No matter what his motives were, what cannot be doubted was that he helped recruit many supporters for me in England; that is, until the executioner's axe fell on him, and they fled in terror.

*   *   *

One humid, airless August day, the Duchess and I crossed the city to the court of Maximilian's young son, the Archduke Philip, to welcome two important ambassadors from England. They had arrived the previous night, but the Duchess was in no hurry to meet them: more likely than not she revelled in the idea of keeping them waiting until the next day!

It was now almost noon, and the ambassadors were clearly annoyed over the delay as when we arrived they were pacing up and down. We delayed them further by making ourselves comfortable in a downstairs chamber. Eventually we asked that they be escorted in. A shocking display of bad etiquette followed. They neither knelt nor bowed; then they started speaking before it was their turn, even before they had been introduced. The Duchess immediately brought them to heel over this, and they mumbled a condescending apology before they were allowed to go on.

From what they said, King Henry had sent them to renew some trading agreements between England and the Netherlands which were shortly due to expire. The Duchess was sceptical about this from the start; and she was right, for it quickly became clear that the real reason King Henry had sent them was to protest against the Duchess's harbouring me on her soil.

The older of the two ambassadors proceeded in uncompromising fashion. 'Your Majesties. This lad who calls himself Prince Richard.' He looked across at me. There was an expression of contempt on his face. 'Your Majesties, he is an impostor. He is no more genuine than that other rogue who cheated and lied a few years back. What was his name now? Lambert something or other - Lambert Simnel, that's it. Pretenders, both of them. His Majesty, King Henry, is only prepared to renew his agreements if you banish the lad *at once*.'

The secretaries - their quills, ink and parchment all ready to draw up the trade agreements - now stirred, visibly uncomfortable at the ambassador's rudeness. They looked towards Philip, expecting him to send them away. But he did nothing other than raise an eyebrow. His young age and inexperience had let him down: for he did not look more than fifteen years old, and his council tended to do most of the talking for him.

Then the other ambassador said his piece. The tone of his voice was bitter: 'It is true what my friend says. There isn't a nobleman in England who doesn't hold this man here in complete and utter contempt. They know full well who he is.' He stared directly at me. 'He is just the son of a boatman from Flanders.'

Philip's ministers were now beginning to get restless, showing

48

signs of concern. They were probably wondering whether this man might just be right. Perhaps this was the true identity of the man who had come with the Duchess, who was so highly regarded by her, had been paraded so much in her own court.

Still getting no reaction from Archduke Philip, the first ambassador turned to the Duchess and began to insult her to her face: 'Ma'am. You've now produced two great big babes, not as normal women do, but fully-grown in your womb - first Lambert and now Perkin here! Banish him from your kingdom. You're being ridiculed abroad, Ma'am!'

Well, you can just imagine how angry the Duchess was to hear this. Her forehead creased, her dark grey eyes shot a look of hatred at the ambassador who had dared utter such words. Before she could say anything, however, Philip's council intervened, threatening to imprison the ambassador at once if he did not withdraw his remarks at once.

There was a long pause. I wondered whether the silence was ever going to be filled at all. Finally, the ambassadors mumbled another condescending apology before being sent outside to calm down. A lengthy interval followed while Philip consulted his ministers; and after much discussion, the ambassadors were brought back into the room. A spokesman stepped forward to give them Philip's answer. 'Gentlemen, the Archduke assures you that he is a good friend of King Henry, and he wants to remain so. He will do nothing to aid one of his enemies.'

I gasped. I had expected Philip's support. Fortunately, the minister had not finished. 'Nevertheless, the Archduke has no power to intervene in the Duchess's lands. What happens there is a matter for the Duchess to decide, and for her alone.'

I sensed a triumphant smile behind me from the Duchess. Revenge not merely against King Henry but against his two rude ambassadors, who would now have to return to England shame-faced and break the bad news to their King.

The ambassador who had well and truly overstepped the mark earlier, began to bluster on again. 'Very well, if you don't believe us, we can prove that this man before you is an impostor. We can show you the chapel where the *real* Richard of York lies buried!'

Some of Philip's ministers who were nearest us were unable to conceal their amazement, and for a while there was a stony silence.

This was my moment. Determined to play my role to the full, I let my jaw drop, conveying a mixture of horror and shock at the report of my own burial. 'I shall remember your words when I become King of England!' I retorted, in an acid tone. For a moment, I glowed with satisfaction at my quick thinking.

The ambassadors cast their eyes down to the floor. They realised it was pointless now. If Archduke Philip was unwilling to intervene, they knew that their mission could not meet with success. Disappointed and aggrieved, the embassy returned to England to report back to Henry; and within two weeks of their departure, relations were cut off between England and Flanders, and all trade came to a stop.

★   ★   ★

But, if truth be known, the meeting had been disappointing for me too. I had learnt that Philip was not, after all, prepared to help me directly, so making it more urgent than ever for me to obtain the support of other countries, all enemies of King Henry. And so, back at court, I decided to write a letter to King Ferdinand and Queen Isabella of Spain. I began by describing how, by good fortune, I had survived a terrible ordeal:

> 'Although my brother, Edward, was cruelly put to death, the lord who was instructed to kill *me* had compassion, and placed me instead with two friends. One of these friends died and the other went abroad, allowing me to go free. Ever since I have had no home and been forced to wander through Europe. First I went to Portugal, then Ireland, afterwards France. Finally I arrived here, at Malines in Burgundy, at the court of my dear aunt who promises to support me. I have also been promised assistance from the Holy Roman Emperor, the Archduke of Austria, and the King of Scotland. I beg Your Majesties that you add your support so that I may be returned to my rightful kingdom.

> RICHARD.'

Even before I had set my seal and Yorkist coat of arms to the letter, there was a smart rap at the door. The steward beckoned in a flustered messenger, who bowed and promptly handed me a despatch, saying that it was from Archduke Maximilian of Austria - the man with whom I had passed such an agreeable evening some

50

weeks previously. Quickly, I broke open the seal and unrolled the letter. Its contents were so extraordinary that I just stood there, frozen to the spot, unable to summon up any words with which to reply. A few hours later, even before it was fully dark, I had gathered up all my things and had left Malines.

Chapter 5

The magnificent cortege was decked in black silk and cloth of gold. By its side, heading the procession, were the late Emperor's young widow, Eleanore, and Archduke Maximilian, their son. Following behind, at a very slow pace and in strict order of seniority, was a party of important mourners and myself, who had been invited from near and afar to Vienna for the state funeral of the late Holy Roman Emperor, Frederick III. To be present at the funeral of so powerful a man was a great honour, and in spite of the solemnity of the occasion, my spirits were boosted to know that I was thought of so highly by the greatest princes of Europe.

Normally there would have been a great flurry of activity in the city, which since the days of the Crusades had been an important centre for trade. But today, as a mark of respect for the late Emperor, it was completely silent, and the shops were all closed and shuttered, as if it were a Sunday. The merchants who usually thronged the markets with their wares were nowhere to be seen; like most folk they were at home grieving. By all accounts, much of this grief was real - for Frederick had been a much-loved leader.

The funeral procession meandered through the old cobbled streets. We passed a monastery of Dominican monks and another of Augustinian, before turning sharply into the main street. From here, a plethora of dark little passages between steep-gabled houses led to some of the oldest parts of the city. Clustered within the high grey walls were dozens of churches, most very old but a few recently rebuilt following the periodic fires with which this city has been cursed.

As we edged our way forward, we could just make out in the distance, beyond the walls, the muffled cries of boatmen on the River Danube which skirted the city and brought in its trade. Eventually, the massive defensive gateway and high steeple of St Stephen's Church loomed up before us. The procession paused. I strained my neck to look up. Watching over me, I saw a sculpture of Christ in stone, seated on a simple rustic stool. His right hand was raised, as if to stop me. His left one clasped a book, the Bible - the guide to a good life through truth and wisdom. His eyes seemed to stare at me, judging me, peering into my very soul; it made me feel ill at ease, and I was glad when we edged forward again.

We squeezed our way between the two lofty towers, and filed into the great church. Along either side of the spacious interior were massive pillars, richly decorated with tracery; while in between the soaring arches of the nave were more sculptures that revealed terrifying images of lions and dragons struggling with one another in deadly combat.

When all the company was seated, a mass was held and psalms were sung. Then the mourners passed alongside the coffin in single file so as to pay their last respects to the late Emperor. After this, the coffin was placed in the tomb which sculptors from Strassbourg and Vienna had spent forty years fashioning out of Salzburg marble - red, brown and white. Above the coffin had been carved an effigy of the Emperor as he would have been in his youth, clad in full armour, clean-shaven and with long, flowing hair. When he had died he was an old man, he had reigned for over fifty years and had been the only ruler who all but the very oldest people could remember. By all accounts, his court - usually held at Frankfurt rather than Vienna - had been like one great family to him.

Eleanore had been used to having her separate court with her own chancellor who had come with her to the funeral, along with her court barbers, physicians, astronomers and musicians - several drummers, trumpeters and even a lute-player. Being the daughter of the King of Portugal, it had been only natural that she should employ a number of Portuguese servants; and, having spent a little time in Lisbon myself, I warmed to them immediately, even understanding a word or two of what they said.

*   *   *

I assumed that when the funeral was over, I would be expected to return to the Duchess's court at Malines; but not a bit of it. Instead, Archduke Maximilian offered to accompany me to

Frankfurt. I accepted the invitation at once, for I already knew Maximilian as a friend. After all, only a few months before I had been walking arm in arm with him around the palace rose gardens at Malines. He would show me something of Bavaria, its castles and thickly wooded hills; and Saxony, well known for its fine woollen garments.

After only travelling a short distance we came to a village - one of hundreds of sleepy little places. However, right in the centre of the village, there was great activity. Something important was going on which involved most of the village folk. Keen to be seen taking an interest in his new people, the Archduke insisted that we stop and take a look at whatever was happening. I must confess that I was less enthusiastic, for the journey had only just begun, and to take a break so early on seemed unnecessary. Surely this was not going to happen in every village.

Our two grooms helped us down from the coach, and Maximilian and I went over to see what was going on. As we drew near, we saw the workers shielding their eyes, looking up to where a great slab of stone was being raised by ropes. All around us there were people busily working - masons carrying levels and set squares, carpenters moving timber posts into position, stones being laid out on the ground ready to be hoisted up to a band of workers in a tower high above our heads.

Our approach seemed to have gone unnoticed, until one of the carpenters working right at the top of the tower spotted us and cried out. Within moments all activity had ceased. A bearded, middle-aged man, who appeared to be directing the work, came over to us. Apart from his confident air of authority, the master mason was distinguishable from the other workers by his saffron-coloured robe. He managed a toothless grin, knowing that he was face to face with some important people, but he was not sure who we were, and the Archduke's groom ended up having to tell him. When he realised who it was - the emperor elect, no less - he fell to his knees with apologies for not recognising him immediately. Maximilian asked him to stand up, then introduced me.

'Yes, yes, the Duke of York, Duke of York,' repeated back the master mason, mechanically.

'So, how is the building progressing then?' asked Maximilian.

The master mason gazed upwards. 'Oh, pretty well. We are up to the task, more or less.'

'And, tell me, how many men do you have working for you?'

The master mason rubbed his beard thoughtfully. 'There would be several hundred on the books.'

'As many as that!' I said, amazed.

'Oh yes.' 'That's if you include all the masons, carpenters, polishers . . . Then there are the smiths making all our tools. It's a great undertaking, building a church tower.'

'You must have every man in the village working for you!' I exclaimed.

'And more besides! Some come from many miles away. See that lodge over there, that's where they live,' he said, pointing to a wooden hut in the distance. 'We did have more - but we've lost a few since the beginning. Sickness and accidents, you know. We lost two masons only the day before yesterday.'

'What happened to them?' asked the Archduke.

'The damn rope broke. When they were hoisting up a stone. Came crashing down on them.'

The Archduke frowned. He spoke quietly. 'I'm very sorry to hear it. Were they married men?'

'Yes, and all with young families too, sir.'

'Please give my sympathies to them all,' said the Archduke softly.

'Oh, many men are bound to perish when you are building something like this. We cannot become melancholic. We just have to carry on as usual.'

As he spoke, he was looking up at the doorway in the rising tower through which a mason was passing with a hod of very liquid mortar that was dripping down behind him.

'One of our biggest problems is with the mortar. It takes such a long while to set. You see the doorway over there? The wooden scaffold propping up the arch. It'll have to stay like that for the next year or more. It needs patience, you see. And sometimes a carpenter or a mason just doesn't have it. And that's a man lost.'

We thanked the master mason, gave the men our blessing and let them continue with their work; but the master-mason's tale had stimulated thoughts about what a frail thing life is, thoughts that gnawed at me for the rest of the journey. I wondered what sort of life the two dead masons had led. Good lives? In that case they had nothing to fear. But perhaps they had planned to repent in their old age for their misspent ways. If so, they had been robbed of these years, denied such an opportunity, and were surely now destined for the tortures of hell.

*   *   *

And so we continued our journey. Wherever we went I was well received, introduced and exhibited as the Duke of York, the rightful King of England. Several times Maximilian repeated his offer to give me his full support to recover the crown of England. I also heard from one of his ministers who accompanied us (though Maximilian never raised the subject himself) that he was prepared to offer me in marriage his beautiful fourteen-year-old daughter, Margaret. What a boost to my fortunes that would be, what proof of the new Emperor's confidence in me.

One evening we came to a desolate village. There was only one light, and that light came from the inn. The innkeeper explained that the smallpox had visited the village and that many had died. He poured us great tankards of ale, and brought out all he had for us to eat - cold meats, cheese and bread. Then he beckoned to a couple of girls to make rooms ready for us, apologising as he did so that neither was really sufficiently comfortable for the Emperor.

Next morning as we set off again, I felt unwell, feverish. My throat felt sore, I found it difficult to swallow. Maximilian ordered the driver to turn round and take us back to the village inn. The innkeeper summoned the doctor, an elderly gentleman, who pawed his chin and tutted a lot. After a while he rolled up the sleeves of my cloak and placed my arm in hot water. This, he said, would make the veins stand out more. Then he drew from a small jar two leeches that he applied to my upper arm to drain away a little blood. As I was feeling so ill, the pain and discomfort that the leeches brought seemed a small price to pay for the promise of good health.

After what seemed a very long time, the doctor removed the leeches by applying salt to their backs. Thankfully, this resulted in them loosening their grip, and he could easily scrape them off. After this I rested, for I felt a little faint.

The next day we continued to Frankfurt but I still felt frail and took little interest in the journey.

*   *   *

After some weeks we arrived in Frankfurt. One day, one of King Henry's most senior ministers, his Garter King-of-arms, arrived from England. We listened with courtesy to what this grey-haired, rather dull looking man had to say. But it was soon clear that his mission was the same as that of the unfortunate ambassadors who had been sent to Archduke Philip's court several months earlier - namely, to prove that I was an impostor.

With little life or enthusiasm in his voice, he recited a prepared speech. It was almost as if he knew that his mission had no hope of success. Eventually he droned to an end with the words: 'Englishmen know only too well that the Duchess has been using witchcraft. She has ensnared not only this young dupe, but many of the leaders of Europe too into her schemes.'

He had said what he had come to say, but neither the Emperor Maximilian nor anyone else took any notice of him, and when he had finished he was immediately sent away.

*　　*　　*

Having travelled in all for some six months or more, we arrived at Antwerp, where I was given a large merchant's house to stay in, the house being empty because of the trade embargo I mentioned. I was also provided with a guard of twenty archers - all, appropriately enough, with white roses in their hats. Sensing that I was in congenial company in the midst of my supporters, I began to relax, tired after the long journey. But almost as soon as I had moved into the house, there were demonstrations by Englishmen loyal to King Henry.

One night, several hours after I had retired to bed, I was suddenly awoken again. I sat bolt upright in bed, breathing fast, my forehead pouring with sweat. Something was wrong but in my confused state it took me a long while to work out what it was. Was it just mice, scrabbling around in the thatch above that had awoken me? No, it was something else. Then I realised. Drifting up from below was the smell of burning wood. Something was on fire. My first thought was that the servants had failed to damp down the kitchen fire. Perhaps a spark had shot out and caught a beam alight.

In my haste, I donned my outdoor cloak instead of my night-gown, and quickly descended the ladder from my room in the attic to the upper floor. By this time, the burning smell had become much more intense, and thick grey-black smoke was swirling around the ground floor rooms. Where were the archers which Maximilian had given me? Why had they not sounded the alarm? Then I remembered that the previous night they had been loafing around idly with some girls in the street, very much the worse for drink. Had they gone off with these girls, I wondered? Were they now abed with them in one of Antwerp's many taverns?

Suddenly, a bright yellow flame shot along one of the beams at the top of the ladder leading down to the ground floor. A moment later, the whole beam started to smoulder. My chest tightened. I was ready to run, but run where? Would I be able to reach ground level at all, now? The most important thing was that I tried to remain calm.

I quickly considered my options. I could jump from a window, provided I could open one, for it had taken ages for me to ease open the one in my bedchamber. In any case, the house was exceptionally tall, and in the drop I would run the risk of breaking a leg, if not my back. No, I had to go down the ladder, and I had to do it straight away. If I hesitated, who knows what would happen? A burning beam might fall, sealing off my way completely.

A thick cloud of black smoke was swirling around below. But I had to go down that way. I started to choke. What could I cover my face with? There was only my cloak. So, with my face buried inside it, I climbed down the ladder as fast as I could. Dense acrid smoke was now pouring upwards from the entrance hall. But the fire could not have begun there, for I had not lit the fire there that evening.

I could not see a thing. Where was the front door? Surely, it ought to be right ahead of me. But keeping going that way would be like walking into the fires of hell itself. So I had to turn right round and head instead for the door at the back of the premises. It was like groping my way through a terrible fog but much worse.

My eyes were now smarting, I was struggling for breath. As I got close to where I imagined the door to be, I stubbed my foot on something and almost fell right over. At first I thought it must be a bundle of old clothes, and I began to curse the servants for having been careless enough to leave it there. But as I reached down to move it aside I was shocked to find that it was a body, presumably one of the guards.

My first instinct was that he must be dead, as he lay sprawled out, oblivious to the smoke and the ever-growing heat. But when I touched him he began to groan. I sat him up and vigorously tried to shake him awake. It was clear from the smell of his breath and his limpness that he had passed out from too much drink.

As flames leapt up to the rafters in the hallway, I dragged him outside, free of the fire, and shouted out to neighbours for help. Shutters were flung open in the houses opposite, and moments later a small group of men, still in their night-gowns, had organised a chain of buckets from the river to the house. From their manner it was clear that they had done it many times before. But it was useless: the fire had taken too great a hold, and we all had to withdraw for our own safety.

Next morning I returned. All that remained were charred beams and some traces of tarnished thatch. My fears that it had been done deliberately were confirmed when I discovered a scrap of parchment on which had been drawn my coat-of-arms back-to-front. It was smeared with shit and fastened with an arrow to what had once been the right hand door post. I could only assume that the men who did it had been working for King Henry. The bastards!

Already angry with the English for making a secret peace with the French, Maximilian now saw it as a personal insult that the house he had given me had been so vilely desecrated, and promised to punish the perpetrators. But they were never caught: I am sure they were being shielded by the citizens of Antwerp.

*   *   *

Soon after this, I returned to Malines alone, where I was welcomed back by the Duchess who was anxious to talk to me further.

Our conversations over the next few days soon turned to money. Up until that time she estimated that she had spent some 800,000 crowns promoting my cause; she had even written to the Pope on my behalf. Understandably enough, she now wanted some return on the time and money she had invested.

And so, some legal contracts were drawn up between me and my 'very dear and very beloved Aunt Margaret of England.' These said that when I was crowned King of England, I would agree to pay the

Duchess 81,666 crowns still owing on her dowry. I also promised to repay all the expenses she had incurred on behalf of her supporters in Ireland, and a further 80,000 crowns she had lent me for my venture. I agreed to hand over to her the manor of Hunsdon and the town and castle of Scarborough; as well as pledging to restore all the English trading licenses which she had been used to when her brother Edward was King, and which King Henry had taken away on his accession. The Duchess had the foresight to insert one other provision into the agreement, namely that if, by chance, I died without children, I would have to give up to the Emperor Maximilian, and to Philip, the Archduke of Austria, all rights of succession to the Kingdoms of England and France, the lordship of Ireland and the principality of Wales.

The signatures were barely dry on the papers when word was received from the Dean of St Paul's, one of the Duchess's most loyal friends in London, that the situation in Ireland had changed for the worse. The earl of Kildare had been ousted from office by a new lord deputy, Edward Poynings. This was a great blow, as, given time, I had hoped that Kildare would prove a loyal supporter of my cause. Now, our position in Ireland appeared to be hopeless. Indeed, with no support forthcoming from France or Ireland, it seemed that our project had almost no chance at all of success.

When all seemed lost, we suddenly received another despatch from the Dean of St Paul's. King Henry had just left London to visit Lancashire where his mother was unwell. This might be my moment to act. Perhaps I had no need to go to Ireland after all. I could seize this unexpected opportunity, and strike against England itself.

Then I heard Rosita's warning, as clearly as if she were standing next to me. Was this the madness of which she spoke? There could only be one outcome if I failed. The penalty for treason was well known. It would be a gamble, but despite my worries I decided it would be worth it. After all, it might be my only chance.

Chapter 6

My plans for the invasion of England were well advanced. The Duchess and Archduke had requisitioned fourteen merchant ships for my short sea crossing, and the town council of Vlissingen recommended to me five excellent sea captains. The most experienced of these was William Gemyne, a stocky and well-respected man from the town, whom I took an instant liking to because he was always cracking jokes and keeping the men in good spirits as the ships were being made ready. Then there was Simon Montford who had already taken ambassadors to Ireland and Scotland; and Peter Corbet who I warmed to straight away as he came from my home town of Tournai. Finally, Martin Quintyn and John Whitebolt who I found difficult to tell apart in their sea cloaks, both being equally tall with their faces partly covered by bushy black beards, streaked with grey.

Nearly three hundred strong brave men were conscripted to man the ships. Some were disbanded soldiers and sailors, with long experience fighting to extend the frontiers of the Duchess's dominions, but now eking out a living by hawking pots and pans from house to house, or helping to run market stalls.

Others, including several French and English sailors, were serving long sentences in local gaols for debt, petty theft or brawling in the streets. Most of these were only too willing to come with me, and escape their present condition - incarcerated as they were in a dark, miserable and stinking cell, sleeping on straw, and with only bread and water to eat and drink. As well as the pardon which volunteering brought with it, they doubtless hoped that a successful invasion of England would earn them sufficient riches and favours to satisfy their wildest dreams. Though somewhat swarthy in their appearance and uncouth in their speech, they were the only men available. I had no choice. I had to take them.

As there was no way of knowing how long King Henry would be

away in Lancashire, we had to make our preparations as fast as we could. The sailing ships that had been fitted out for us were almost ready. They had received fresh coats of blue and white paint, their holds had been brushed and scrubbed, and their worn and hole-ridden sails renewed.

We began to load the battle equipment. Our weighty coats of mail were taken on board first. Then came our weapons - long, gleaming swords and lances forged by the smiths of Burgundy, deadly pikes, three times the height even of Quintyn and Whitebolt, my tallest men. On came powerful crossbows and bulging quivers of arrows, some of the new arquebus guns and a quantity of powder produced by the factories of Antwerp. Last of all, my own clothes were brought on in a large wooden chest.

Within three weeks, all our preparations were complete. It was now almost the end of June, though the weather was still more like that of April - cool and showery. A lot of rain had fallen during the past few days, and our clothes had not properly dried out and smelt musty. But we could not delay our departure further. We had to sail the next day at first light, which was soon after four o'clock at this time of year.

Crowds lined the quayside to see us off - leading aldermen from the town, boat-builders and dockers, the sailors' girlfriends. As the people of Vlissingen sat in their houses eating breakfast, our ships were slipping silently through the docks, out into the open sea. In the pocket of my cloak I could feel a black leather pouch containing copies of the agreement which the Duchess and I had signed some weeks before. It was a constant reminder of all that the Duchess had done to help me: the introductions she had arranged for me at the great courts of Europe; of all the money she had spent on my behalf; and now the ships she was supplying for my crossing to England. To her I owed everything. When I became King of England I would quickly repay her with all the things I had promised, and more besides.

I looked around at my men - some twenty-five or thirty of them in all, including a dozen or so crew, easily distinguishable from the others as their skins had been tanned by constant exposure to the sun, wind and driving rain. So different from my own skin which was still fair and pasty, despite all my travels, my outdoor life.

It was still barely light, but I could just make out one of the sailors adjusting the rigging; a couple of others were standing by the rudder. Several men I found just idling about playing dice or telling one another bawdy stories; others were lolling around at the bow of the ship, waging bets on who would see the coast of England first. I set them all to watch immediately; for I could not have an ill-disciplined, work-shy crew.

We were now well out to sea, and the coast of Flanders was disappearing into the distance. As the sun came up it seemed to herald a bright day - and a glorious one for me and for England. I began to dream of the grand court I should have in London, the visits I would receive from princes all over Europe. But before my coronation, I should be betrothed to a beautiful princess - perhaps Maximilian's own daughter - who would provide for the succession of the House of York by bearing me strong male heirs.

At that moment, a stretch of rope became detached from the port side of the ship, and hit me full in the face with a nasty blow. I lashed it down and rejoined the group of sailors at the bowsprit, several of whom were English.

'We're sure to get a right welcome in Kent!' said one.

'Aye, Kent folk have guts' joined in his mate. 'They'll stand up against injustice, just like they did for Wat Tyler and Jack Cade.'

'Too right. And there are plenty of wicked things this king has done to stand up against! *Taxes* for one.'

The other sailors let out a great cheer of agreement.

The weather kept calm for our crossing, and just after noon we approached the Kent coast, the white cliffs glistening in the sunlight. But it was too difficult to make a landing there. So we ventured further along the coast in a north-easterly direction. The English sailors, who knew the area well, told of the many shipwrecks caused by the sands in these parts; and as a precaution against going aground kept on dropping lines over the sides to check the depth of the water. As they were doing so, I looked up: the sun was now obscured by cloud, and there seemed little prospect after all of the beautiful day that had been promised earlier.

Soon we came off the small fishing village of Deal. This looked a much more inviting place to land. Ahead of us, the beach was completely open as far as the eye could see, and the land was mostly flat. The waves roared and crashed ferociously onto the stones, and jets of cold white spray shot up into the air with a great hiss. Overhead, the clouds were fast becoming darker as though a storm was gathering, but there were more hopeful chinks of light, too. A few small fishing boats bobbed around in the distance; while beneath us shafts of sunlight gleamed on the water, revealing traces of broken fishermen's nets enmeshed with pieces of black and brown slimy sea-weed. Gulls squawked above us chillingly, circled for a while, then dived down for fish.

Suddenly, one of the English sailors caught sight of a small band of men on the shore, and shouted out at the top of his voice: 'We're the Duke of York's men!' There was a pause. Then a great cheer went up from the Kentish men, who started to come right down to the water's edge. It seemed that they were overwhelmed to see us.

Another great cheer went up, even louder than the first. The men beckoned vigorously to us to come ashore, to set foot in my rightful kingdom. All this was a better welcome than we could possibly have hoped for.

In fact, everybody's spirits were boosted to such an extent by this that several of my men in their enthusiasm mistook the depth of the water - which was about two fathoms as we were still some distance from land - and attempted to clamber ashore. Their recklessness wasted time, some going under the water and needing to be rescued.

While they were being brought safely back to ship, I started to make plans. Upon landing, we would, of course, celebrate; but then quickly (while the advantage was ours) assemble a great force from the surrounding towns and villages. Armed with whatever weapons they had, and those we had brought from Flanders, we would march directly inland towards the city of Canterbury. I could just imagine the terrific welcome we would get when we arrived there - the cheers and rejoicing that would greet us as we marched through the streets. I would stay either in the house of the Archbishop of Canterbury, or at some great inn or other in the city. Then, the next morning, without delay, we would head for Rochester, the other great cathedral city of Kent. And so on, towards London on the third day. Coming into the city I would be transferred to a fine new coach driven by six white horses, and we would then drive to the palace of Whitehall, through streets lined with crowds twenty people deep. Finally, the Lord Mayor of London would escort me into the Abbey at Westminster to be duly enthroned and crowned King of England, to the satisfaction of all true loyal Englishmen born and bred.

Leaning against the bowsprit, shielding my eyes and surveying the land that would soon be mine, I ran over the plan several times in my mind, until it was no longer just a romantic dream. It was now all within my grasp. Surely, it was only a matter of time before the whole country could be taken out of King Henry's control.

I stayed at my post aboard ship while about half of my men went ashore. After a while, there were great whoops of delight, and I looked up to see the Kentish men dragging a tun of ale from the road down onto the pebbles; and using a couple of tankards and several clay pots they doled out the very welcome refreshment. Some of my own men told me later that they were completely unused to its taste; but this did not seem to bother them as they quaffed back the draughts in the peaceful warm sunshine.

Most of the sailors were now sitting down, and the atmosphere was very relaxed. They had unbuckled their armour and were chatting enthusiastically in groups, save half a dozen or so who had gone off to fetch even more refreshments from an ale-house nearby, so that we could continue to celebrate well into the late afternoon. Some of the men were wrestling playfully on the stony beach, others were lobbing pebbles down in the direction of the sea, their aim not at all helped by the large amount of ale they had drunk. From time to time, a peel of laughter went up. Perhaps a good joke had been cracked, perhaps it was just the drink that was making them so merry.

About an hour passed, and I was just about to disembark from my own ship to join the revelry when one of the sailors high above me who had been repairing the rigging, gave a shout. The alarm in his voice alerted us all. He was pointing inland. We concentrated our gaze. I heard the sailor's voice from above shouting again: 'Henry's soldiers!'

Some of the sailors scrambled up the rigging to get a better view. They yelled out: 'Yes. It's the enemy!'

I had been tricked and cheated. The men obviously had no intention of bringing ale. Instead, they had gone to fetch the Mayor of Sandwich who now arrived with a militia of some two hundred well-armed men, ready to force a fight. How could they have done this, the Kentish men who I had been assured had such a fine fighting reputation? Their conduct was cowardly. It made me sick to think about it.

I left my ship at once to join my men. But our arquebuses, pikes and crossbows were still stowed in the holds of our ships, and were too difficult to get out at such short notice. So that before we were aware of what was happening, the Mayor of Sandwich's men had drawn up in formation along the roadway and began to fire down a torrent of arrows on us from their crossbows.

Using as many of our swords as we could lay our hands on, we put up a gallant fight from the shifting pebbles beneath our feet. But because we had been so badly tricked my men were taken entirely unawares. Many had their armour off and laying beside them, and the majority were the worse for the drink they had been so liberally plied with by the men who had deceived them by taking them into their confidence.

I would have made a greater stand myself, but a glancing blow badly pierced the skin of my upper arm, and forced me to retire early on. Ripping off a piece of my shirt, I tied it around the wound to stop the bleeding as best I could. But the pain was shooting up and down my arm, and I had nothing to ease it - as the ale that might have dulled it had all been consumed. I did my best to oversee the fighting from on board ship; but it was no use, as their superior numbers and better weapons gave the Kentishmen too great an advantage.

In all, on that grisly day, I calculated that some one hundred and sixty-nine of my men were taken prisoner, to endure almost unspeakable cruelties. For, showing no hint of humanity or fellow-feeling, the mayor's men tied them to the back of farmers' carts, and dragged them along the road to the town of Sandwich - some five miles or so away - with their backs bleeding horribly. After that, they were taken to London: some to be locked away in Newgate Prison, others to be thrown into the depths of the Tower to await trial and sentencing. In due course most of them were hanged at the gallows in Tyburn or Wapping. They included my friend Peter Corbet from my native town. But for some, the agonising ordeal was delayed even further. These were the ones who were taken all the way back to the coast again a few weeks later to be made a horrifying example of. Here, strung up on gibbets, their bodies were left swinging in the sea breezes along the shores of Kent and neighbouring counties. It was a terrible warning to other would-be invaders.

I told one of the older men who was tending to the wounded, to leave them for a moment, I would stay with them. 'You raise the anchor. Get them to let the sails down!' I shouted, pointing to some men who had gone up the rigging to escape capture. 'We must get away! We can do no more. If we don't get away now, we shall all be killed!'

The man went off. It seemed like an eternity before I heard the sound of the anchor grating against the side of the ship. Sails came hurtling down, and a sudden gust of wind played into our hands. The ship began to move. As we gathered speed and were out of danger, I sank to my knees and thanked God for my safe delivery.

Chapter 7

Early the next day, after an anxious crossing, we anchored off the French coast. William Gemyne and Simon Montford, the most experienced of my sea captains - both mercifully spared at Deal - had warned me that King Henry would most likely mount an all-out attack from around the north coast of Kent, and that I had best beat a retreat to Flanders at once. My only concern was to get back to the Duchess's court as soon as possible. But what should I do about the ship? I decided that I would leave it in the hands of my loyal crew, for them to make what use of it they could. They were delighted at my generosity; but little did they know I had no choice. What could I do with a ship in the present circumstances?

I put on a brave face when I bade them farewell, but my spirits were low. I made for the village of Dunkerque on foot, where I was able to purchase a horse.

After three days solid riding, I was back at the Duchess's court in Malines. However, from the moment I set foot in the palace I sensed there was something wrong. The guards were brusquer, the ministers less obseqious. It soon emerged why: the Duchess was away on a progress around her dominions.

At first I was dismayed, angry even. Then I began to calm down. After all, why should she expect me back so soon? If her plans had gone as they were supposed to, I ought at this moment to have been entering London, ready to be crowned King of England.

The initiative now lay with me, and I decided to hold a council of war. As usual, there was no shortage of suggestions from my advisers, though not all of them were very practical. 'Suppose we gather together as many men as we can. All the exiles from the English court . . .'

'And?' I asked.

'Return to England straight away.'

I frowned, extremely doubtful about this idea. 'I don't think we'll find enough men here at court. Besides, even if we left as soon as we could - say, in three or four days - by that time the King will have returned to London and assembled an army against us.'

John Taylor of Rouen, ever the wise one, came up with a far better plan. 'Why don't we recruit as many as we can from Flanders and then head for Ireland. We should get lots of support there. We'll be able to build up a big army.

There was a pause. A few of my men still frowned - perhaps contemplating the length of the journey ahead of them, but more likely because they were envious of not having thought of the scheme themselves. No matter, as by far the majority had raised their eyebrows in interest, and their excitement sent a sudden rush of colour to my cheeks.

Emboldened by their enthusiasm, John Taylor was only too happy to continue. 'It has to be the right moment, sir. Ever since Kildare was dismissed, there's been trouble. Cottages have been looted, crops burnt. You'd be welcomed there, sir. As a friend.'

Everyone thought about what had been said. 'After that, when we're ready, we'll cross to England. It'll only be a short crossing to Cornwall,' Taylor finished.

'Yes,' joined in another: 'and we'll get plenty of support from those parts. People there are sick to death of the King's taxes. I've heard that they're planning to break away from England altogether. So, plenty of discontented men to join our ranks!'

Everyone nodded in agreement. The council was unanimous: there could be no doubt that our best hope now was to cross to Ireland. Preparations were hastily put in hand for the journey, and we arrived at St Malo within a few days, ready to embark as soon as the weather was favourable.

★   ★   ★

All the way to Ireland we met with heavy July squalls. At one point there was such a violent outburst of rain and thunder that the deck was flooded and the sailors were at full stretch trying to sweep the water off.

Towards the end of the month my small fleet neared the rocky coast of Munster, and soon afterwards we limped into port, very much the worse for wear. But at last we had the protection of a safe harbour.

Surrounded by rolling hills and swathed in mist, the city had lost none of its mysterious charm since my previous visit. Flowing peacefully through the very centre was the river, divided into two streams, making this area of the city an island; it reminded me of part of Paris I had seen. Most of the buildings were clustered on this island which was connected to the rest of the city by rickety wooden bridges. Along the riverside, the streets doubled up as quays; while further back stood several beautiful churches, a splendid abbey and two castles.

I had hoped for a sympathetic reception, though what I got was far more, for the people welcomed me as something of a saviour, offering protection from the harsh hand of the English. When they saw me some of the council fell to their knees, overjoyed. An eccentric looking old man with straggly white hair, who I supposed was the council leader, spoke for them all. 'Oh sir, it is a miracle,' he exclaimed. The others kissed the ground before them. 'The founder of our city, Finbar, was fair-haired - just like you. It is such a wonderful sign.'

At noon the next day, I was received enthusiastically by the Earls of Desmond and Lincoln. They backed my claim to the throne of England without reservation, and joined their force of some two thousand men to my own army.

Before long, no doubt on account of my still not fully disguised foreign accent, I came to be known affectionately among the citizens as the 'French lad.' My self-confidence began to return, and once again I felt at ease and more secure.

*　　*　　*

Late one evening a few weeks later, we were sailing northwards up the coast under cover of darkness, ready to lay siege to the town of Waterford. What a blow to the English its capture would be. Apart from the ship in which I was sailing, there were ten others - seven provided by John Waters' brother, the rest by King James of Scotland.

A short distance up the coast we lay anchor and waited until dawn came up. The men had strict instructions not to make a sound. Not a voice was to be heard above deck, nor a lamp lit for fear of alerting the people of Waterford.

As the first glimmers of light appeared on the horizon, we pulled up anchor and sailed the last league or two. The wind was favourable, and we hoped by our early arrival to take the inhabitants by surprise. But as we sailed into the harbour, beacons were lit and there was a great commotion ashore.

A very lengthy siege ensued, during which the enemy used their cannon to very good advantage. Three of my ships fell into the hands of my enemies, and another was completely sunk in the harbour by the constant fire coming at it from the town.

As if this was not bad enough news, worse was to follow, for soon after I heard that Lord Deputy Poynings was marching with an army against the city. My greatest concern was that I should avoid any further losses, so I decided to retire while I was able to do so with honour.

Disappointed, I withdrew to Cork where I knew I could expect help from my loyal friend John Waters. While my companion John Taylor stayed at an inn, Waters gave me a room in his fine tall house. Here I was waited on by his servant, and was even offered the services of a personal groom and secretary.

John was in his mid-forties, with a weathered face, piercing blue eyes and a warm smile. I had always found him easy to talk to, but I sensed that something had now changed, and as I entered the house seemed quieter than before.

'What's wrong?' I asked, as we went and sat in the large front room that bordered on the river.

He fetched us both a tankard of ale; then, drawing his chair closer to me, he quickly took me into his confidence. 'My wife died last year of the fever.' There was a quiver in his voice. 'I'm on my own now, with this big place all to myself.'

I touched his arm. 'I'm very sorry to hear it,' I said softly. I had liked his wife very much. She was a very kind woman with a wonderful sense of humour, and her peels of laughter had filled the house.

'Do you have any other relatives in Cork?' I asked.

'Yes. My brother lives a few streets away. It was partly his ships we used against Waterford.'

'What about your children?'

'Philip, the oldest one, he's now a priest in Limerick, more than forty miles away. But I still see plenty of John. He lives in Cork. Training to become a legal secretary. He's found a lovely girl and is engaged to be wed next summer. God bless him.'

'And what about your daughter?'

'Mary? . . .'

He hesitated. There was clearly something wrong. 'About four years or more ago she took up with a gentleman from Waterford - much older than she, he was. They were quickly wed and have now got a little one - a baby boy.'

'How proud and happy you must be!'

'I would be, if only I could see them both more often. This is why it's so good to have your company. Please treat this house as your own.'

He called to the servant to replenish our tankards of ale before continuing.

'You'll notice that I have kept on my old servant. He's been with us for about ten years, and deserves better than to be thrown onto the street. But really there is not sufficient work for him to do. I had to let our other servants go.'

In spite of this, the house never really seemed completely empty. This was because the upper floors (that once contained the bedrooms of the sons and daughter) and the servants' basement were full of wares - mostly fine linen cloth, some of it lying on tables in rolls, some single lengths draped like tapestries on rails from ceiling to floor. John had clearly become very successful at his trade, enough to keep his family in considerable comfort, luxury even, had he so wished. However, he was not an extravagant man; besides, experience of the uncertainties of his own trade had taught him to be prudent.

Two or three evenings each week he would spend with the mayor and leading aldermen, working on council matters of some sort - drafting orders, attending to petitions. He worked very hard (sometimes not returning before midnight had rung out), hoping that one day he would become mayor of Cork himself. During those evenings when he was at home, we often talked into the small hours, often about the state of the cloth trade in which we shared an interest. As we talked, I taught him how to play chess, trying all the while to be as patient as my own mentor, the Bishop of Cambrai.

As the weeks passed we became close friends, and I decided that I valued his friendship sufficiently that I wanted it to be on the basis of trust rather than deception.

One evening we were sitting in the front chamber, overlooking the river. It was mid-August, very humid, and the servant had been asked to leave the windows open so as to let a little air circulate.

Darkness was beginning to descend, and the lamps along the

river were making little dancing lights on the surface of the water.

'John . . .' I faltered.

He took no notice, and continued to place the chess pieces on the board, polishing each one carefully in his large blue silk handkerchief as he did so. 'It's my turn to be white this evening, so it's my first move I believe!' he said triumphantly.

We opened our game and played for some quarter of an hour. But I found it difficult to concentrate.

I could keep my secret no longer. I had to interrupt him there and then. 'John . . . there's something that you ought to know. Something I should have told you long before now.'

'Oh?'

'The fact is that I'm not who I said I was.'

I got no further before he stopped me. 'I already know!' he said softly, his blue eyes twinkling.

'How?'

'The Duchess Margaret told me.'

I was so surprised that I made a bad mistake on the board at that point, and John was able to capture my Queen's Knight. Recovering my composure a little, I came straight to the point:

'Are you still willing to help me?'

'But of course. I hate Welsh Harry as much as the next man. What loyalty do I owe the man? He has raised our taxes and is led astray the whole time by his favourites. I am only too happy to make his reign a mercifully short one!'

I clutched his arm, delighted to hear him confirm his continued support, now that my disguise was an open secret.

Nevertheless, our terrible experience in Waterford had made me doubt the prospect of a successful uprising in my favour in Ireland. It seemed, after all, much safer to attempt a landing in the southwest of England where the people were already disaffected to King Henry for raising taxes for his campaigns in the remote north. My arrival would be well timed: I would be able to offer them hope, and an end to oppression and injustice.

★   ★   ★

A few evenings later, an hour or two before curfew, John gave me his blessing, then helped me and my chest of possessions onto a

73

market wagon that took me to the docks. Here, shortly after midnight, I was smuggled out of the city in a small fishing boat. That night I slept very little. The people of Waterford had already given me a scare - for I had not expected them to remain loyal to Henry - and I was now anxious that I might come up against his fleet at any time.

To my great relief, we escaped down the coast unchallenged, and I was troubled by nothing more than the stench of rotting fish in the bottom of our boat.

As dawn came up the next day we sighted the Old Head of Kinsale, a great rugged rock with white waves crashing about its feet. The fishermen told me that close by was a good safe harbour. Here I would land, recruit an army, and sail to England.

No sooner was I ashore than I was surrounded by the townsfolk of Kinsale, who told me that they had an urgent matter to discuss with me. From the quay I was led up murky winding passages, lined with small fisherman's cottages, the shutters of which were still closed, most people still being in their beds.

Before long we came to a moderate sized inn, and I was taken inside, into the front chamber where a log fire blazed in the hearth. A small band of men sat at a table over in one corner. As I came in, two men rose and came forward to greet me. They spoke in a curious accent that I had never heard before. It certainly was not Irish - for it came from further back in the mouth:

'Your Grace, our master, King James of Scotland has heard that you carry letters from the Holy Roman Emperor and the Duchess of Burgundy, letters which vouchsafe your identity, and pledge their support on your behalf.'

'That's true, but what of it? Was it really necessary to bring me here, to this inn so early in the morning when I need to get some sleep?'

'Sir,' joined in his companion. 'Our King would happily welcome you into Scotland. You will receive there all the honours that are due to you.'

I was not sufficiently awake to think clearly. Besides, the offer put me in a great dilemma, as I had intended to go from here directly to England. I told the messengers that I needed time to consider, and they left me alone to think.

Should I change the plan that my wise counsellor John Taylor had proposed at Malines? It had been strongly approved by my other companions, and would surely have had the approval of the

Duchess herself if she had not been on one of her progresses. Nevertheless, the situation had changed. When I had originally agreed to the plan, I had fully expected the support of the Irish - support which, as it turned out, had not been forthcoming. Could I rely on the people of the south-west of England on their own to rise up in my favour? Of course I could not. The extent of their support was uncertain. On the other hand, going to Scotland would delay me reaching London by perhaps as much as a year. And yet, assuming that everything these heralds said was true, it would bring me the unquestioned support of the Scottish King, and therefore the backing of a powerful army.

What is more, I had heard many great things said about King James, who had already proved his allegiance to me a few weeks before by providing ships to besiege the town of Waterford. Evidently he was an ambitious man, with plans to expand his northern lands. Already on bad terms with King Henry, he must have found attractive any scheme that enabled him to get revenge - and doubtless some land in the north of England by way of reward from me. Perhaps he also believed that I still had support in Ireland, and expected to gain some land there, too. A difficult decision, so many things to weigh up.

After about an hour the messengers from Scotland returned, and I gave them my answer. All things considered, it seemed wisest to accept King James's invitation to go to Scotland. The messengers were unable to conceal their delight; and in spite of the early hour (for it was still only just dawn), the landlord began to serve great tankards of ale, and we made a toast to 'Scotland and King James.' After this I was shown to a room high up in the inn where I slept until after midday.

The next day, three Irish chiefs - Shane Burke, Patrick O'Donnell and Feargus O'Neill - arrived with offers to accompany me through the interior of Ireland, all the way to the point where we should make the short crossing to Scotland. Such is the nature of men that they are so easily tempted by material gain. I knew full well that these men hoped to further their own ambitions every bit as much as my cause; but so be it.

Together we made our way slowly westwards in the persistent rain, through the oak forests and across the bogs of Connaught, at times having to skirt dark lakes of vile and muddy water.

One evening we came to a great river, and the only way to cross it was by a poorly maintained wooden bridge. In the driving rain and half-light we edged our horses forward. The bridge groaned under our weight. O'Neil's horse put his hoof right through a plank. The horse reared up and he was thrown off but survived more or less unscathed.

As the autumn rains beat down ever more furiously, we battled across some of the very poorest farmland I have ever seen, past houses which were no more than huts made of dried mud, without a chimney or even a window.

Every so often, rough tracks led off to remote villages. I imagined I could smell their food, simple tasty stew. The village folk would take us in, share with us all they had. But we rode on, with the rain lashing against our faces all the way up to Donegal in the extreme north-west, where heather and gorse from the moor lands and hedgerows crept into the fields of cattle.

Once we had to stop for a child's funeral, the tiny coffin being carried on a plain wagon; behind, the sad procession, the weeping mother.

Eventually we reached the northernmost coast with its grey rocks, battered by the constant ravages of the sea. It was now almost dusk, the sea stretched into the distance like a dark mass, there was a taste of salt in the air.

We were almost there when we saw directly ahead of us, blocking our way, the silhouette of a figure on a horse. We slackened our pace at once to a trot. As we approached, the figure dismounted, clutching a scrolled document in his right hand.

'Sir, I have ridden all through last night and today, hoping to intercept you before you cross to Scotland.'

Now that I was close, I could see that his horse carried an emblem, the Duchess of Burgundy's own emblem - the chained falcon. The messenger must have come from her court at Malines. Surely there was not another change of plan. Could the Duchess be calling off the whole expedition? His expression was sombre. He primed me to expect bad news:

'It is from your mother, sir.'

'My mother?'

I had assumed that the message must be from the Duchess. My mind started to be filled with memories of my early years in Tournai, such happy times. Hurriedly, I broke the seal and unrolled the despatch. My father was dead.

Chapter 8

What should I do? Here I was, on the brink of crossing to Scotland at the invitation of its king. Should I return to my mother in Tournai, as a dutiful son ought to do? I stared out across the dark mass that was the sea, deep in thought. Shame to say it but I felt no grief, not then, only a little since. I had not been close to my father. So little did I see of him that I felt I scarcely knew him.

The letter certainly said nothing about expecting me back; and my mother did at least have many relatives and friends in the town. So, it was not as though I was leaving her to grieve alone, I told myself.

Besides, if I went back now I would have to give up everything - the prospect of attacking England with the aid of a powerful Scottish army, being crowned King of England, being in a position to restore the Duchess's fortunes. I could not return to Tournai. I *had* to go on to Scotland.

It was a bitterly cold day towards the end of November when we approached Stirling in a wagon that had brought us all the way from the little port of Ayr. This was one of the King's two homes in Scotland - the other being Edinburgh. Surrounding the town, and far into the distance, stretched bleak, rugged hills. Cradled in a valley between these hills lay the town, at the intersection of all the great routes that crossed the country. On an imposing granite rock above the town stood Stirling Castle. As the King resided in Stirling at that time, the town was the capital of Scotland, and this castle was his palace.

The extreme dreariness of the misty day was only penetrated by the weakest of sunlight, shining sickly over the castle's grey ramparts. Although it was now almost midday, thick frost still lined the hedgerow, and underfoot the puddles were covered with layers of ice which crackled under our feet.

As we drew nearer to the castle where I was to meet the King for the first time, young page-boys blew trumpets heralding our coming. Crowds of spectators lined the sturdy arched bridge which spanned the river, awaiting our arrival, jumping up and down on the spot to try and keep warm. As I passed, they greeted me in the same strange language which King James's messengers had spoken on my journey through Ireland. I nodded back solemnly as befitted my position as a prince.

An echo of hooves rang out as we passed under an arch in the outer wall, and I recall seeing a portcullis raised high above our heads. Then we clattered under a larger gateway flanked by turrets, and emerged into an inner court. People thronged the court on all sides; though judging from their fine clothes, they were from a much wealthier class than those who had been on the bridge. At last we came to a halt, and as I stepped down from the wagon, a great cheer went up.

One of the King's ministers, a portly and rather nervous man, bowed before me, then led me into the palace. Our feet resounded on the cold stone floor as I followed him down a wide corridor and into the Great Hall. The hall was full of guests dressed in thick cloaks and gloves, and there were more people up in the galleries. At the far end was a high dais. Here, seated behind a massive oak table, was the King himself. A shimmer of very pale sunlight managed to glance in through two large bay windows behind him, sufficient to make the heavy iron chain around his neck sparkle.

The King rose and came towards me. I got the impression that he was a year or so older than myself, tall and handsome, with long red hair and a ruddy complexion. He addressed me formally and respectfully, just as he would address the greatest of princes no doubt, and thrilled me by referring to me as his 'cousin.' From his confident manner, he was clearly well practised at receiving foreign ambassadors, and I was told that he could speak Latin very well, and could make himself understood in most other European languages, too.

I looked around at the very well dressed ladies and gentlemen (even more numerous than I had at first realised) standing in the galleries which ran all the way around the hall, applauding my arrival. It was just as well that I had been taught fine manners at the Duchess of Burgundy's court, as I should certainly need them to impress the gathering here. But more than this: when I spoke I was able to do so, not as a hesitant and nervous commoner, but with all the confidence and bearing of a prince. 'Your Majesty, I know you will have heard tales of what has befallen the children of my father the late Edward, King of England . . .'

Although my voice was soft, it had caught everyone's attention. The ladies and gentlemen in the galleries leaned forward on their elbows to hear better what I was saying. A promising beginning, I thought.

'As you know, my father appointed his brother Richard, the Duke of Gloucester, to watch over my brother and me, and be our guardian. But our uncle, a cruel man, was seized with ambition to be king, and ordered our executions.'

I could hear exclamations of horror and sympathy, followed by a few words; but (as I have said before) the language here was so different from English that I found it impossible to understand what was being said.

When the commotion had died down, I continued with my story. 'My brother Edward was killed, only twelve yet his life was at an end. For months afterwards I was distressed, I felt that I could not go on. But the man who was given the job of killing me was so affected by my terrible state that he decided to spare me. So, I was able to escape abroad, wandering from place to place - with all the uncertainties and dangers this brought with it.'

There were more exclamations, this time of wonder and surprise. I waited until they had subsided. 'Eventually, I reached my aunt's court at Malines. When she saw me, she was overjoyed to know I was safe. She wanted to help me, but she only had her dowry to support her, so advised me to look to others.'

I paused, as I had now reached a delicate point. In the room there was rapt interest, amazement even. My eyes were drawn upwards to the skilfully crafted timbers of the hammer-beam roof above our heads. I took a deep breath, plucked up my courage and completed what I had to say. I had to please the King, even though it might mean bending the truth a little. 'She advised me to come to you, Your Majesty, as you are well known for your understanding and generosity. If you are able to help me regain my kingdom, I shall be in your debt forever.'

There was silence. How would the King react? His face was solemn and revealed nothing of his inner thoughts. Surely I could expect a favourable response. Why else had he brought me here?

Could it be a trap? Had he made a secret peace with the English King?

After a while, he nodded and smiled, then got up and came forward to embrace me. There was a knowing expression on his face. Somehow, I felt sure he did not really believe who I said I was; but it suited him to appear as though he did. England and Scotland were still bitter enemies, so James was more than willing to give me the assistance I asked for.

A great many courtiers now edged forward and bowed; and their ladies curtseyed before me, as though I were more important even than their own fair prince. Then they presented me with a gift - an emerald green gown made of the finest wool and decorated with a border of white fur. After that, one of the King's poets read a short verse in my honour. Finally, everyone toasted my good health with the finest whisky - a truly remarkable drink that burnt my throat and left a curious sensation in my stomach.

What with the enthusiastic reception I had had that afternoon, and now the effect of the whisky, I felt an unusual lightness in my step as I left the palace and was escorted by a steward to a special lodging prepared for me in the town below. The King had offered me a place at his table for dinner that evening but I was so exhausted by my journey all the way from the southern tip of Ireland that I had to politely decline.

As tired as I was, I found it difficult to sleep that evening, reliving instead that extraordinary day, my first day in Scotland. I could never have dreamed I would be so well received, for I had, in truth, been given nothing short of a state welcome from the King. Furthermore, his pledges of support for me surely meant that my prospects of success were now better than ever before.

*   *   *

Over the next few weeks, in spite of the cold, many splendid tournaments and festivals were staged in my honour. As well as jousting (which I knew well), there was a short display of Highland games - strange activities to my eyes. One game involved the tossing of an enormous tree trunk that the Scots called the caber. The King himself joined in this, and there was great applause; he was obviously a popular man.

One morning, we arose early as James said he had a surprise in store for me. Having breakfasted, we went out onto the ramparts to watch a greatly entertaining attempt at human flight. James had selected an impressionable young lad for the display, and had agreed to pay him in advance. The boy seemed nervous as feathers were attached to his arms to act as wings. He was then hoisted onto a high perimeter wall. There was hushed silence when he was ready to launch himself off, just like a great bird. Off he leapt, and he appeared for a while to rise up.

But shortly after this it became all too clear that the attempt was a dismal failure. So far from soaring to great heights, the lad was dashed down to the hard earth below, incurring terrible injuries as he did so - injuries from which he died in the palace infirmary a few days later. It had presumably been the money that had attracted him, for it seems ridiculous to imagine that man can fly.

★　　★　　★

In recognition of what they believed to be my great status, I was always placed for dinner next to the King, at high table. This was a special table set up on the dais at the far end of the Great Hall for the most important guests. Here, I attempted to grapple with the strangest of food.

The King, like myself, was still unmarried, and some of our conversation at dinner was spent discussing eligible brides. James was most insistent that all kings should get themselves wives at the earliest opportunity, so as to provide strong sons who would ensure the succession of their dynasty. We had known each other for only a matter of days but already he had plans for me:

'I must introduce you to the Earl of Huntly's daughter, young Katherine Gordon. By my troth, I think she would suit you admirably well,' he said, with a broad smile.

I asked my steward to find out more about the Lady Katherine; and the following day he reported back that she was everything the King had said she was - a lovely young girl with long, flowing chestnut hair, hazel eyes and a beautiful milky complexion. That she also had my dear mother's own name, Katherine, warmed me to the idea of her even more, and made me think that this was a sign of our entwined destinies. I asked him when I should be able to see her, and he promised to arrange a meeting very soon.

*   *   *

It quickly became clear from my many conversations with King James that he was an intelligent man with an enquiring mind. He had highly varied interests, the most fascinating of which had to be the turning of lead into gold through the process of alchemy. He showed me a special room in the palace, full of tubes and containers and powders devoted to it. Was this how the King managed to maintain his expensive lifestyle? No wonder the palace was so rich!

A little further along the passageway was a room where he kept bottles of leeches. James was interested in medicine and surgery, and he preferred to use these for blood letting rather than the time-honoured method of letting the blood trickle into bleeding cups.

Noticing the wound in my arm that had been inflicted in the skirmish on the beach at Deal, he offered to apply leeches to drain away what he called the bad blood. Recalling how faint they had made me when the doctor from the deserted village had used them, I shook my head, and attempted to change the subject by pointing to a worn oak chair. As I drew closer I could see that it was stained with blood, both on the headrest and the seat.

'What are these for?' I asked innocently, fingering several clamps and knives lying on a little table beside the chair.

'Oh, I do a wee bit of dentistry. Every week I draw a few teeth.'

'Whose teeth do you draw?'

'Why, those around us here at court, though some come from outside too, from the town. I always offer them a fee, but many volunteer freely.'

I tried to restrain a sudden impulse to feel my own teeth, several of which were loose. Although I did not like the idea of sitting here to have them pulled out, it seemed infinitely preferable to letting the tooth-puller in the street do it.

Besides all these interests over and above his state duties, the King still found time to play football. The game was played in the grounds of the castle, beyond the outermost defences. It caused great excitement, not to mention lost tempers, as a rabble of men tore at each others' clothes as they chased and kicked the ball from one end of the grounds to the other. James would sometimes watch and bellow at his team to do better; but more often than not he would participate himself, and he proved a most energetic and able player.

His agility with the ball was helped by his fitness. In fact, one of the first things I noticed about him was the vast amount of time he spent outside in the bracing air for which this land is known. Apart from his many hunting expeditions, there were his various tours around the Kingdom. He would also delight in physical feats of all kinds, and boasted that he could ride from Stirling to Perth, and then on to Aberdeen and Elgin in twenty-four hours, a remarkable achievement by all accounts if it be true.

*   *   *

One by one, I came to be introduced to all the leading noble families - beginning with the lords and barons of Strathearn and Atholl, and the Earl Marshal and barons of Angus. Before long, it was the turn of the King's own kinsmen, the Earl and Lady Huntly, together with their daughter, Katherine, whom the King so clearly reserved for my bride.

It was late afternoon when I saw her for the very first time. James had asked me to accompany him in his own private apartments. Some of his rooms were still in the process of being built; but two spacious retiring rooms, lit by handsome windows, and reached by a wide spiral staircase at one end were already complete.

The retiring room where we sat was strewn with all kinds of souvenirs that the King had brought back with him from pilgrimages. They included a small flask of sacred blood from Walsingham and a scallop shell from Santiago de Compostela in Spain.

An awkward silence pervaded the room. I cleared my throat. The King smiled nervously. Then, from a tall jug beside him, he poured two glasses of whisky. He passed one to me, but drank his down in one gulp.

Suddenly, footsteps were heard on the stairs. It was the sound of two, possibly three people. Then there was silence again. A valet knocked. The King called for them to enter. I waited, anxiously, for the door to open.

Chapter 9

The gleaming doors of the King's new apartment slowly opened, as if by their own accord, to reveal the Earl of Huntly and his wife. The Earl, dressed in a thick grey winter cloak, was in his late forties, stocky and bearded, his forehead wrinkled, his hair turning grey. Lady Huntly, who followed a step or two behind, was younger by perhaps as much as ten years, slender (almost to the point of being fragile) but very attractive, with a rosy complexion. She was wearing an elegant gown made from dark green velvet, and a long black head-dress, reaching down to her upper arms.

Then, their daughter, a slim young woman, stepped nervously into the room. She was several years younger than I was - maybe no more than sixteen or seventeen years old. I stared at her, transfixed. If anything, my steward had been too modest in describing her loveliness. Her milky white complexion was fairer than that of any girl I had ever seen before or since; and her chestnut hair flowed down her back like a shiny stream of spun silk. Her rose-pink dress was patterned with flowers and leaves, and bordered with intricately embroidered lovers' knots. Around her neck she wore a gold chain to which was attached a small crucifix.

As soon as the doors closed behind them, the King got up, stepped forward and made the introductions. 'Earl and Lady Huntly, Prince Richard.'

The Earl bowed; his wife curtseyed. When the Earl spoke, his accent was broad, his voice seemed to come from the back of his throat. 'We are very pleased to meet you.'

Then he stood aside.

'And their daughter, Katherine,' continued the King, as if his introduction had been unbroken.

Katherine stepped forward hesitantly, and made a well-practised curtsey. Her wide hazel eyes shone up at me as she repeated her

84

father's words. 'I'm very pleased to meet you, Prince Richard.' What a gem she was, so innocent and pure.

That evening we were placed next to one another at dinner. From time to time we caught each other's eye; but the conversations around us were so noisy that when we tried to speak we could not make ourselves heard. Both of us found this very amusing, and started to laugh. She had a wonderful laugh, a light playful giggle that sent a tingle of happiness down my spine.

After dinner I invited her to dance. Now was my opportunity to speak to her alone. I had expected the musicians on the balcony above us to play something slow and elegant, as I had heard in the courts of Paris and Burgundy. Instead we danced a reel - fast and energetic, making squares and circles with the other couples, until, by the end we were both completely exhausted. But the vigour and pace of the dance had melted our reservations, and brought us together, so that we began to talk more freely.

*　　*　　*

In those first few weeks after we met, we spent every afternoon at Stirling together. How quickly the hours passed as we got to know one another better. Whenever the weather permitted, while the King was out riding or playing football, we would leave the confines of the palace to stroll in the charming knot garden that adjoined the Great Hall. Although it was now winter, Katherine still managed to describe to me the flowers and their different hues so vividly that I could imagine I was there on a gloriously warm day in June. At the far end of the garden we would stop and gaze together out over to the west, watching the sun set behind hills cloaked in mist.

On cold or wet days we would stay inside, and walk up and down the Long Gallery, deep in conversation, her arm gently resting on mine. We would talk about anything and everything - what we liked to do, the food we enjoyed, the weather, anything - it really did not matter.

There were many tapestries, statues and paintings in the gallery; but so enchanted was I with her that I scarcely noticed them. I felt a warm glow burning within me as she clutched my arm and pressed her head towards me, as if to share my most intimate thoughts; and her hair felt so soft and smooth against my cheek and the roughness of my chin.

She was as eager to hear about my life as I was to hear about hers; and what were to me the most ordinary little things about myself, seemed a source of endless fascination for her. I told her how happy I was when we were together, how beautiful I found her.

About this time, my steward suggested I write to her, as a declaration of my love. I had done nothing of this kind before. As I read back the little poem I had written, I wondered whether I was saying the right thing, as my words seemed so stilted and awkward:

> *My love, the brightest ornament in Scotland.*
> *Your beauty is so divine*
> *That some believe you were not born here at all,*
> *But descended from Heaven.*
> *You are so beautiful.*
> *Your eyes, your neck, your forehead.*
> *Whether waking or sleeping*
> *I cannot find rest or happiness*
> *Except in your affection.*
> *All my hopes rest in you, and you alone.*

Everyone in the palace now saw her more and more often. They stopped referring to her as the Lady Katherine, and began to call her 'The White Rose,' so impressed were they by her fair looks. The name was doubly appropriate, of course, the white rose being the symbol of my own cause - the House of York. But I was soon calling her Kate, just as her father did.

In the first few weeks of our courtship we were always together. From the very moment I got up, I could not wait to see her, to catch sight of her radiant smile, her temptingly protruding lips that I dreamed to kiss.

Sometimes we would go into the forests, hunting hare and deer with the King. He would ride before us, his tall and muscular frame cutting an impressive figure. It was my first experience of hunting, and I found it at once exhilarating and terrifying. The horses travelled at such speed, and the ground was so unpredictable and uneven, that many an experienced rider was thrown from their saddle, one poor man a spear's throw behind us dying from his injuries, and the King himself badly hurting his leg. Thank God that Kate and I were preserved unscathed.

When it was not too cold, we would go fishing for salmon in nearby rivers and lakes. What a contrast this pastime was to the rapid pace of the hunt; but how I loved the peace and stillness, sitting at the water's edge, just Kate and I - my followers having to make their own diversions so that our conversation might not be overheard.

Now completely on our own, and far from prying eyes in the palace, I had plenty of opportunities to get to know Kate better. I complimented her again on her good looks and lovely complexion. She blushed. 'I've not always been healthy,' she said, her words ringing out softly on her breath.

'Oh?' I replied, concerned.

'No, when I was little I used to be very sickly. At eight years old I was stricken with the smallpox and almost died. I was in bed for many months.'

Instinctively, I reached out and wrapped my right arm around her slender waist. But she made light of the ordeal.

'Oh, I spent the time reading. I was lucky. We had some of the new printed books in our library. I started reading tales of chivalry, and still like them now - when I am not busy with my embroidery, or playing the lute.'

'Did your parents teach you to read? It's a very rare thing for a girl to be able to read.'

'No, a tutor came to the house. He taught me to write as well as read. My father also made him show me how to behave, as *the daughter of a nobleman* should.'

Then she gave one of her little laughs that I liked so much.

But I had started to go off into a dream of my own. 'Nobleman, the daughter of a nobleman,' I mouthed, remembering the conversation I had had with my grandfather when I was little. His words echoed back at me: 'It's up to you my lad if the de Faros are ever to become great again.'

'Richard! Richard! Are you all right?'

I was still so unused to the name that at first I did not respond at all. There was a pause while I grasped for an excuse. 'I'm sorry,' I replied finally. 'I was imagining what you must have been like when you were little.'

★   ★   ★

One mild day as we sat together on the banks of a loch, I started to tell Kate much more about my own great adventures before arriving in Scotland - my visits to Paris, Vienna and Ireland - and she seemed enthralled by what she heard.

'I already know a lot about you,' she said softly in my ear.

I was intrigued. 'How is that?'

'Why, I got Jane to find out as much as she could.'

'Jane? Who's Jane?' I asked.

'My maid,' she smiled.

I visualised the middle-aged woman who had accompanied her that morning, pleasant enough, though somewhat staid.

'She said some lovely things about you.'

'Oh?' I replied, embarrassed.

'Yes, she said that you are very kind, intelligent, ambitious.' She smiled again and added 'no more than what is true, of course.'

Hearing this, the first sign of any feelings she might have for me, I drew her slowly and instinctively to me and kissed her for the very first time - to begin with on the forehead, a light brotherly kiss, then on the mouth. I drew her out from me, so that she was at arm's length, and gazed across into her cool, hazel eyes. Then I drew her in again, and kissed her once more. Three times or more I did this. I told her that I loved her, and that if she only returned my affections and agreed to become my wife I would adore her for ever more, and would share with her the glory that I hoped to achieve in my life.

I tried to tell her that cares and worries about my business in Scotland had made me anxious, and hoped that I appeared loving enough towards her. Blushing, she said that I must not worry myself on that account, that she found me very kind and sensitive; and quite apart from it being the wish of her cousin the King that we be wed, she would be very happy to marry me from her own choice.

Of course, my mother, like all mothers, had hoped that one day I would court a local girl, a daughter of one of the Tournai tradesmen, and that we should be married and settle down; and, despite my grandfather's fantasies, in my heart I had expected to do exactly that. Never could I have possibly envisaged that the King of Scotland, of all people, would arrange a marriage for me into a noble family, his own family.

So, you can imagine how disappointed I was when, some days later, my steward told me that Kate's father had serious misgivings about our match. 'Sir, the Earl feels that your interests and backgrounds are so different from those of his daughter. He doesn't believe that your marriage can be a happy one. That it is some wild notion of the King's.'

I was furious. 'Interests! Backgrounds! Wild notion! What the hell does he mean?'

He scratched his chin nervously. I noticed that his face was horribly pock marked.

'More than that, sir.'

'There's more?'

'I fear so, sir. The Lady Katherine is already spoken for. The Earl has another suitor in mind for his daughter.'

'Another suitor? Who is he?'

'Lord Dalyell.'

'Never heard of him! What do you know about him?'

'Very little. He's meant to come from a good family, though. And he's a distant relative of the King, I believe.'

I screwed up my face and with a dismissive wave replied 'Oh, isn't everybody!'

For a moment I felt that this was the end, that the Earl would simply block my marriage with his daughter. However, his loyalty to the King (or was it his fear of him?) was such that, at last, he came to agree to it. Admittedly, it meant that his daughter would not, after all, have the secure and certain future that he had planned for her in the home of a great Scottish noble family. Instead, she seemed destined to become the future Queen of England.

Chapter 10

Throughout the twilight days of December and January, as the old year passed away, and a new year, 1496, was born, all the preparations were completed for our wedding. At first it had been uncertain whether we should be married in Edinburgh or Stirling, but at length Stirling was settled on, as it fitted the King's busy itinerary better. The ceremony would be performed in the Chapel Royal at Stirling Castle, two days after the King had returned from a visit to Edinburgh.

As the first few light snowflakes of winter fell, every messenger at court was employed in despatching wedding invitations to all the leading noble families. A score of extra seamstresses was brought in from the city to take frantic measurements for the wedding gowns. Cloth merchants carried in bright new tapestries for the state bedrooms, and woven carpets to put over the rushes on the floor. Meanwhile, a corps of caterers and vintners plied their way up to the castle from their little shops, to take orders for the wedding banquet which was to be the largest Stirling had witnessed for many years past.

*   *   *

Almost as soon as Christmas was over and the festivities had ended, a great many leading nobles, clergymen and prosperous merchants began to crowd into Stirling; all the inns were full, and the streets bustled with life. Some well-wishers, who were not fit enough to attend in person, commissioned others to go in their place. They had been instructed to bring them back detailed descriptions about what had gone on - the costumes everyone was wearing, the dishes that were served, how the company had been entertained after the meal.

As our wedding day drew closer, my dreams were full of our

future life together as King and Queen of England. I thought back also to our courting days, sitting in peace side by side on the banks of a loch, shielded all around by soaring mountains; our afternoon walks together in the palace gardens, watching the sun set behind the distant hills.

I had tried hard to show my best side, to impress Kate with all the things I had done, my plans for the future. After all, I had had an intriguing life up until then, and my prospects were excellent. She listened so attentively; and when she told me she was proud to call me hers, I was thrilled.

Yet, I was still tormented with doubts. What would happen after our marriage, as she got to know me better, to know my weaknesses as well as my strengths? Would she become disappointed in me, think me ignorant and uneducated? Would her love for me last?

*　　*　　*

Eventually, the day of our wedding arrived - 13 January 1496, which is St Mungo's Day. From first light, the guests started to arrive at the castle - not just noblemen and gentlemen, but people from all ranks of society. Soon, the castle grounds were full of retainers, some travelling hundreds of miles down to Stirling from the Highlands so as to take part in the feasting and jousting.

Kate's father (now won over to the marriage) agreed to provide a generous dowry. When this was added to the allowance the King had already granted me, I worked out that it was about adequate for my needs at that moment, to maintain Kate and me in the style of a prince and princess. For my part, I promised my wife that when I was crowned King of England she should receive one third of all my worldly goods.

By noon the King's party had arrived, dressed in splendid robes of purple and green, trimmed with ermine and decorated with golden belts and buttons. Many of the leading gentlemen, who they called lairds, were dressed in scarlet; and their ladies in cloth of gold, embroidered and trimmed with gold and silver lace. At a distance stood poorer people, with little better (so it appeared) than rags to keep out the bitter chill of the day.

When it was time, my young bride and I made our way slowly towards the chapel. We came from different directions, as convention did not allow us to meet until we reached the heavy studded door.

As a mark of respect to the people of Scotland, I wore the special emerald green gown that I had been presented with at court on the day of my arrival. Kate wore her hair long and loose as a sign of her maidenhood, and on her head she wore a garland of delicate wild flowers. She was dressed in a gorgeous high-waisted, wide-sleeved gown made from blue velvet, with trimmings of fur. A sparkling gold brooch with the Virgin Mary at the centre hung on a pendant from around her slender white neck.

Outside the chapel door we made our vows to one another. As the chaplain to the royal household joined our hands together, I gazed across at Kate. She looked lovelier than ever. Then I handed her a gold ring and a gift of gold coins wrapped in white linen. Any moment now we would be betrothed: I was indeed a very fortunate man. A marriage such as this to a nobleman's daughter - the King's own kin - would surely make me more worthy of support from the princes of Europe. Our union would also, God willing, provide me with a healthy male heir - so important to any king.

Then, side by side, we walked into the chapel for the wedding mass. Everywhere was decked in scarlet and gold. Big bunches of mistletoe and holly had been placed all around, their bright berries shining out like lamps in the half-light. If only my mother and my grandfather could see me now. My mother would surely have to take back her critical comments about her over-ambitious son.

When the short ceremony was over we knelt, and the priest stretched cloth of gold over us both. From this moment we were betrothed: I had been married into one of the country's leading families, and had the blessing of the Scottish King in doing so. It was more, much more, than I could ever have dreamed of.

Now man and wife, we climbed into a well-upholstered wagon, and led a procession of noblemen and their ladies all through the town and then back to the castle again. The streets were lined with expectant citizens, all jostling for a good view of us. Poor people at the back surged forward, pressing against each other, trying to see what was going on. Those who briefly caught sight of Kate as we swept past were thrilled, and sighed: she looked so beautiful in her blue velvet dress.

At one point, as was the custom in these parts, a poor young woman came out of the doorway of an inn and placed her child in my bride's arms, just for a few moments. This would bring her many strong sons, she said.

Then the woman produced a small coin. Kate, who was clearly familiar with this custom, happily took off her shoe, and the woman placed the coin inside it. 'Twill bring you riches,' she told her.

My wife smiled. I wondered what riches meant for her. A secluded castle in the Highlands, packed with servants and cooks? Or much, much greater things, the stuff of dreams?

It was already growing dark when we returned to the palace, and time for the banqueting to begin. As we entered the Great Hall, I looked up to find that the roof had been draped from beam to beam in blue murrey. Cooks bustled in and out, carrying silver dishes of fresh salmon and trout that they set out with studied precision on long buffet tables. Then, two kitchen boys carried in a great boar's head on a huge silver platter, and soon a rich assortment of roast meats and fowl lay alongside it - venison, pork, lamb, chicken and pheasant. Underneath the tables, dogs were already roaming freely, hoping that one of the guests would throw them a juicy bone.

On the platform at the far end of the hall, the sturdy oak table that we were used to dining on had been decked in purple, black and gold, and the dishes were made not just from silver but from gold, too. Kate and I were placed to the right of the King, and Lord and Lady Huntly seated to the left. As we ate and drank in the flickering shadows of the hall, we were soothed by the gentle lull of minstrels singing ballads on the gallery above. A dwarf, clowns and jesters moved clumsily in between the tables, performing tricks, while dogs sniffed our boots below.

After several hours of merriment, many of the guests were becoming very drunk and the conversation, even of the leading lairds, was getting extremely bawdy.

As the evening wore on and the revelry became louder and louder, the priest who had married us, and my bride's female attendants, stood and came forward to lead her away to the marriage bed. Slowly, she rose from her seat, clutching the table to steady herself. As she did so, the other guests turned round to look at her. I wondered whether she, too, had perhaps drunk too much. The noise died down. I noticed how a few of the drunken young men nearest me were nudging each other and muttering a few words behind their hands. Several began to chuckle with laughter, some of the bolder ones teased Kate by calling something out. I did not catch what they said, but I suspect that it was rude because she blushed.

Eventually Kate rose from her seat and curtseyed first to the King, then to her parents. Lady Huntly brushed away a tear from her eye, no doubt at the thought of her daughter leaving her family home and going to her bridal chamber. I stretched out and lightly touched Kate's hand to reassure her before she left. Little tremors began to run through my body.

She walked hesitantly towards the door, pausing several times; and as she did so the minstrels tuned up again in the gallery above. Her attendants (all married women themselves) gave her words of encouragement, though the priest, torch in hand, remained silent and solemn. His task, after all, was an important one: he was needed to bless our bed, so that our union might prosper and we have good healthy sons. My bride disappeared through the door: it was the last I should see of her before we were one.

As soon as they were gone the festivities got wilder and more drunken. People started to glance at me. When was I going to join her? There was more muttering behind wine-cups, ribald laughter. I tried to make polite conversation but my mind was only on my lovely bride and the night before us.

At last, after what seemed an eternity of waiting, I was summoned to join her. A few of my bolder guests insisted that they escort me to the door of the bridal chamber. This was surely not normal routine but I did not want to spoil their fun. One of them, who had had far too much to drink, tripped on a stair and spilt wine all down the front of my gown, letting out a great guffaw of laughter as he did so. I tried mopping it up with my sleeve but it made no difference and left a nasty red stain. I asked them to leave but they said they wanted to see me go through the bedroom door first.

When I hesitated, one of them dared to bang on the door. 'Ready in there?' Another whoop of laughter from all three of them. By now really annoyed, I pushed him aside and straightened my gown. Here I stood, on the threshold of my new life with Kate.

Slowly I turned the handle and went in. The delicate scent of roses greeted me, a bowl of rose petals in water having been placed by the door. My bride was already sitting on the edge of the bed near where the bolsters were piled. Her long white night-gown gleamed in the candlelight, its soft folds clinging to her shapely body. As we looked into each others' eyes from across the room, I dreamed of the night ahead, and prayed I would be everything to her - tender, loving, passionate. Would she be the same?

She averted her gaze as I undressed clumsily and put on the robe that had been set out for me at the foot of the bed. Then I went across and sat down gently beside her. Her face was near to mine. As I began to stroke her long, streaming hair she smiled.

'How lovely you are,' I whispered.

She came towards me, soft and yielding. Her long fingers caressed my back, and a warm glow spread throughout my body as I clutched her tightly in my arms. My hand trembled when I touched her cheek, and a quiver shot down my spine, making my whole body tingle with excitement.

Her lips parted, just for me, and I tasted the softness of her mouth again and again. Moments later, enveloped in each other's arms, we were rolling over impulsively into the bed. There had been no time to close the drapes around us. Nervously, I pulled up the sheets over us, and our bodies melted into one another.

Chapter 11

The days passed too quickly. Winter receded and spring came. Kate and I grew ever closer, both in body and mind. Yet I knew I would soon have to leave Stirling on my campaign to England. How could I bear to be parted from her, now that she had come to mean so much to me?

Every night we held each other, reliving our love; but there was already a dark cloud on the horizon. Some of the Scottish lords were warning that King Henry was deeply unhappy with our marriage, that his advisers were urging him to kidnap me and bring me to London.

One morning, King James summoned me to the Great Hall. There had been a feast the night before, and the hall stank of sweat, smoke and damp wool. As I entered, I was forced to step over a small puddle of congealed vomit in the rushes.

James was seated as usual at the long oak table on the dais, working on some indentures. I stood before him while he dipped his quill into the ink to sign one final set with a great flourish. Then, as he applied his seal, he looked up. His expression was serious, and when he spoke the tone of his voice was grave. 'King Henry has offered me his daughter the Princess Margaret as my bride.' He paused, then looked straight at me. 'On the condition that I give you up.'

I was astonished, speechless. But worse was to follow:

'And King Charles of France has promised me 100,000 crowns.'

I thought back to my days in Paris - to the French king, his bulging eyes, his great hooked nose, spindly legs. Why had I put so much trust in that man? I began to despair.

But James had been teasing me. Seeing my look of horror, he put a friendly hand on my shoulder and chortled heartily. 'Don't worry. I've no intention of giving you up, old fellow.'

I drew a great sigh of relief. Then I looked up, right up towards the soot-blackened rafters, and said a little prayer to God in thanks.

'Fear not, Richard. I'm not one to break a promise. We shall be going ahead with our plans.'

But I was still not fully convinced. 'Your Majesty. Forgive me for asking, but our expedition is going to be expensive. And I've no money of my own. That's why I came to you in the first place.'

The King's quick answer went some way to reassure me. 'This should not present any difficulty. I'll raise a tax on spears right away.'

'Your Majesty, won't that take months to collect?'

'No, my men will go out at first light tomorrow and begin.'

There was a pause. I looked up, straight into the King's eyes. 'What do you ask of me in return?'

The King smiled. 'All I ask from you is that when you become King of England you give me the town of Berwick-upon-Tweed. The town lies on the border between England and Scotland, and is really mine in any case.'

'Berwick-upon-Tweed,' I repeated the words, entranced. The place meant nothing at all to me but it had a fascinating sound to it, made more interesting by the sheer length of the name.

'Oh, and 50,000 marks. But you can have two years to pay me that,' he added, as he rolled and tied the documents.

*　　*　　*

During the following weeks, my young bride and her maidservant, Jane, begged me to let them accompany us to war. I understood their concerns, but the suggestion really could not be entertained, and I stayed firm.

'Kate, I'm going off to fight. It's a war, not a tournament.'

'I know that, my lord, but spare a thought for me. We've been married for so little time. To be separated so soon is such a cruel blow.'

She stared up at me with her appealing hazel eyes, imploring me to change my mind; but I begged her to see reason. 'I know we've had little time together, but a battle is no place for a woman.'

She raised her eyebrows at this.

'And besides, it won't be a long campaign. As soon as we've won over the northern earls, I'll return to fetch you. You'll come with me to London as my queen.'

Kate did not reply. Tears shone in her eyes as she turned away abruptly and left the room, her head tossed high in the air. I had never seen her like this before - behaving not like a grown up woman but a little girl who had failed to get her way - and I prayed I would never see her like it again.

The day before we were due to leave, the Spanish ambassador arrived - an inconvenient time to see a visitor from abroad if ever there was one. But so eager was he to talk to us that instead of waiting until we returned, he said he was happy to follow us into battle. Why had he come? He said his King and Queen were interested in supporting me. But was this the truth? Would he influence King James against me?

We had mustered over 1,400 men, all outlaws and mercenaries from foreign parts. To these, King James added all the forces he could from his native land. The royal armourer in Edinburgh despatched a supply of arrows to Stirling; and new doublets, gowns and thick winter hose were made. I was assigned a strong brown war-horse, and provided with a standard and a special banner of red and blue taffeta. How delighted I was to see my own coat of arms emblazoned on both.

It was now the very night before we left. Alone in our bedroom, Kate told me that she thought she was with child. I held her in my arms, showering kisses on her, saying how overjoyed I was to hear such wonderful news. I told her how Jane would be able to look after her during the next month or two, and how I would return long before the confinement.

She was not convinced. 'My lord, I know it's only a few hours before you leave, but won't you let me come with you?'

'Kate!' I said, stroking her hand and doing my best to soothe her. 'We've gone through all this before. I've told you. A battle is no place for a woman - least of all a woman with child.'

She wept on my shoulder. 'But my lord, I fear I may never see you again! I would rather die with you than live without you.'

'We must think of the child,' I persisted. 'You are in no state to travel.'

'But if I stay, if I am left here alone, worrying over your safety, I'll lose our child.'

'Kate, if you come with me my mind will never be at ease. You must stay. You have our child to live for as well as me.'

At last she appeared to calm down, she saw that I had made up my mind. But still she was determined to have the final say. 'Promise me that you'll take care and return quickly. Send me messages to let me know that you are well.'

'Of course I shall, Kate. Of course I shall.'

*   *   *

Early the following morning I tore myself away from her clinging arms. She pressed a lock of her lovely hair into my palm. 'Carry it with you always!' she sobbed.

I kissed her tenderly and walked slowly away to where my warhorse stood tethered to a post, not daring to look back in case my resolve weakened.

In the depths of winter, and armed with only crossbows, pikes and spears, I set off, riding side by side with King James at the head of our combined army of a little less than two thousand men. Banners fluttered in the chill breeze and drummers beat out a marching step. We headed off towards Berwick, where we hoped to storm the castle on Sunday when the lieutenant was at church. The baggage trains trundled along the muddy roads behind us, heavily laden with our weapons, tents and food.

At the head of our army rode a herald carrying a trumpet, ready to proclaim my true identity as King Richard the Fourth, and to call upon every Englishmen to take up arms to defend my cause, the true cause, their cause. They were promised handsome rewards for their troubles: even the humblest man would receive £1,000, and land for him and his heirs forever.

Darkness was descending as we pitched our tents close to the northern bank of the River Tweed. There was an icy chill in the air - it felt as though it was going to snow. The wind was rising, tugging at the tent folds. We lit fires, and soon the smoke blowing about, and the dark and the shadows began to play tricks with our eyes.

We slept as best we could but by now the wind was becoming stronger still, lashing and whipping at our tents all the while, until some of the posts began to sway.

At last the sky began to grow lighter again in the east, and we took up our tents and loaded them with our other possessions onto the baggage trains. The first real chinks of light now began to be seen above the horizon; but the sky remained unusually dark.

We advanced slowly towards the river, the one obstacle that lay between us and England. However, before we reached its banks it started to snow - just a few powdery flakes at first, then, after a while, more steadily so that our boots were soon crunching into a thick white blanket.

As we continued to edge forward down the bank of the river, it began to snow harder than ever, making it difficult to see what was going on even a stone's throw ahead of us.

Several men lost their footing, a few fell from their horses and (I am sorry to say it) were swept away. But (with God's blessing) the rest of us were successful, and reached the border with England, my England.

Snow was still falling, though now less heavily than before. Shielding our eyes from the dazzling white mass, we peered out at the countryside all around, but strangely enough it seemed that the English had made no preparations to oppose us. So I ordered two of my men to go on ahead into the town of Berwick, to find out what was happening.

★   ★   ★

Soon after dawn the next day they returned, excitedly. 'King Henry is having the utmost difficulty collecting his tax,' one chuckled. 'And those men who are paying up do so resentfully. It will be many a long month before he has levied sufficient to pay for an army.'

'But before long he *will* have an army then.'

'Well, maybe, sir.'

This teasing was more than I could take. I could put up with it from the King; but coming from one of my own men, it was damned cheek.

'Speak plainly. What do you mean?'

'Well, his people down in Cornwall - a remote western county - are refusing point blank to pay up.'

'Indeed!' I was unable to suppress a smile. The news was consistent with everything that John Taylor's mate had told me about the wayward Cornishmen, and served to greatly boost my spirits.

'Yes, they say they're damned if they'll pay to protect the Scottish border when it's so far away from them. And they're thinking of marching on London to tell the King exactly what they think of his Godforsaken taxes.'

Our army continued to march south unopposed, fording streams and descending into tree-lined valleys. We got about four miles over the border and captured a couple of watchtowers. I am convinced that we would have managed more if it had not been for lack of support from the English. It pains me to admit it but not a single Englishman in these parts rallied to my cause, not one sword was unsheathed in my defence. I could not believe the response would be so poor. I was staggered. If the English up here in the north did not rally to me, what hope of success had I?

To make matters worse, King James started to behave very oddly: he began to seem tired and disinterested, his expression glazed. To pass the time he began to gamble and drink late into the night (one night he lost £70); then he would stay in bed until late next morning. It was a poor example to set the men who were themselves now becoming lethargic, and we were travelling a shorter and shorter distance each day.

Though I did not relish the prospect, I decided that I had to confront the King, and I arranged to see him the very next day.

★   ★   ★

I was awake next morning even before the first pale glimmer of light. After breakfast I went to the King's tent. But he had completely forgotten that I was coming, and was sprawled out on the ground, sipping whisky from a silver bowl. Beside him was a small leather-bound book, open and face down.

As he seemed to be unaware that I was there, I decided to break the silence: 'Your Majesty, is there something wrong? Have I done something to offend you?'

There was no reply.

'I feel that your attitude has changed,' I continued.

The King prevaricated: 'Oh, I have much on my mind, that is all.'

He picked up his little book and thumbed through it, until he found the page he was looking for. He stared at it and frowned.

I went on, the tone of my voice becoming more urgent. 'Your Majesty. We must take advantage of the fact that King Henry is finding it difficult to raise an army against us. We must press on. Look, suppose . . .'

But he cut me short in mid flow. He put his whisky bowl down beside him and belched quietly. 'I fear you must continue alone.'

His words were cold, and I was shocked into silence. I could not believe what I had heard, and neither of us spoke for a good while after this.

As he began to realise what an awesome effect his words had had on me, King James tried to soften the blow. 'Rest assured that you still have my support. I wish you well. But I must return to Scotland at once. I have matters to attend to which cannot wait.'

He held up the book. I saw that it was an astrological calendar. 'These next days are not good ones for me. But I wish *you* well.'

His best wishes were of precious little use to me: I needed the support of his army!

There was another long pause. I was dumbfounded, my mouth dry. At last I managed to put a few words together. 'But Your Majesty. Without your support, I've no hope of success.'

'Not so! I am in your way. You do not need me. You have made a good start in England. Take courage!'

I said no more. It was the King who had the last word, and once more it was to soften the blow. 'If ever you need help, send me a message. I promise I shall help you - always.'

It was clear from the slow, deliberate way in which he said those last few words that he had finished all he had to say, and that I was now expected to leave.

Trying to disguise my deep disappointment, I bowed before him, kissed his hand and thanked him. Then, just as I turned to go, a thought struck me. The King was returning to Scotland, that was a blow, and I could do nothing about it - matters of state must come first. But at least I might salvage something from the situation. 'Please give a message to my dear wife at least. Tell her I am well and that I shall soon be back with her.'

The King did not answer.

Crushed with despair, and with an icy heart, full of resentment, I bade farewell.

Shortly afterwards, James returned to Scotland. The Spanish ambassador went with him, which only confirmed my suspicions all along that his visit was merely to poison the King's ear against me.

When I heard later that the King had not returned to Scotland for business reasons at all, but had ridden on to Perthshire to go hawking, I felt still more cheated, full of melancholy. All I could think was that he must have become bored not just with me, but with the whole English campaign.

Despondent by their performance in battle, and without their leader, the Scottish soldiers began looting and pillaging the country all around. Sadly, I was unable to stop them, as they refused to take orders from me. They broke into houses, cursing and swearing, searching in every corner for money, terrifying the poor women to hand over their purses, threatening to rape them.

'How dare you wantonly destroy my country!' I yelled at them. 'These people have put up no resistance against us. They don't deserve to be treated like that!'

The men's expressions were surly, they would not look me in the face. I thought I heard someone mutter 'coward' under his breath but could not be sure.

'Did you hear what I said?'

One of them farted loudly. His mates fell about laughing, they knew I must have heard. Another spat on the ground, inches from where I stood. I was furious. There was nothing I could do with this rabble. But I vowed they would pay for their misdeeds later. In the meantime, I would have to follow King James back to Scotland.

* * *

A few weeks later, weary and despondent, we arrived back at Stirling. Unlike on my wedding day, there was no one in the streets to welcome me this time. On we rode, up towards the castle.

But before I had a chance to dismount, a servant rushed out to greet me: 'News, sir, news!'

I sensed a sharp pain in my chest. I clutched the servant. 'What is it?' I stammered. 'Has something happened to my wife? Is she all right?'

'A child, a child!' he shouted, pointing towards the castle.

After my long ride north I was tired, and slow to make sense of what I was being told.

'What about a child?'

'Your son, your son!'

'A son!' I looked up and recited a prayer in gratitude. But my thoughts turned quickly again to Kate. My wife, was she all right?

Leaving a groom to tether my horse, I pushed the servant aside and hastened inside towards her room.

The voices of several people could be heard from within. Opening the door, I quickly took in who they all were in one sweeping glance: the maid-servant Jane, a maid and an elderly woman who I assumed to be the midwife. And there was Kate, seated in a high-backed chair with our baby in her arms.

I flung down my cloak and knelt by her side, grasping her hand in mine.

'How are you my love?'

Kate's face glowed as she beamed up at me. 'I'm glad you are back,' she said. 'Just look!'

A great wave of happiness washed through my body as she passed our baby to me, all swathed in beautiful white silk. I held out my arms and very slowly drew in the warm little bundle to my chest. And there, cradled in my arms, I began to rock him gently to and fro. Large hazel eyes stared up at me, not knowing what to make of me. His cheeks were rosy and he looked in every respect a healthy little boy. I was so very, very happy. My face felt flushed with colour as I gazed around the room, from my wife to the faces of the maid, the midwife, Jane, then that of my own dear wife again.

After a while, I pulled back my baby's little woollen shawl, just very slightly, and kissed his forehead ever so delicately, just as my own wife had kissed me for the very first time on the bank of a loch when we were courting. Then I gave him my little finger to suck on. He burped and I patted him on the back; but when he began to cry, I thought I had better return him to his mother.

To think, that we had been blessed with a baby boy. We called him Richard. He would inherit my title and become King Richard V of England. Apparently it had been a difficult birth, but both my wife and child were now well, spared by the generous hand of almighty God. It was indeed a providential sign.

*   *   *

It was now July and my wife was pregnant with child again.

One morning I was called to the King's new apartments. A brilliant ray of sunlight poured in through the oriel window behind him, bathing the interior of the room and making the polished oak gleam.

The King came across to me, and taking me by the arm, just like an old friend would, led me over to the far corner. His face was almost as grave as the day I had visited his tent when we were camped outside Berwick. The news was going to be bad. Resting a hand on my shoulder, he began. His tone was hushed and solemn:

'My friend, I have done all I can to restore you to the English throne. Sadly, you did not find among the English the friendship and support you had expected. I must be honest with you. Over the last few months I have been seeking terms with the English, and I am now on the verge of coming to a settlement. Naturally, if King Henry came to hear that I was harbouring one of his enemies here at court, it would put my negotiations with him in grave jeopardy.'

He paused. Even kings need to summon up courage at times. 'It is against my wishes, but we must part company, Richard. You must leave Scotland, my friend, and try your fortunes elsewhere.'

And so, reluctantly, James dismissed my wife and me from court.

At first I considered going to Spain, where I had great faith in the King and Queen. But my advisers were quick to confirm my worst fears - that the Spanish ambassador's mission had indeed been to urge King James to abandon me.

My only hope, therefore, was to see what support I could muster for my cause in the rebellious south-west of England.

Chapter 12

Although Kate had never supported my project with anything remotely like enthusiasm, she had until then at least given me a lot of moral support - even wanting to accompany me on my winter campaign into England. Now, however, her true feelings about my ambitions began to surface.

We had retired to our comfortable chamber one night, it was late, almost midnight, and I was looking forward to getting some rest. I was really too tired to argue.

'It is a mad scheme,' she declared, as she sat in front of the mirror brushing her hair. 'What makes you think men in Cornwall are going to help you any more than those in the north who so badly betrayed you last winter?'

'I've got every reason to think they'll support me. Don't you remember, I told you how angry they are about having to pay taxes for Henry's Scottish war.'

'But what in heaven's name can you offer them for their support?'

'I'll see that they get their reward, and that their country is restored to the House of York.'

Kate frowned. She was not convinced. 'Do you really think they will be willing to wait for their reward? Won't they want something from you straight away?'

'They'll be rewarded soon enough. When we reach London, when we are crowned King and Queen.'

'My lord, can't we wait until I am safely delivered of my child?'

'Kate, I understand your fears and concerns but we must go now, while the resentment of the Cornishmen is at its height. If we delay we shall lose their support. I'll make sure you are given every comfort and attention on our journey.'

Kate turned angrily towards me. 'You're thinking only of yourself. Don't you care about our child?'

I tried to reassure her, and put my arm around her. But she shrugged it off. 'It is too risky! Let us wait.'

'If I believed it was too risky, I would not do this. You are in good health. There is no time like the present.'

At length, my wife gave in; but we had quarrelled again, and it left me sad. Would our love survive?

The arguments brought back to mind the warnings of Rosita. Was it all those years ago when I held Rosita in my arms? So different was she from my own fair skinned wife. Although I had known her for such a brief time, I had loved her as I love Kate now. How curious it is that the only two women I have loved felt the same way about my plans, thought I was mad.

*   *   *

We set off from Stirling on a beautiful June morning - Kate, my young son Richard and myself, accompanied by our maid-servant Jane and our advisers. The sun was rising over the hills, the air was still and there was not a cloud in the sky.

Gradually we made the journey through Glasgow and Kilmarnock, to Ayr on the west coast of Scotland. I rode on horseback, in front of the wagon that carried my wife and son.

Every few hours we stopped at an inn for refreshment and a change of horses. One of my advisers went on ahead to tell people we were coming, so that when we entered each village there was a hearty welcome awaiting us. I can remember how in one place, the country folk came out of their cottages with little gifts of cheese and whisky in earthenware jars.

We passed many small stone churches on our way, and stopped at one which had a particularly attractive little bell-tower. The driver helped Kate down from the wagon. She was followed by Jane who clutched baby Richard in a blanket.

I remained outside. I do not like churches: the statues, inscriptions, stories in the glass always seem to be speaking to me, trying to teach me (just like my mother used to) about the right path in life, warning me against the terrors of Hell.

As I waited, I ran over the plans in my mind - meeting up with a congenial crew in Ayr, a safe passage to Cornwall, a triumphant march on London.

My family seemed to be in the little church for above half an hour, and I was beginning to get impatient. The sky had turned dark and it was starting to rain.

When they eventually came out I asked them what they had been doing all that while. Kate told me that she had lit a candle, and had prayed for the good health of Richard and the safe delivery of our new baby.

* * *

It was late at night. The rain and wind were beating against the sides of the wagon. Suddenly, something darted out of the undergrowth. I managed to steady my own horse. But the horse behind me reared up and began pulling the wagon, hell for leather, with my wife and child inside it. I spurred my horse, drew alongside and grabbed the halter. The horse reared up again, and the wagon nearly tipped over on its side. Thank fortune that my wife and child, although shaken, were unharmed.

At last we arrived at Ayr where we were lodged in the best inn and treated with considerable courtesy and respect. The food was wholesome and plentiful, and our rooms were a good size, though naturally much less comfortable than our whole suite of rooms and great chamber at Stirling. Nevertheless, the company was good, as the inn was much frequented by sea captains and travellers with a tale or two to tell.

Next day I rose early, eager to inspect the four ships that I had been promised for my journey. But they were not nearly ready; and as for Robert Barton - the experienced mariner appointed by King James to captain my vessel - there was no sign of him at all. Nor, for that matter, did he take the trouble to meet up with me for several days.

Eventually he showed up, not at all as I had imagined him but a surly type, with a thin, sour-lipped mouth and small, piggish eyes. He was full of insincere apologies. 'I'm sorry, Your Highness. I had business of my own to attend to.'

'What personal business was so urgent that you kept us waiting for so long?' I demanded angrily.

'Well . . . I needed to settle an account with a wine-merchant in Glasgow; but when I arrived I found he was out of town.'

I reprimanded him for these poor excuses, and made it clear that if he was sailing with me he had better make sure that he got his priorities right in future. He looked down, and began picking his nose, so I could not see his expression; but I thought I had made my feelings on the matter clear to him.

So, when he dared to go on complaining I could scarcely believe it. 'My ship has been seized for this passage wholly against my wishes,' he protested.

'Come on man! You are receiving a handsome enough sum for your troubles.'

'Handsome? Sir, it's not nearly enough!'

'Then you must take that matter up with the King on your return. It is no business of mine.'

'You can rest assured that I shall. I shall indeed!,' and with that he turned abruptly and walked away in a huff.

*   *   *

While the ships were being refitted and receiving fresh coats of paint, the men King James had recruited for my journey (some one hundred and twenty in all) were put up at inns in the town. With nothing to do other than wait, they soon became thoroughly bored, and began to acquire a bad reputation in the town by their constant brawling and foul conversation.

To try and pacify their impatient spirits, I summoned a band of the men together on the quay one morning, and gave them instructions. 'When the ships are ready, we shall sail directly for Cornwall. 'We can expect to get plenty of support there . . .'

I got no further before I was interrupted by Robert Barton, the resentful ship owner, who acted as spokesman for the others. 'Sir, we have not undertaken such a long journey before. The furthest the men have been is Ireland . . .'

'And may I ask what are we going to get for all our troubles?' joined in another sailor with a long face and straggly red beard.

'Keep your place!' yelled Barton, angry at being interrupted by one of his own men.

'Is personal reward your only concern?' I asked.

The sailors scowled.

'I expect my men to fight for justice, for the House of York. That'll be reward enough for any man with principles.'

*   *   *

It was by now the middle of July. As the delays to the ships continued, costs were increasing, as all this while King James had to pay for my men to be lodged and boarded in the local inns. I began to wonder whether we would manage to get to sea at all.

The uncertainties were making Kate still more anxious. She was getting very big with child and finding it difficult to get about. More desperate now than ever, she urged me to call off the expedition.

'It is a flawed scheme my lord. No good can come of it, and I am now in too poor a condition to travel. I have had an awful premonition that something terrible is going to happen to us.'

'Be strong, Kate,' I urged. 'We can't stop now. I know the next few weeks will be tough. But the years ahead will be great ones for us. Our children will see us being crowned King and Queen of England.'

'But the men freely admit they have never undertaken such a long journey before. They are just local sailors and fishermen. And what do they know about laying on provisions for a journey all the way to Cornwall, without stopping? I simply do not trust them.'

'That is not their business. My agent, Roland, is seeing to all that. He will not let me down. He will provide all four ships with everything we need - cauldrons, drinking vessels, candles, the lot. There will be seventeen carcasses of beef and twenty-three of mutton. Bread from the cook-shops in the town, and freshly caught herring. There will be plenty of ale, cider, beer and four tuns of wine. Surely that will be enough?'

'And what about my health, and the health of our baby?' Kate persisted. 'As for that midwife you have found me, I don't like the look of her at all. She is nothing like the one I had at Stirling. Has she ever delivered a child before? Look at the state of her, she doesn't even seem to know how to look after herself, let alone a bairn. My lord, I am full of fears and doubts.'

Again I did my best to reassure her. 'Kate, she is a married woman of mature years, and her character is good. She has borne many children herself, and I have it on good authority from the townspeople here that she has delivered countless others.' I told my wife again and again that my first concern was her well being; but she continued to worry.

*   *   *

As we neared the day of departure, Kate tried to concentrate as best she could on her embroidery and reading. However, one morning her routine was broken when some of the town council came to our inn and presented her with a black cloak and a special tawny coloured sea-gown made from Rouen cloth. While several of the ladies made a fuss over our baby, a grey-haired, heavily bearded gentleman stepped forward to demonstrate the new garment. 'You see Ma'm. This is how the gown is worn, like this . . . and it is done up here . . . like so. It will protect your fine clothes from the elements while you are aboard, Ma'm.'

Kate put on a brave face so as not to offend the little group, even forcing a smile and thanking them for their thoughtfulness.

'Don't thank us, thank His Majesty the King,' replied the gentleman, bowing as he withdrew, 'for it is *he* who asked us to make you the garment.'

After they had all gone, Jane inspected the gown more closely with an air of disapproval, for she knew at once that it was not nearly full enough for her mistress's present condition. Anyone else would have laughed out loud, but Jane took things seriously and could only manage a 'tut tut.' 'I shall let it out for you!,' she said finally.

About this time, a despatch arrived from the King. I asked the messenger to wait while I read it out to Kate. 'He sends us his blessing . . . He says he would like to have helped us more . . . that we, more than anyone, deserve to have success . . .'

'How is the King? Was he well when you left him?' Kate asked the herald.

'The King is very well, and sends you his greetings and blessing. He is planning a second expedition into England.'

The answer struck me as odd, for I thought that the King was trying to make peace with England. But I put such thoughts aside. 'Oh, that's good news. I am delighted to hear it. Please send him our greetings, and thank him for everything he has done to help us.'

'I shall with pleasure, Your Highness.'

Then a thought struck me. 'Is there any news from the King's astrologer about the day it would be safest for us to travel?'

'Your Highness, he suggests you sail on the fourteenth or the fifteenth of the month, no later.'

★　　★　　★

It was on the latter date, St Swithin's day, cool and drizzly, when we boarded our small flagship, 'The Cuckoo.' The pleasant smell of recently sawn timber and fresh paint filled the morning air. Roland had lived up to his word - and all our provisions for the journey were already on board; what was more, his thoughtfulness and attention to little details seemed to have set an example to the men who to all appearances were ready to depart and were actually in good humour, civil even!

As we prepared to embark, the people of Ayr flocked out of their houses down to the quay. Kate was helped on board by Roland, her condition being now very delicate. Around her neck she wore an eagle stone which was believed to help during pregnancy. Once she was safe on board, our maid-servant climbed on, cradling our precious young son and heir in her arms.

Although new cabins had been built out of storage space, the ship was still very cramped, most of all below deck where, being so tall, I found it impossible to straighten myself up; and I kept banging my head against the rough beams above.

And so we sailed out of the harbour at Ayr to the cheers of the townspeople gathered on the quayside. Even the fishermen stopped unloading their catch and mending their nets to watch us.

My plan was to sail directly to Cornwall and attempt another invasion. You will recall that we had earlier had hopes in the men of Kent, but these hopes had been misplaced and a tragedy had occurred on the shore at Deal. But the men of Cornwall had to be more dependable. Already angry about the King's high tax demands, they would surely be only too pleased to assist us.

On the very first day at sea the weather turned foul and the ship began to roll. Some of the sailors began to talk about terrible whirlpools that could suck in ships and smash them to pieces. Others muttered about the kraken, a sea-monster with jaws big enough to hold a man and a horse, and teeth so sharp they could crunch bones into tiny pieces.

Then Kate was taken unwell, screaming, clasping her hands over her belly. Soon afterwards, she collapsed onto the deck, convulsed in pain. I ordered that she be taken below deck to her small cabin so she could be looked after properly by the other females.

When I was allowed to go below, I found Kate calmer. She had been given a special drink of dwale to ease the pain, but she was still moaning. Around her bed, partly obscuring my view of her, were Jane and the midwife. As I drew closer I could see that her attractive milky complexion had turned an ashen grey. There were beads of sweat on her brow, which the midwife was dabbing at with a cloth. Her lovely long hair had become tangled and greasy. It was clear that she could not withstand the uncertainties of the journey to Cornwall. As I returned above, I knew that I had to change our plans: we must head instead for the coast of Ireland.

*　　*　　*

However, long before we ever reached there I was summoned below again urgently. As I got to her cabin, Kate was being carried from her bed by our maidservant and the midwife, and was lowered onto a delivery stool. By her side was a jug of water and a basket containing some towels. Our young child lay crying in a little cot in the corner.

The eagle stone that Kate had been wearing around her neck as she boarded ship had been tied around her left thigh: this was supposed to make labour easier. The psalm that she had been writing out a few days before was now strung from her neck where the stone had been, and our maidservant whispered that Kate had drunk the ink washed off the parchment, for it would bless her and bring good health to the baby.

As soon as the midwife caught sight of me she sent me away, saying that this was no place for a man to be. I protested, but it was no use, and I was forced to go back up on deck. As I paced up and down, waiting for news, the waves were rolling more violently than ever.

Perhaps an hour passed, though it seemed much, much longer. The red bearded sailor, who claimed to know something of astrology, looked to the sky to forecast the baby's future.

Suddenly the midwife emerged on deck, her head bent down. 'I'm afraid I have got bad news, sir. Very bad news.'

'What is it? What is it?' I asked, grabbing hold of her wrist. 'How is my wife?'

'She has bled badly, but is otherwise well.'

'And the baby? How is our baby?' I pressed.

'I did my best, sir.'

'You mean our baby is dead?'

'I am very sorry, sir. I did all that I could. Your wife is very distressed. She is being comforted by her maid-servant. It is better that you wait a while before seeing her, sir.'

Utterly distraught to hear this terrible news, I started to blame myself for having insisted we come in the first place. Ignoring the midwife's instructions, I quickly scaled the ladder to my wife's cabin, where I found her ghostly white and weeping.

'This is a punishment from God!' she cried.

'God would not punish *you*! Not you who love him so.'

'I am being punished for taking part in your stupid schemes. They must be against God's will.'

I tried once again to comfort her. 'God is on the side of justice and truth. He will see to it that we reach London safely, that we are restored to our rightful kingdom.'

But Kate would not have it. Tears trickled down her cheeks. She buried her face in the pillow. 'All I can do now is pray,' she wailed.

★　　★　　★

We anchored in the harbour at Cork. It was to be my last visit there. We had hoped to receive a warm welcome from the Earl of Desmond but there was no sign of him, which caused my advisers to become gloomy and dispirited. I tried to allay their disappointment by reminding them that we had not intended to put in at Cork, that the Earl could not have expected us. But tiredness was getting the better of them: some doubted whether it had been wise to stop over at Cork at all; a few went further and began to question the whole enterprise.

Fortunately, my good friend John Waters, who was now mayor of Cork, once again came to our aid, and put up Kate and myself in his house. There was no shortage of space, and he gave us the room at the top of the house that he and his late wife had shared. Jane and little Richard were allotted a smaller room that one of John's children had occupied when they lived at home.

That evening he beckoned me into his own quarters at the back of the house. I knew by his expression that he had something serious to say. Before beginning, he handed me a tankard of ale. Then he bent his head forward and looked me straight in the eye. 'Just after you left for Scotland I received a summons to appear before King Henry's Lord Deputy at Dublin.'

'A summons? What for?' I asked, bemused.

'For aiding and abetting you!'

I drew a sigh of relief: 'Why, thank God you were spared.'

'Spared yes, but pardoned no. I was warned in no uncertain terms that if I ever became involved in any other deceit I would be arrested immediately and tried for treason.'

'You mean you can no longer help me?'

'I am not saying that. I *can* help you - for a little while at any rate. But I fear for my life. I cannot be seen with you. You must make your plans quickly and go from here.'

And so, while Kate stayed at home with our child, I spent the next few days wandering the streets of Cork, deep in thought, contemplating what to do next. When I was there last, these streets had provided such a source of comfort and inspiration; but now they seemed cold and lifeless. I noticed many beggars - beggars with open sores, beggars who had lost limbs. It was a distressing and pitiful sight. I suppose they had been there on my earlier visits; but then I had been in such high spirits and my mind so occupied that I had simply failed to see them.

On one quay, a beggar on crutches approached me. He had his foot all bandaged up. 'Battle wound, sir! Battle wound!' he pleaded, his hand outstretched and cupped ready to receive money.

I had seen beggars like this in Paris as well as in Tournai where my mother had warned me that many were frauds. Suspecting that there was nothing wrong with this man's foot, that he was just work-shy, I turned away.

Suddenly he started to moan. I looked back to see his eyes rolling in a fearful way. Then foam started to ooze from his mouth and dribble all down his chin.

I urged one of the fishermen mending his net nearby to fetch a doctor; but to my surprise he scorned the suggestion. 'There's nothing wrong with that man. He's not having a fit at all. The rogue's put a little tablet of soap in his mouth. That's all that froth is!'

The fisherman turned round to face the beggar. 'Piss off you! You'll have none of this gentleman's money! Do you hear me?' With that, the beggar spat the soap out on the ground, glared at the fisherman who had revealed him for a fraud, and made off on his crutches. Feeling foolish, I left the quay myself soon afterwards and returned home.

When I arrived home there was yet more bad news. I could scarcely believe it. Was there no end to all this? John waited until Kate had gone up to bed before breaking it to me. 'I am afraid that Desmond and Kildare have deserted us and gone over to Henry.'

'What? No wonder we had such a poor welcome when we arrived here,' I replied quickly. Then, sensing I may have offended him, I promptly added, 'apart from *your* hospitality, of course.'

However, John had not yet finished. 'There is more - and worse, Perkin.'

I fidgeted in my chair. 'Please don't call me that, even when we are alone, for fear you should say the name in front of my wife; for Kate knows nothing of this.'

'I see.' He looked surprised, shocked. 'I'm sorry. I had not realised. I thought you had told your wife everything.'

'So, what is this worse news?'

'Desmond and Kildare are hot on your heels. They're riding towards Cork with all speed at this very moment.'

Ever since the death of our tiny baby - barely formed - I found myself sinking periodically into low spirits, a melancholy mixed with the kind of awful self-pity that I so scorn in others. Now was such a time. But I could not let these feelings get the better of me. I *had* to go on. There was no option for us now other than to make for Cornwall without further delay. I only hoped that I would be able to convert the Cornishmen's hostility towards Henry into active support for my own cause.

However, even escaping from the shores of Ireland would be no easy matter. John's friends warned him that the citizens of Waterford - being ever loyal to Henry - were preparing to attack us, and had been given orders by the two turncoat earls to fit out four ships.

So, in the stillness of the night, and at great personal risk to himself, John agreed to take my family and me secretly in a small fishing boat to Kinsale. It was to be his final act of kindness towards us.

*   *   *

What a relief that we had evaded the Waterford fleet, I thought, as we sailed south in the cool night air, away from the enemy, and back to the old head of Kinsale and safety.

116

But still our problems were not over, as when we came into the harbour at Kinsale three more ships were awaiting us - not English ones but Spanish!

As we moored, one of these ships drew alongside ours, and before we knew it a score or more soldiers had boarded. The hilts of their long swords glistened menacingly in their sheaths as three of them lunged towards me, flung me against the side of the boat, and pinned my arms behind my back. The oldest of them, who I imagined to be one of the captains - a very tall red-haired man with a moustache - took out his sword and held the blade right against my throat. Much of what he then said I failed to understand at all, other than that he had orders from King Ferdinand of Spain to arrest me and take me back to Spain.

While all this was happening, the other men were staring at us wide-eyed, and I could not help feeling that our fine clothes had impressed them. With that, an idea came to me. Sensing that they might be susceptible to a bribe, I took the risk of offering the crew a reward of three thousand nobles if they took us safely to the coast of Cornwall. By a stroke of good fortune they agreed.

How easily we had been saved from the jaws of death! My wife was more suspicious, though. Ever more melancholic since her awful ordeal, she said that they were not to be trusted, that we should probably all end up in Spain, and she vowed to stay awake at night until we reached safety.

$$\star \qquad \star \qquad \star$$

This is how we came to set off on the final stage of our journey to England in a Spanish ship! We sailed due south, making for Land's End in Cornwall. The weather was now much improved, the wind had abated and the water was smooth. Little did we suspect that King Henry had already been warned of my intentions, and had sent ships to patrol the route from southern Ireland to the English coast.

It was late afternoon the next day when, suddenly, on the distant horizon, we saw a small fleet of warships. A cry in Spanish went up from the crow's nest. 'King Henry's ships!,' shouted out one of my followers.

'We've had it now!' yelled another.

Without delay we held a council of war. One possibility was to

117

turn round and sail back to Ireland again; but Henry's ships were gaining on us fast in the southerly wind. It was extremely doubtful whether we would make it. We could hear war-like shouts in the distance, and could see their cannon.

Much against my will, I was finally persuaded that my wife, my young son and myself should be hidden away for safety's sake in some empty barrels below deck in the hold. There were dozens of barrels here, and they singled out three at the very back.

The barrels stank with the remains of sour wine slopping around in the bottom. But we had no choice. Kate and baby Richard struggled into one barrel, Jane into a second. I urged them to be as still as possible, reassuring them that all would be well.

The sailors hammered over our heads, nailing on the lids. Would we be able to breathe inside? What about my son, and my wife? I felt sick with worry. Their job done, the sailors returned above. All was still.

The barrel's sloping sides prevented me from straightening my back, and my neck and head were bent forward awkwardly. The smell of bad wine was so pungent that I thought of pinching my nose, but my hands were pinned against the sides of the barrel; and as I tried to ease my right hand free, I felt something clammy wriggle across it.

Suddenly, there was a juddering. My barrel began to lurch and I thought I was going to overturn. I could only imagine that one of the enemy ships must have come alongside ours, and forced us to lay anchor. A squall was beginning to come up. Rain beat fiercely against the deck above me. Then, some of King Henry's men boarded. All I could hear was the sound of loud but indistinct voices overhead.

Evidently, they were questioning the Spanish captain and crew about their movements. There was a lot of shouting, perhaps Henry's men were not satisfied with the answers they were receiving. Then the sound of crates scraping the deck. They were searching the ship! At that moment my heart failed, for I thought I detected a muffled cry from baby Richard.

From above I could hear the thud of heavy footsteps, crates being tipped over. There was a lot of swearing, as the search was getting nowhere.

By now the rain had turned to hailstones, and the ship was beginning to rock in the wind. My barrel began to sway and tilt, and I became giddy. My ears were blocked, and so I swallowed hard; but the congestion would not clear. I was terrified that at any moment we were going to overturn and be washed out to sea.

Then silence. The men seemed to have gone. Not even a muffled sound from anywhere. Hurry and get us out of here! Surely the crew hadn't forgotten us?

At last there was the scraping of boots scaling the ladder down to the sleeping quarters close to where we were. But no friendly Spanish voices. Instead, English ones. My God! Henry's men must have just been having a rest. As they had found nothing up on deck, they had presumably now decided to search below.

Moments later, footsteps seemed to be approaching the very casks in which we were hiding. We should surely now be detected. I knew that Jane at least would remain calm; but I was terrified in case our baby son began to cry again.

My breathing stopped, and I had to tell myself to start breathing again. At any moment I thought I was going to faint. A dull ache stretched across my forehead, and I felt first hot, then cold.

The whole of my chest began to tighten. I knew I was going to be violently sick. I tore my hands away from the sides of the barrel to clasp my stomach, and started to bring up everything I had eaten. Some of the thin watery vomit landed in the folds of my cloak, the rest streamed down the insides of the barrel.

Henry's men must surely have heard me choking. We would doubtless now all be caught. Despite everything I had said to my family about keeping still, and all the reassurances I had given them that all would be well, I was the one who had let them down.

Chapter 13

Suddenly there was a strange wrenching sound, like timber smashing to pieces. Most of the commotion seemed to be coming from the enemy ship - for I recognised the sailors' curses in English. Then orders were shouted across to our ship. Still more confusion followed. I could hear more curses and a lot of scrambling about on deck. Could the ships be sinking?

My heart began to pound so loudly that I felt it was going to unsteady the barrel. I was terrified that we were all going to drown. Were my wife and child never going to see the light of day again, but going to perish inside their barrels?

Without warning, the ship lurched violently and began to roll. There was a dull thud against the barrel in which I was hiding. Another curse, a scuffle. After that, the sound of retreating footsteps. Silence. A lot more noise, some movement. Several of Henry's men were still on board, down here in the hold, coming this way.

Footsteps were now approaching. I was terrified, expecting the worst. They must have forced my crew to tell them where we were hiding. I was shaking with fear. Sweat was pouring off my forehead. I felt sick inside. At any moment I would be face to face with Henry's men, swords in hand. Would they strike my head off there and then?

The lid of my barrel was wrenched off and torn back. A shaft of light dazzled me. It was so strong that at first I could not see at all. Then my eyes began to adjust to it, and gradually I came to make out a familiar Spanish face smiling down on me. You can imagine how relieved I felt. Even then I was trembling as he helped me out of the barrel. After all, perhaps Henry's men were still on board, giving instructions to the Spanish crew to fetch us up on deck to deal with us.

To my great relief, this was not the case. It turned out that the grappling irons which the enemy was using to fasten their ship alongside ours, had become dislodged in the squall. One of King Henry's men had been completely thrown off his feet, and the thud I had heard was his head striking my barrel. Quick to take advantage of the confusion, the crew of our ship had pulled up anchor and made off into safety.

Soon afterwards I was mercifully re-united with my wife and baby son. What a relief it was to see that they were safe! As I suspected, our maid-servant was the only one of us to have stayed calm: incredibly, even her gown showed no signs of disarray. So different from my wife and I who had been terrified.

'I felt as though I was going to suffocate. There was so little air, and that was rancid,' I said.

Kate held Richard close to her and stroked his hair. 'I had to put my hand across our poor bairn's mouth to stop him from crying. My lord, won't you reconsider? For how much longer are you going to make us suffer like this?'

I listened but I did not hear. We had been saved, and I could scarcely believe our good fortune. It had been a miracle, and I sent up a prayer: 'Thanks be to God!'

'Kate. Don't you see? The fact that we have been saved is proof that God is on our side, on the side of justice.'

This time she did not answer me, just gently caressed our child's back. Better that than another quarrel, I thought.

I went back up on deck to see the captain, for something was puzzling me.

As I scaled the ladder I had to steady myself, as the episode in the barrel had turned my legs to quivering jelly. Heavy drizzle hung in the air as I emerged on deck. The captain was at the bow of the ship, staring out to sea. 'What made you keep our secret?' I asked him. 'Didn't Henry's men offer you a reward if you told?'

He smiled wistfully. 'Why yes, they offered a reward all right, but only two thousand nobles. You'll be paying me *three* thousand when we reach Cornwall. So you see, it made sense for my men to, how do you say, *keep their mouths sealed!*'

Chapter 14

We continued to sail in a south-easterly direction, towards Land's End, at the tip of Cornwall. After a few leagues, the wind abated, and before we reached our destination it had become quite calm. The coastline ahead was rugged rock, the grass lining the cliff tops dark and shadowy, flecked with grey.

Navigating carefully around a small rocky island lying off the shore, we came to a little cove, then entered a bay that the local people called Whitesand Bay. The whole place looked deserted apart from two bright red little fishing boats moored in between the rocks.

We laid anchor and waded ashore. Our feet sunk immediately into the deep white shimmering sand, so pure and clean, tarnished only by the occasional piece of black seaweed, a few traces of fishermen's net and some solitary footprints.

I picked up a handful of sand and let it trickle slowly through my fingers. It was like a wonderful dream. We had landed in England. I felt elated, even Kate managed a smile.

Slowly I looked around, taking in the delights of this desolate spot. Stretching down to the sea over to our left was a mass of orange-red rock, covered by a sparse weed-like grass; while behind the wide strip of sand in front of me were scattered very large grey and black boulders, the height of four or five men; then smaller stones. Cliffs rose up behind us, great streaks running across them in places, like the steps of a giant's staircase. How different from our landing place in Kent, which had been flat and open, and dull. Here, tracks snaked their way intriguingly down to the beach in between the rocks. I was told that fishermen used them, to take their catch of pilchard and mackerel home to their little huts that lay dotted around the cliff-tops.

I sent a small band of men ahead, armed with knives and cudgels. When they signalled that the coast was clear, the three of us followed them slowly up one of these paths. Occasionally, when the path became very steep, we had to scramble up it on all fours. Waves crashed against rocks in the distance, their roar echoing like thunder around the bay. As we climbed, every so often shouts could be heard from some of my men playing the fool somewhere on the beach below.

We stopped to rest. I looked back, out to sea, a vast expanse of sea. Sunlight glistened attractively on the waves. A lone seagull screeched above. My thoughts raced ahead of me: I knew that from here the journey to London would be a long one - possibly many hundreds of miles, and that there were bound to be difficulties ahead; but we had at least reached England's shores, and no army lined up against us.

After a while, small groups of fishermen began to trickle down the winding paths that stretched from their huts to the shore. They must have been watching us arrive. As they came closer to the place where we were resting, they stopped, afraid.

My men told them not to fear, that I was their friend, their true king. With that, they began to bow, and one of them fell down clumsily on his knees before us. I told them how I needed their support, how those who helped me now would receive rewards of money when we reached London.

All the while they listened attentively, and as soon as I finished speaking, a great cheer went up. Spurred on by the others, not a single man hesitated in pledging his support. One of them, a confident type with a tanned face and piercing blue eyes offered us a ride in his ramshackle ox cart. We climbed on, first Kate, then me. Jane passed Kate our child who was now beginning to cry. Then she climbed on board herself, helped by the fisherman who I thought for a dreadful moment was going to pat her on the bottom. God forbid how she would have reacted if he had dared to.

Together we made our way inland along muddy tracks, steep in places and often winding. So jolted and shaken were we that before long we all felt thoroughly sick.

Thankfully, after about an hour, we arrived at the nearest town that went by the name of Penzance, meaning holy headland. On one side of the town there rose steep sloping hills, on the other side a broad bay.

High up in the centre of the town the roads crossed. Nearby was a small fish market, and here I read my proclamation in full, with my wife and son beside me. The townspeople listened with interest, and before long I had managed to recruit into my army nearly two thousand men from the town and some of the coastal villages.

Two of these recruits stood out from the rest. Their names were Nicholas Astley and Edward Skelton, and they soon became my close companions.

I met Astley first. He was about the same age as me, though much shorter and with dark curly hair and beard. His confident and helpful manner pleased me.

'Sir, if you are looking for someone who knows the area well, please look no further. I can guide you to Exeter and beyond. I can also read and write, sir.'

I was very interested, and smiled. To be able to read and write was a rare enough quality; and to have a man in my army who could do this would be very useful. For a start, I could get him to keep records of the men and supplies. Better still, I could get him to write all my despatches.

Other men were now trying to interrupt us, bragging about their own experiences; until, before long there was so much noise I could hardly think. I held up my hand, signalling them to be quiet. When the noise died down I turned again to Astley. 'What sorts of things have you been used to writing?'

'All sorts of things, sir. You see, I'm a scrivener by trade.'

'What was the last thing you wrote?' I asked.

'I have just copied out a long list of Cornishmen who want the King to know that they will not be paying their taxes.'

'And what are your views on that subject, Mr Astley?'

'I'm proud to say that my name heads the list, with that of Thomas Flamank the lawyer.'

'Really!' I beamed in delight. The man really impressed me. He had skills as well as the will to fight for my cause. What good fortune to have met him.

Little could Astley have suspected that his abilities were just about to be put to the test. For he had scarcely finished his sentence when a despatch from King James of Scotland was handed to me. I had not heard the messenger's horse arrive because of the row the men were making.

Without hesitating, I handed it over to Astley to read aloud.

Assuming what he said was true, that he was a skilful writer, then he should be a very fluent reader, too, for tutors always teach their pupils to read first.

He clutched it a few inches from his chest. I wondered for a moment whether he was going to make it. But he had paused only to draw breath, and when he began to read, he did so with ease:

'Sir, King James says he has launched a second attack on England. His army has reached Norham Castle, not far from Berwick . . . [he skimmed the page] . . . his men have fought tooth and nail, but were beaten back by the Earl of Surrey's army which came up from Carlisle.'

This would have been disappointment enough but there was much graver news from the man who stood beside Astley:

'Be advised, sir, that a merchant just arrived in town from Exeter reports that King Henry already knows of your landing in Cornwall. Even as we speak he is assembling an army against you.'

The speaker was Edward Skelton, a stocky, good-humoured man with plenty to say. I took to him straight away, for I admire a man who is not afraid to speak up.

'How long will it take the King's army to reach us?' I asked.

'The King's army travels fast, sir. It will surely meet us by the time we reach Taunton, and may even be facing us at Exeter.'

'Sir, you must see to the safety of your wife and child,' cautioned Astley. 'You dare not let them accompany you to London.'

'What do you mean? Their place is in London. Katherine is my queen, Prince Richard my heir.'

'It's too risky, sir,' he warned, fingering his beard.

'Too risky? In what way? They will be travelling under escort.'

'There is still a risk of them being captured, sir.'

There was silence. I sighed. 'You are right. I cannot risk that - anything but that! What should I do?'

'They must be held in a secret place, a place of safety.' Astley's tone was soft and mysterious.

'Do you know of such a place?'

'I do, sir.'

'Where? Where is this place?'

'Not far from here, near the market town of Marazion, is a little island. It lies just off the coast, but is cut off and isolated when the tide is high. Locally it is known by the name of St Michael's Mount. There your wife and your son will be safe.'

There was nothing more to be said. With our little boy fast asleep, we set off at once for this little isle.

*   *   *

It turned out that the town of Marazion was even closer that I had imagined, and we were soon standing on the shore looking out towards the little island that was to be home for my family over the next few weeks. There it lay, at a short distance out to sea, a lofty isolated crag - a solitary spectacle, thickly forested on all sides, a pyramid of rock crowned with a great pinnacled castle bathed in bright sunlight.

We could not cross to the island by foot because of the high tide. So one of my men borrowed a boat from some fishermen. Although the crossing was brief, it was long enough to be noticed by any possible spies, lying in wait on King Henry's behalf.

Mooring the boat at one of the little jetties on the island, we went ashore, passing some small cottages and monastery buildings. Then Kate, my baby son, our maid and myself followed the Cornishmen up a very steep, rocky path to the top. In places, the path was strewn with boulders that we had to scramble over as best we could.

We continued to climb, keeping as close to the rocks as possible, knowing that over on our right hand side there was a sheer drop to the cliffs and the sea below. We passed batteries of guns half way up and again near the summit.

As we climbed the last stretch, the pathway narrowed suddenly, and I noticed several well-tended herb gardens over to my left. By this time we were within sight of the entrance to the castle where there was a rusty iron portcullis, not fully drawn up.

Outside the entrance we were welcomed by a cross-bearer and a small group of monks of the Benedictine order, hardly distinguishable from one another as they were all dressed in their black habits. Almost without realising it, we were being whisked up a short flight of steps and through a low doorway. The door closed behind us with such a thud that it echoed all over the castle. Behind us, heavy long bolts were drawn across to secure it.

Then the abbot appeared, full of smiles and more welcomes. He went over to Jane and made a big fuss of our child. From their friendly, relaxed manner, it was obvious the monks were used to taking fugitives into sanctuary here, and they had prepared themselves for our coming.

After this we were taken up another short flight of steps and along a rickety walkway. Mounted on the wall about half way round, I saw a lantern cross containing a picture of a pilgrim and a king. My mind started to wander. I thought about all those kings and princes I had seen in my own pilgrimage through Europe - the disappointments I had had, the moments of triumph.

From here we were led into a small chapel where prayers and a mass were said for our safety. As I mentioned, I have no liking for churches and chapels: the burning incense, the mournful chanting, above all the scenes of hell depicted in the stained glass making me feel ill at ease.

This chapel was different, though. An ornate brass chandelier caught my attention. It was hanging low enough over our heads for me to notice that on one side was depicted the Virgin and child, and on the other St Michael slaying the dragon. I had seen something very similar in Flanders, and its familiarity reassured me that this was the place that had been marked out for my wife and child, as I was forced to continue alone to London.

After we had said our prayers, Kate, her serving-maid and my little boy were shown their sleeping quarters, high up in one of the towers. As they disappeared up a spiral staircase, I stayed behind for a moment looking out to sea, deep in contemplation. I was on the threshold of the final stage of my enterprise - the long journey to London where we should be crowned King and Queen of England. Sadly, for that last part we were to be separated. I was shortly to leave my beloved wife and child - for how long I did not know.

Before we said goodbye to one another, we were led into the refectory, a low room where I had to stoop the whole time on account of the exposed roof timbers. A long oak table that must have seated a good twelve persons ran the length of the room; while at the far end was a large fireplace with a comfortable looking chair by the side.

The monks ushered us into our places at table. The abbot said the grace, and, as it was Friday, we were served fresh cod. All the while we ate in complete silence, as this was the custom. From where I sat at the centre of the table I had a good view, and spent much of the time staring out to sea.

Soon the glare of the sun became too strong, and I averted my gaze into the room where Jane was absorbed in feeding little Richard. I looked across at my wife. She was quiet, her face sad. What might the future hold? Could I be sure that I would ever see them again?

We finished our meal, and as silently as possible got up from the table. Once outside the refectory, I thanked the monks for everything they were doing to help us, for providing my family with a safe place to stay. I think they were impressed by my manners. Thank goodness I knew how to conduct myself in company, and could show myself to be a man worthy of their support.

My emotions were now very mixed. I felt sadness at having to part from my family. I had lost a baby. Would I now lose my son and wife too?

Yet, I could not suppress the thrill of achieving my ambition to rule, an ambition surely now within my reach.

But what if I did not succeed? The consequences of being caught, captured by Henry's men, were too awful to think about. I was nagged constantly by worry and terrible self-doubt.

* * *

It was our final meeting, alone in her small, bare room at the top of the castle. Our child was crawling about in the corner, playing with some shells that the Cornishmen had given him. The two of us stood by the window. The sea had now receded and it was possible to cross to the mainland by foot.

Even now Kate urged me to reconsider. 'My lord, I beg you to think again about your plans. You know how I feel about them. Please, I beseech you, think again.'

I held her closely in my arms, trying to calm her fears and reassure her. But I saw the tears welling up in her eyes. She clung to me desperately, the crucifix on her chain dug into my chest.

'We have lost our baby. Let's not lose each other!' she cried.

'Pray for me,' I implored her. 'The hours will pass, and soon we shall be reunited again. Only this time as my queen, not just my love.'

Yet it was clear she felt I was abandoning her again. I could see the sadness in her hazel eyes; and as we embraced, I felt her tears against my cheek.

'We shan't be separated for long. God has meant us to succeed. We have suffered so much. Don't give up now, my love.'

It was time I left. Before we parted I gave my blessing to her, and to my son Richard. The monks were waiting to receive her. She turned towards them and they quickly led her through the gaunt grey archway, and she disappeared from view.

Treading awkwardly, I made my way along the uneven stone causeway to the mainland. The sunlight shimmered on the water. Overhead the clouds were patchy - it looked like rain. I turned around to look back. High above, from a solitary grey tower, I thought I could see a figure waving to me. Could it be her, I wondered?

Chapter 15

The sun was slowly rising into a cloudless sky as we took down our tents and began the journey eastwards towards Bodmin, the most important town in these parts. It promised to be a very warm day, and long before noon the men were using their sleeves to wipe sweat from their foreheads.

I had in my ranks some three thousand men at this point, mostly fishermen and tin-miners, yeomen farmers and peasants. Astley was still faithfully recording their names and places of birth - their ages, too, if they knew them. The oldest may have been fifty, though he did not look it; I think he had added on a few years here and there to impress people. The youngest was a black-haired lad of just twelve years old, bright, fresh-skinned, eager to fight. Many were family men who had left their wives and children behind; though the girlfriends of some of them persisted in following.

Having only a few pikes and scythes which they fetched from the fields to fight with, we were reduced to picking up anything which could be used as a weapon - splinters of wood, nails and sharp stones to hurl at the enemy. All these we concealed in our pockets ready, for we did not know when King Henry's forces might strike a blow.

We made our way in single file along narrow tracks, slipping in the mud, while the fishermen sang about the sea to keep up their spirits. As we went, we were joined by hundreds more men who came out from villages along our route - a motley assortment of types, but united by a common cause. The conversation behind me was proof enough of that:

'Why should we pay for the King's soddin' wars up in Scotland?' complained one of the young fishermen from Whitesand Bay.

'Yeah! Sheer bloody greed. That's all it is!' shouted his mate. 'What 'ave we to gain from 'em, us down here in these parts? What's the King ever do to help us?'

'Not a damn thing!' roared one of the farmers. 'We must stand firm and fight the bastard. We owe it to Michael Joseph and Thomas Flamank who gave up their lives.'

'Here here!' shouted his mate.

It was clear that what spurred the men on most was to get revenge for these killings and for the heavy fine that the King had placed on the county of Cornwall by way of a punishment. My cause was of no interest to them - that was understandable enough. Nevertheless, they were still only too willing to support me; my arrival had been an opportune one for them, I was someone they could rally around.

I did my best to drill and marshal them, tried getting them to listen and obey instructions without always questioning them. Yet to little avail - they simply could not see the purpose of it all. They preferred to waste much of their time when we were camped, not in training but in gambling and telling one another dirty stories. So I just had to put up with them the way they were, much less well-disciplined even than the motley assortment of soldiers I had been used to up in Scotland. It made me all the gladder that I also had my trusted advisers at my side.

One evening, after a day on the march, and when most of the men only wanted their sleep, we were disturbed by a really vicious brawl between two of them, ploughmen by occupation, over one of these hangers-on. She was an attractive enough girl with striking long red hair and an ample figure; but she had persisted in following her young man all the way from Penzance, and was now being chased by one of his mates. The two men - youngsters they were, only just out of their apprentice - tore at each other like wild dogs, swearing and cursing as they scrapped.

I could not put up with this right in front of my nose, for all to see; besides, I was concerned that they might do one another some permanent harm. So I ordered Astley to pull them apart - he had the strength for it. Then I gave them a good talking to; but they just scowled back at us, full of resentment. In fact, the one who had just taken a fancy to the girl went straight off and broke into a cottage nearby, stealing ale and money. A terrible thing, to steal food from local people who were hungry themselves. I had him hanged as an example. We left his body on the gibbet for the crows to pick at his skin. The men looked suitably subdued. If only I had been able to exercise the same level of authority over King James's soldiers up in Scotland, the outcome of my expeditions there may well have been different.

At Bodmin, a busy market town, full of trade and manufacture, I was escorted through the streets to the square where I was again proclaimed King Richard IV of England, and was soon joined by close on a thousand men from the town itself and the villages around.

By now my army was some six thousand strong, and I was told that there was not a single home in these parts which had not provided a father or a son. Now there were tradesmen and shopkeepers in my ranks, side by side with fishermen and farmers - all determined to avenge the awful slaying of their kinsfolk by the King's army some months earlier at Blackheath, outside London.

Before we went any further, I held a council of war to decide on our best course of action. Edward Skelton was the first to make a suggestion. 'We must wait here until we can gather a force together. We need ten thousand men, the strongest force that England has ever seen, well-armed and well-trained.'

Little could I have guessed that an intelligent man would come up with such a futile scheme. I cut him short. 'There's nothing like enough men in these parts for such a great army! And even if there were, training them would take months. Before we know it, winter would be fast upon us. By delaying like that, King Henry's forces will gain great advantage.'

Astley nodded sagely. 'Time is of the essence. The King has many retainers he can turn to, and he can mint coins to pay them regularly.'

This worried me, as I knew what regular payment could do for a soldier's morale and discipline. I could not pay my troops at all; and although their desire for revenge against the King remained as strong as ever, tiredness was beginning to take its toll on their spirits.

Then a despatch arrived from a cloth merchant who worked the road between Bodmin and Exeter. I unrolled the parchment eagerly. It turned out to be more bad news: the Earl of Devon was heading towards us with a force of fifteen hundred men. Only about half the size of my own army, I know, but the weapons they carried were far superior to ours. I urged my men against being complacent.

A few miles outside Bodmin at a place called Cardinham, many yeomen farmers swelled our ranks and helped to strengthen our confidence. And so, in good spirits, we crossed Bodmin Moor, a very wild stretch of upland, its black tops strewn with granite.

The scene reminded me of the carefree days I had spent in the Scottish Highlands with Kate when we were first courting. I expected to smell the scent of heather in the air but could not; indeed, all that seemed to grow on the moor was a poor quality grass and a few gorse bushes. Kate. Kate. How was she? Were the monks keeping to their word? Would they be able to protect her? And what about our child? I missed hearing his playful gurgling, his happy laughter.

The still warm September days were now beginning to draw in, which caused us to march fewer and fewer miles each day. Progress after dark on the uneven ground of the moors was becoming very difficult, and several of my men had sustained injuries, one twisting an ankle so badly that he had to be helped along by his two companions. The Cornishmen constantly reminded us to watch out for bogs, some deep enough to drag down both a man and his horse.

All this while my men had kept together well - all, that is, apart from the headstrong Nicholas Astley. Ever since daybreak he had been playing the fool. Now he had taken my cloak as a prank and put it on:

'Don't you think I'd make a fine prince? Look, I've even got the cloak for it . . . and the badge!'

Playfully, he strolled up and down, showing off my Yorkist crest with its big grey falcon.

'Come on. Give it back!' I laughed.

With that, he leapt on his horse and rode off.

Tedious though this was, I had no option other than to follow him.

All the way across the moor he kept at some lengths ahead, and before long he disappeared from our sight altogether. On the edge of the moor, I can remember passing a little stone church set back from the way, all tumbledown and derelict. After this we descended through a steep, dark wood, crossed by a myriad of small, bubbling streams.

Suddenly, a great cry went up from somewhere ahead of us. It was a piercing, desperate cry, a cry for help, the cry of someone in trouble - perhaps lying injured, perhaps being attacked. The voice sounded like Astley's.

I gave a signal for my men to halt. Our horses trembled and stamped, sensing that there was danger ahead. Any attacker must surely have heard our thunderous hooves as we approached, but may now have thought that we had turned off in a different direction.

I strained my ears to listen. The cry came again, even more urgent than before. As silently as we could, Skelton and I eased our horses forward in the thick undergrowth. At that point I was still not sure exactly where the yelling was coming from, as the wood gave off an eerie echo.

All of a sudden, over to our left in a clearing, I saw two shadowy figures, wrestling on the ground. I beckoned Skelton to stop, and we quietly dismounted. One of the figures was Astley all right; but his horse was nowhere to be seen. It must have bolted in fright.

As we watched, his assailant - a man of an indeterminate age with long, scraggy black hair - dragged him over and pinned him tightly to the ground with his knees. The man was no soldier, he had no armour on, just rags.

Astley was spluttering and coughing, thrashing his legs around in an effort to get away; but his assailant was stronger, he was managing to hold him down, and was now rifling through Astley's pockets.

I told Skelton to keep a good hold of my own horse, dismounted and ran across to where the two men were fighting, hoping that the element of surprise would scare off the attacker.

When I was only a few yards from them, I inhaled deeply and roared at the bandit. But he took not the slightest bit of notice. So, I approached, wrenched him away and flung him to the ground. In his left hand I could see that he held Astley's purse. Before I could seize it from him, however, he had sprung up again, and it was then I saw he carried a dagger.

Stepping backward a few paces, I drew my sword and ordered him to hand the purse over at once. Still there was no reaction. So I tightened my grip on the hilt to make it clear that I was ready to kill him if he did not obey me.

Thank God the bandit showed no inclination to go on, and instead began to cower and plead. I wondered what had caused his sudden change of heart; and then I saw the rest of my men coming into sight in the distance.

I ordered him to stand up, and he did his best to do so. Two of my men held him, his hands twisted behind his back.

'Kill him!' yelled some of the others.

I looked at the man. He was a pathetic, defenceless specimen with his head bowed low. Noticing something odd about his face, I gently asked him to turn around. It was then I realised why he had not heard me coming, nor had responded to my shouting: both his ears had been cut off, right the way down to the stump.

Slowly, he turned round again. He was desperately thin and bony, probably starving.

Really he was no threat to us. It had only been his weapon that had given him strength.

'Kill him!' shouted the men again, even more insistent than before.

'No, let him go!' I said. 'And give him a piece of bread. Look at him! Can't you see he's got nothing in the world apart from the clothes he stands up in? And they're just rags!'

Reluctantly, my men released him: it was clear from their disappointed expressions that they had been looking forward to slitting his throat there and then. One of them tore off a crust of bread and handed it to him; but some of the others spat in frustration after the bandit as he limped off into the wood, which presumably was his home.

Astley's horse had not got far (he found it drinking from a brook close by), and we were soon able to set off again. Was Astley attacked in mistake for me, I wondered, as I retrieved my cloak and crest from him? No, it couldn't be, I reasoned. After all, what would my crest mean to this poor man?

I continued to dwell on this thought as we were welcomed into the town of Launceston.

*   *   *

The next day we reached the river Tamar that separates the great western counties of Cornwall and Devon. I was surprised not to see the forces of the Earl of Devon lined up against us on the opposite bank. I asked the local people, who told me that he had come the day before, but when he heard of the strength of my army (more than four times larger than his own), he had decided to withdraw to Exeter.

Buoyed up by news of his retreat, we made good progress, and three days later reached the substantial walled city of Exeter ourselves. In an hour or two it would be midnight. The air was full of the smoke of wood fires, and the smell of burning pitch lingered on the soft breeze. Within the walls I could see the silhouette of a castle, together with many churches; one of them, larger than all the others, I imagined to be a cathedral church.

The curfew bell must have rung more than two hours before, and the inhabitants would now be in their beds asleep. We found many gates along the city wall, but every one was closed and bolted for the night. It was evident that the citizens had not expected us to arrive so soon. The question now was - would they remain loyal to the Earl of Devon; or could they be tempted to support my cause?

Chapter 16

The two guards patrolling the wall needed a lot of persuading before they agreed to get me a parley with the mayor and aldermen. With their torches blazing fiercely in the night breeze, my advisers accompanied me around to the city's north gate where the parley was to take place. Here they listened with polite interest to what they had heard many times before, as I once again proclaimed my identity as the younger son of the late King Edward the Fourth - cruelly sentenced to death by my wicked uncle, King Richard.

When I had finished my well-rehearsed speech, I pleaded with the citizens of Exeter to support my cause, to help me gain my rightful inheritance, as the fourth King Richard of England. The company before us was completely silent - there was not even a murmur - What did their silence mean - attentiveness, or disinterest? Please God, not the latter. I *had* to win them over to my side. A new note of urgency entered my voice: 'We have much in common, above all a common enemy, the usurper Henry.'

There were cheers from a band of my own men, but still mostly silence from the leading men of Exeter. Not knowing what to make of them, I decided to continue in any case:

'Henry - I loathe to call him king - Henry has taken my throne from me, he has levied taxes on your city, harsh taxes. And when you asserted your rights and resisted payment, he punished you with a huge fine. Are you prepared to put up with this any longer? Surely not! We must stand together and fight back, fight the oppressor!'

By this time, swarms more of my men had joined us outside the gate. When I paused for breath, they started to cheer loudly and clap their hands wildly against those of their mates. I shouted out to them to stop at once: for I had had enough of their ill-disciplined outbursts.

All the while, the mayor and aldermen - spineless men in their dotage - continued to listen to me, with faces of stone. I had finished all I had to say, done all I could to raise their interest. I had spoken with conviction, recalled many of the details I had learnt many years before at the Duchess of Burgundy's court. All I could do now was await their response.

When eventually that response came it was not as I had hoped. The mayor informed me that far from the inhabitants of Exeter being likely to support my cause, they would stand out resolutely against me, almost to a man. They were weary with marches and campaigns and battles, and wanted a period of peace to be with their families.

Although disappointed, all was not lost. The citizens may well be weary and suspicious but perhaps they could still be stirred if only I appealed to them in the right manner, chose the right words to sway their consciences, and gain their confidence. But I had to persuade them to give up their warm beds and come out to listen to me.

Many came, still in their night-gowns, lamp in one hand, cudgel in another, to form a great arc around me. I coughed to clear my throat. 'Gentlemen, respected citizens of Exeter. I bring you great news. Freedom from oppression and tyranny is within your grasp. Don't let it pass you by. Reach out and seize this opportunity. I shall not forget you if you help me now. Your loyalty will be rewarded next month when I am crowned King of England at Westminster.'

I had done my best, addressed their grievances, I had offered them rewards - even set a date when they would receive them. Yet all this was to no avail; for at the end of it, most remained unconvinced. Those who spoke said that they so feared King Henry that they dared not join my ranks, and that they would fight to protect their city from my army.

One of the aldermen told me frankly that it was only because we had arrived so suddenly, at night, that they had been caught unawares - many in the midst of their sleep. They did not have a chance to summon those living in surrounding areas to come to their aid. This they now did in great haste: and soon, at regular intervals along the stone walls, I could see messengers being let down by ropes.

The sight of so many of them set my pulse racing: they would soon have reinforcements. For the moment, however, the advantage was still with us, and this spurred me to throw a spear at the iron-studded gate as a formal signal that my army intended to take the city by force.

From this moment, the rules of siege warfare applied; so that anyone trying to get in or out of the city became a legitimate target for attack. (Unknown to me then, some of my men had already started mining the walls on the other side of the city, using picks and axes - the only weapons they possessed. Several had even tried to remove stones with their bare hands!)

The citizens of Exeter were clearly unprepared for an attack, with hardly any means to protect themselves, as most of the city's bows, arrows, chain mail and gunpowder were locked away in the armoury of the Guildhall. As a distant bell chimed the midnight hour, all they could do was keep the gates closed, man the walls and prepare to defend their city as best they could until dawn broke.

The capture of Exeter was vital to my campaign. It was the key to controlling the south-west of England. Now that I had been refused admission to the city, I had no choice other than to attack the gates by storm. So, I ordered that five oak trees near where we were standing be felled and used as battering rams.

Without waiting to be picked, my men began to rush forward to volunteer, shoving and knocking one another over to get to the front. What a rude and disagreeable mob: good soldiers should obey instructions, and do not brawl. Alas, mine were not good soldiers - amassed, as they had been, from all sorts of places, acquiring only what discipline I had managed to teach them on the march from Penzance and Bodmin.

This state of affairs could go on no longer. My army had to be better organised. So I decided to form them into two divisions, and gave them different tasks. One division had orders to scale the high walls using rope ladders brought with them by the citizens of Bodmin; while I set the other division to burn down the North Gate. It was a daunting challenge, as it was protected by a lofty barbican, and a yard surrounded by arrow loops and cannon emplacements, known forbiddingly as the 'killing ground.' Still, for men who had been drinking steadily since light of day, anything would have seemed possible.

Our plan was the more difficult because the great wooden drawbridge was raised, so that the only means of gaining access to the castle keep was across the moat. But the moat - filled with stagnant and stinking water collected from the castle latrines - ran the whole length of the curtain wall.

Undeterred, my men started to work themselves up into a frenzy of hatred, howling abuse as they threw missiles at the gateway from the far side of this stinking ditch. But this proved to be completely useless, as the rocks simply rebounded off the stonework and splashed into the moat. All the while, the citizens catapulted boulders and carcasses of dead animals at us from their siege engines; and our assault was easily repulsed by their far superior equipment.

To scale the walls would first mean swimming the moat, which was a deadly prospect: for if we were not caught by a stone fired from an enemy crossbow as we did so, then the stench of the water would be enough to overcome us and take us under. So I decided to turn our attention instead to undermining the more vulnerable stretches of wall which were not protected by the moat on the eastern side of the city.

Yet even here our progress was held up by disagreements between my advisers about the best means of attack. Skelton, always the impractical one, was keen to weaken the actual foundations of the walls and had convinced many of my men that this is what needed doing; but this would have taken far too long, as the base of the wall was even thicker than the rest.

No, we had to strike at once. Astley suggested we attack one of the less well defended gateways. This was a more realistic solution; but now that they had got started my men were reluctant to change course.

As we wasted valuable time arguing, all sorts of dangerous and obnoxious objects were hurled down on us: large stones with razor-sharp edges, scalding water, the boiling pitch we had smelt in the air when we first arrived in the city. Dead and rotting animals - even the contents of stinking cesspits rained down on our heads. My men cursed and swore like mad, having had no time to build a covering to protect their heads from the missiles.

One man, who had left his young wife and two little daughters at Marazion to join us, was about half way up a scaling ladder when a defender on the parapet walkway above overturned a cauldron of burning pitch on him. The sheer force of the scalding liquid flung him from the ladder and sent him reeling to the ground.

I was at his side in an instant. Heaven only knows how many

bones he had broken in the fall, for he was unable to move at all. His face was scarcely recognisable, his skin bright red, the pitch continuing to burn into his skin and hair even as I tended to him.

I asked that a soothing balm be fetched, and it arrived within the half hour. In the meantime I applied cold water to his skin, but he was so badly burnt that it had little effect in reducing the heat; and before I knew it his skin had completely peeled back, exposing his cheek bones and lower jaw - a horrific sight.

I could do nothing more for him, and I left him in the hands of one of his mates. He died from his injuries and burns a few hours later, a terrible agonising death. I can only thank the Lord that his suffering was not more drawn out.

*   *   *

News was filtering through to me from some of the men that my second division had been more successful. I did not know how much stock to place on what they said, but rumour had it that they had overpowered the enemy and that some of them had forced their way through the North Gate. Unfortunately, that was not the full story, as shortly afterwards I came to hear that they had found the way ahead after that steep and narrow. This gave the defenders a great advantage; so that although there were few men defending the gate, they still managed to overpower my men and drove them back beyond the walls.

Refusing to yield, we next brought all our strength to bear against the East Gate; and this time we were successful, breaking the gate down with our new battering-rams, and forcing an entrance. After that, there was no stopping my men, and some of them continued on - even as far as Castle Street in the heart of the city.

As they did so, a desperate hand-to-hand encounter with cudgels, scythes - even bare fists - was taking place within the gateway itself; and for a while my hopes were greatly raised, as it really did look as though the spirit of the defenders was going to yield to our superior numbers.

It was not to be, however, for suddenly the Earl of Devon arrived, with his son, Sir William Courtenay, and a force of some fifteen hundred men. My lookouts had badly let me down; and it was at this point that our luck began to turn.

Being granted permission to enter the city immediately, the Earl's men fell at once upon my left flank with all the force they could. The two experienced commanders shouted out orders to the men with practised authority, orders that were instantly obeyed.

The defenders were greatly emboldened by the arrival of the Earl of Devon's army, and now came at us with all they could, killing and wounding a great many of my men with pikes, arquebuses and stones. During the fighting, one of my men managed to pierce the Earl of Devon's left arm; but most of the injuries, alas, were on our side.

Tending to these wounds fully occupied a small band of my men. The main problem was bleeding, and these apprentice surgeons stood ready with scalding hot oil of elder and red-hot irons to clamp on the wounds to staunch the flow of blood. I shuddered to think of the tormenting pain they would inflict on the injured patient.

As we saw to our wounded and dying, the citizens of Exeter were trying as fast as they could to breach the gaps we had made in the walls. Then they set fire to faggots of timber so they could see their way around in the darkness.

There was so much noise and confusion, and the smoke was insufferable. We fought on as best we could in the night drizzle, tripping and stumbling over the dead bodies of our men, and some that were not yet dead, hearing them cry underneath our feet.

Realising we were unlikely to secure victory that night, at about two hours after midnight I asked the Earl for a truce, which he granted. This would not give an advantage to either side, as according to the laws that govern sieges, all military activity must be suspended during a truce; defences must not be improved, nor must any siege engines be built or moved into position. The siege would continue in the morning as if there had been no interruption.

Now very weary indeed, I retired with my advisers to spend the night a few miles away at a small village called Minet where they assured me I would find loyal friends who would treat me well.

*   *   *

Although we found an inn, the room they gave me had been closed up for so long that it was very musty and airless. What with

142

this and my fears about what the next day would bring, I slept poorly, my sleep full of bad dreams.

I seemed to be close to a hill, a hill steeper than I had ever climbed before - so high that the summit actually seemed to touch the sky. Around me, however, were some familiar sights: the grey flecked stone I had seen when I came ashore in Cornwall; and the very same wood, near where I had rescued my companion from the bandit, stretched up into the distance like a dark green carpet.

At the foot of the hill, on the bank of a turbulent river, stood my mother - not as she must be now, but as I knew her many years ago in Tournai. A cold northerly wind got up, and my mother took from the leather bag she carried a black woollen scarf to cover her head.

I hugged her and said goodbye, much as I had done when I left for Antwerp in my youth; but this time she clung on to me, refusing to let me go. 'Don't desert your family, Perkin,' she cried. 'Stay here in Tournai. You can be happy here.'

She held me so tightly that I thought my ribs were going to crack, and I had to wrench myself away. After that, I did not dare turn around in case my resolve should weaken.

As I began to climb I thought I could just make out the top of the hill. Something high up above was glistening there: I thought it could have been a rainbow. As I ascended, there were fewer and fewer trees, and those there were had fewer branches. There was also less air, and I found it more and more difficult to breathe.

Before long, I reached a crag where I decided to rest. The sun poured down onto the hill, almost blinding me, pinning me to the spot. I needed to shelter; and looking around me by some stroke of good fortune there was a cave nearby. Here I would be able to find some shade.

It turned out to be further away than I had supposed, my feet seemed weighted down and clumsy, so that when I reached it I was gasping for breath. I put a foot inside and froze. Strung to the wall were four badly burnt human faces, their eyes having been gouged out of their sockets.

Suddenly, I heard a voice. It was a little like that of my wife, but somehow it was shriller. 'My lord, do not go on. Turn back. For the sake of me and our child!'

I heard a baby crying, crying more and more loudly, until the cry became a deafening scream, and I had to put my hands over my ears.

The cave, which had been cool inside when I entered it, was getting hotter with every passing moment. I could not understand why. My cloak stuck to me - I was saturated with sweat. Suddenly, I knew why. I saw flames reflected on the far wall of the cave, first a flicker, then leaping up higher and higher. The whole place was on fire.

Terrified, I ran out of the cave. By this time the sun had moved round, and I was able to cast my eyes up towards the summit. There I saw many trees, even more than at the foot of the hill, all with heavily leafed branches.

Suddenly, there was a rustle in the grass behind me. A wolf dog rushed up to me, as if from nowhere, barking furiously, barring my way down, making it impossible for me to turn back. So I had no choice other than to continue climbing, up towards the sky.

Before long I could clearly see the summit and could make out the object that was glittering. It had not been a rainbow at all - it was a crown.

From this point the scent to the summit was very steep indeed. I had to climb on all fours, picking my way up the last few feet, afraid of falling backwards. I paused to take breath, but it was almost impossible. There was so little air now.

I looked down. To my horror, I could no longer see meadows and forests beneath me. Instead there was a great dark gaping pit.

I dragged a sleeve across my forehead to soak up the sweat, and looked upwards again. The crown glowed in the sunlight more than ever now. It had suddenly got much nearer. In fact, it seemed to be only an arm's length or two away. If I reached out I could probably touch it.

Next to it stood a man, with arms outstretched. I reached out, too, eager to feel the soft metal in my hands. But as I touched it the crown began to crumple. It was only, after all, made of paper.

The shock had upset my balance. I had left myself nothing to cling onto, and the ground beneath my feet was beginning to shift. Then I slipped, and before I knew it I was plummeting downwards, spinning round and round out of control, down into the huge black pit. Wild laughter - the laughter of devils - taunted me from all directions as I was sucked downwards. I smelt blood and burning flesh. Could this be hell, I wondered?

Suddenly, I reached the bottom with terrific force. I sat up and tried to grip the rocks either side of me; but I only clasped rags.

Sweat was streaming off my forehead. I looked down at my hands and gave an enormous sigh of relief: I had the bed drapes in my fingers.

★   ★   ★

I forced down some bread and ale, for I knew I must keep my strength up. We returned to the city soon after dawn to make a fresh attempt upon the North Gate. The drizzle of the night before had ceased, and as it grew lighter it promised to be a fine late summer's day. I could only hope that it would also see a revival of my own good fortune.

As I rode into the still smoky city in the calm of the early morning, a shock awaited me. For, contrary to the rules conducting sieges that I mentioned earlier, the defenders had mounted great guns and moved them into place. Evidently one cannon, a particularly menacing-looking brute on wheels, was so heavy that it had taken two dozen men much of the night to move it into position.

I consulted my advisers. Skelton, as ever, was quick to offer his opinions - just as he was probably used to giving customers glib advice about garments in his little tailor's shop back in Penzance. It is cruel of me, I know, but at times I wished he had stayed there. 'Sir!', he exclaimed excitedly, 'we must trick our way into the castle using some disguise. When we get in, we'll piss on their powder, then set fire to their buildings . . .'

I refused to hear talk like this, and would not let him go on with his schemes of subterfuge. If we took Exeter, it would have to be fairly and squarely, or not at all.

Help for the defenders now flowed in from the neighbouring villages, and we were in danger of being attacked both in front and from behind. I rode along my lines, encouraging my men, praising them for what they had already achieved. 'We must not give in now,' I told them. 'It will take days for reinforcements to arrive on the King's side. Until then it is us who have the greater fighting strength.'

A number of those from Devon were, alas, already beginning to drift back to their homes - tired and demoralised. The Cornishmen, on the other hand, though scantily clothed and even more poorly armed, were determined to fight on; they had now

145

come too far to go back, and vowed (if need be) to perish for my cause. If they stayed, we should still be the larger fighting strength.

Yet, our plans were soon to change drastically. The Earl of Devon's men told us openly that a second division of the King's forces, led by the Duke of Buckingham, was closing in on the city. Moreover, that at only a short distance behind - perhaps no more than a day's riding behind - was the King himself, with a still greater force.

It would have been utter madness to launch my ill-equipped and inexperienced men into battle against such overwhelming odds. Some three hundred men had already perished in the assault on Exeter. I looked upwards to the huge threatening cannon directed at us from the walls; and that single glance was enough to tell me that our only sensible course of action for the present was to withdraw.

Therefore, in the late afternoon, with great reluctance, I raised a badly torn shirt spattered with blood as a white flag of surrender. Shortly afterwards we retreated to the nearby town of Cullompton where my men camped in the fields, my advisers stayed at an inn, and I was put up in an old thatched barn house close to the church.

Chapter 17

Next morning I was awoken early by rain pounding furiously against the window of my little garret room, and the wind making the shutters rattle in the frame. As I got out of bed to look outside, I found that my legs ached and my joints were stiff.

I pulled open the shutters to see rain gushing off the roof into a puddle below. In the distance, on the other side of the church, trees swayed in the wind, their tops sweeping into one another as if they were sharing a secret.

Suddenly, there was a cracking sound as a gust of wind caught the shutters of the window on the floor directly below mine. In the shock I spun round, grazing my left cheek against the corner of a dark oak beam that projected into the room.

I dressed quickly and fastened my spurs. Seizing a hunk of dry, hard bread and swigging back a mouthful of some local brew that was so foul I had to spit it out, I set off to meet my advisers who were lodging at an inn just off the main street.

With the rain beating down incessantly, I skirted the puddles by the church, and wove my way through some little lanes into the centre of the town; here, unlike in Exeter there flowed a good, clean water supply.

It was still not eight o'clock, yet in spite of the bad weather Cullompton was already full of merchants carrying sacks of wool, their cloaks drawn up around their shoulders; others arriving with sacks of wool stacked up high on their carts.

When I reached the inn where my advisers were lodged, I was disgusted to find they were still in bed. I told them to get up right away. As I stood in the front room waiting for them, the weather seemed to be worsening. It was now raining harder than ever, and the wind tore at the great iron jug (the sign of this inn) which creaked to and fro above my head. Each time it did so, it scraped against the timbers, sending a shiver down my spine and causing my teeth to grate.

It was not long before my advisers joined me, still dressing themselves as they came out into the street. I explained how with Exeter untaken, we had no choice that morning other than to make our way directly to Taunton - the next market town on the route eastwards to London.

As our men joined us from their camp, the rain was falling as fast as ever, and the wind lashed it into our faces, causing our cheeks to sting and our eyes to smart. Our progress out of Cullompton was slow, the roads being very bad in these parts at the best of times - and in these conditions much worse.

In places, the road was barely wide enough for a mouse to squeeze round us, so that packhorses travelling in the opposite direction were forced off the track to wait in the fields on either side until we had passed. Two young men, deep in conversation, and carrying what looked like sacks full of turnips on their back, either did not hear us approaching or did not want to move, so that we ended up spattering them with mud. Further on, a plump woman on horseback reluctantly pulled her nag to the side to let us pass. Her basket that had been precariously resting in front of her, tipped over the side, spilling all her vegetables. We did not stop to help her, but could hear her curses as we moved on.

Soon after this there was no road at all. Some farmer had planted wheat right across it. So we went across his field. That will teach him a lesson!

Suddenly, there was a terrific jolt. The wagon lurched forward and I shot off my seat, bruising my knees and bashing my chin against the door. We must have fallen into a ditch. Our carrier cursed and swore like fury. He knew the road well: there was certainly no hole here when he was on the road yesterday.

We all climbed down ready to give the wagon a push out of the ditch. Only the metalled rim of the front wheel on the left was visible, the rest being submerged in a puddle full of filthy water.

'Some rogue's been diggin' up the god-forsaken road again!' fumed the carrier. 'It'll probably be that bloody miller again, after clay to repair his mill.' He pointed to a run-down looking property in the distance. 'Somebody'll break their bloody neck before long, you mark my words!'

Even unloaded our wagon was very heavy. Try as we might, we could not get a grip under our feet so it kept slipping back down into the ditch, with the result that we wasted the rest of the morning while my men went to fetch ropes to haul it up. Soon after noon, we managed to continue our journey.

At one of the inns we stopped at along the way, the landlord reported that the King's army was gaining ground on us, that his men had already left the cathedral city of Wells and were now taking rest in the abbey at Glastonbury. This meant that only the town of Bridgwater stood in their way before they reached Taunton. When I told my men this, I expected them to show alarm, but they seemed to savour the contest ahead, as they let out a great cheer. How little did I know them!

*   *   *

At the end of a second day's marching, our clothes now wet through, we arrived at Taunton, a much less important place than I had been led to believe, far less busy than Exeter.

Here, in the public square before an audience of several hundred inhabitants, I affirmed once more who I was. It was the fourth time I had done this since my arrival in England, but I kept reminding myself that the people of Taunton were hearing this for the first time. I had to make my words seem just as fresh and convincing as the very first time I made my speech at Whitesand Bay.

As inducements to any who might still be undecided, I told them of my intention to coin a considerable quantity of money which I would distribute freely among all those who agreed to support me. With such encouragement, many came to my side - including some of the town's tradesmen, whose lively conversation helped the miles ahead to pass so much more quickly.

It was in Taunton where I met up with John Heron. Until a year or two before he had been a cloth merchant in London. Then, becoming more and more disaffected by the King's ever increasing taxes, he had returned to Taunton, the place of his birth. A serious outbreak of fever had prevented him taking part in the Cornish uprising earlier that summer, but he now relished having a second chance to take his revenge on the King. His local knowledge, as well as his connections with tradesmen and minor officials in

London, would be of great advantage to me, and I was delighted to welcome him into my army.

My new recruits then made off to fetch barrels of drink, and started to toast my good health in a local brew from these parts that they call cider. I drank down a few sips out of politeness more than anything, for it was much too sweet for my liking - much the same as the disgusting stuff I had drunk at the inn back at Cullompton.

Even as we were still drinking, there was a great clattering of hooves, and four war horses galloped into the square. They were Henry's men. How had they managed to get through without our being aware of them? How could my guard have been so stupid as not to notice them coming?

A stout, fierce-looking man dismounted and came forward, introduced himself as the King's Lord Chamberlain, and coolly encouraged me to surrender. 'Sir, I come with a promise from the King that you shall be pardoned if you lay down your arms . . .' He did not even look me in the face as he spoke; and I suspect that he realised only too well, when he saw the expressions of my high-spirited men, that such an offer would never be accepted.

I did not wait for him to finish, dismissing his proposal with a contemptuous laugh. 'Do you really believe I have come this far only to give in now? Give up my rightful inheritance? I have the backing of the courts of Europe and the King of Scotland.'

From my tone it must have been clear there was no point in him trying to persuade me to compromise, to give in; and so the Lord Chamberlain turned on his heel, went back to his three companions, mounted his war horse, and together they rode away. I was glad that I had managed to mask my real feelings, my fears and anxieties, for, in spite of my confident bluster, I have to admit that my heart had failed at the sight of the royal standard - my first encounter with the forces of the King.

For many hours I discussed what we should do with my closest advisers. In the end, I decided that the only sensible action to take was to return to the Duchess's court; but this would have to be kept secret from the rest of the men. I knew our flight would mean delaying the time when I should meet up with my wife and child again; but I would see them soon when I returned from Flanders with a great army. How proud of me Kate would be, when together we would march into London and be crowned King and Queen.

Chapter 18

Soon after midnight, when most of my men were sound asleep under whatever shelter they could find, I passed the word to sixty horsemen to make ready. Quickly, they fastened their spurs and together we left our camp just outside Taunton, bound for Southampton Water. Two of my more dependable men I sent off ahead of all the others, so they could have a ship ready when we arrived.

It was a foul autumn night to be out riding. There seemed to be no end to the stinging, cold rain that had soaked all through my cloak. In the cool breeze, the dampness of the cloak felt icy against my skin, and as I shivered I sensed a chill coming on.

As it started to get light, the two horsemen who I had sent on ahead returned with the disturbing news that the King had set up a blockade all along the coast, that Lord Brooke was at this moment patrolling the Solent near to the Isle of Wight.

There was no prospect of me crossing now to Flanders. We would have to rethink our plans. 'We'd better head for Beaulieu,' said John Heron who seemed to know the area like the back of his own hand. 'It's a sanctuary.'

'A sanctuary?' I was unfamiliar with the word.

'Yes. It's a place where the King has no control, sir. Much like St Michael's Mount where your wife and child are. I know the abbot at Beaulieu well - his name is Humphrey. You will find safety there.'

'Safety from the King's army,' joined in Astley.

I did not answer at first. The very mention of St Michael's Mount reminded me at once of my wife and little son. Were they safe? Were they well?

'Sir!' exclaimed Astley.

I stopped dreaming, and tried to pull myself together:

'Where is this place?'

'It's on the edge of the New Forest.'

'Very well,' I nodded, trying to disguise a sneeze. 'We must go there without delay.'

★ ★ ★

My advisers and I were riding ahead of the others, our horses straining at the bit. Suddenly, when we were still only a short distance on a lonely stretch outside Taunton, we were encircled by six masked horsemen.

Holding their swords to our throats, they forced us off the road. One of them roughly told us to keep still, and put blindfolds around our eyes. Our horses were then led for a short distance.

When we finally stopped, the blindfolds were removed, and I realised we were in some sort of camp, deep in the forest. We were surrounded, roughly roped together, and searched. But if it was money they were after they were sorely disappointed.

They questioned me as they searched us, interested by my crested cloak. They obviously still distrusted any stranger, no matter how plausible he might seem. When they realised who I was, at first they laughed in disbelief; but after they questioned the others, whose stories confirmed my account, they appeared to be convinced, their mood began to change, and they became less threatening. They even shared their meagre rations with us - a few chicken bones and some ale.

As we ate, it became clear they were not the dangerous ruffians I had imagined outlaws to be: their tale was one of injustice and oppression. They described in bitter terms their treatment by King Henry - the taxes they had been forced to pay, their lands confiscated when they could not pay.

After we had rested, they led us back to the road, but once again we were made to wear blindfolds. I wondered whether they had really believed my story. As soon as they had ridden away, we removed our blindfolds to discover we were back where they had captured us.

After another two hours riding we arrived at Beaulieu Abbey, or, to give it it's full name, the Abbey of St Mary of Beaulieu Regis. It appeared to be a peaceful, solitary spot, surrounded by cornfields - a place that encouraged contemplation. All around were large fields of sheep, hundreds of sheep - needed to supply the abbey with wool and skin for making blankets, hoods and parchment. I had not reckoned on there being so much activity - for I had expected an abbey to be a quiet, restful place, with everyone at prayer. As it was, there were a great many little buildings within the perimeter wall. Apart from the church and the monastic buildings themselves, there was a busy little mill, a brewery, a pungent-smelling tannery, and a clattering forge that made ploughs and tools for the abbey.

Our wagon skirted a stinking brown pond as we neared the abbey building itself. When I was told that fish swam in it, I could not believe my ears; for judging from the smell I assumed it was a cesspit full of sewage.

We entered the abbey precincts through an outer gatehouse with a simple stone cross above it. However, there was some confusion, as the porter who opened the gate was not sure who we were; noticing only our drenched and disarrayed clothes he mistook us for poor people trying to claim food, clothing and firewood.

The matter was soon cleared up with the arrival of the abbot, a friendly and concerned man, followed by a small group of monks in their white habits. As soon as the abbot set eyes on his friend, John Heron, we were immediately welcomed inside the white walls. Stable boys led our horses down a tree-lined path while we were ushered along cold, stone passageways into the hall. Here, the abbot made us surrender our weapons. All I had was a cudgel, a knife and a few sharp stones, all of which I handed over to the abbot who placed them in a leather sack, then beckoned to another monk to take them away. I felt naked and vulnerable without them; but was reassured when Abbot Humphrey solemnly promised to feed and protect us in return.

After this, we followed him along a narrow corridor that ran next to the infirmaries. Moaning sounds could be heard from within. 'Some of our monks are having a course of bleeding,' explained the abbot. 'Every quarter of the year, all the monks are bled - not just those who are sick, but those who are fit, too.'

I raised an eyebrow, but then recalled how the Duchess Margaret was bled each month.

'Oh, we treat them well here, they are given good food. In fact, those staying in the infirmary for some weeks have liver, pigeon and duck to eat - things normally we have vowed not to touch.'

Noticing some sacks in the corner of the room, I asked him what was in them, and he said they contained almonds, liquorice and sugar for the sickest monks. 'What's wrong with them?' I asked. 'Mainly breathing difficulties, and problems with their joints,' the abbot replied, rubbing his own elbows before beckoning me on again.

Passing by the lofty Chapter House, we entered the great abbey church, where monks would be summoned eight times every day by a bell housed in a special tower high above our heads. Inside, the sacristan was replacing candles, made by the monks themselves from wax produced in the abbey's own hives; while he did so, another officer counted out service books on a large oak table.

I was taken to an adjoining chapel where I was asked to kneel and confess my sins in silence. Instead of doing anything of the sort, I spent the time gazing up at the stone carvings and towering pillars, reflecting on what had happened, making plans about how I might still escape back to Flanders.

After this, an officer who they called the hosteller took us to our rooms. As we went through the cloisters, monks were at work - some seated at benches teaching the novice monks in small groups. Others were in their carrels, small rooms set aside from the cloisters; all that could be seen of them being the tops of their heads as they knelt in contemplation and prayer. The rooms had been deliberately set into the north wall for protection from the wind, and to take advantage of any sun; but there was little enough of that around on this dull late September day.

A few monks had come out of the gloomy scriptorium into the sunlight where they were laboriously copying charters and accounts onto sheets of parchment. I watched them for a few moments. Every stroke of the quill they made with painstaking care, every letter they formed was uniformly even in size, almost as if they had been printed on one of the new printing presses. It must have been very pleasant to have worked here, so peaceful, and with the sweet scent of nearby herb gardens in the air. Eventually, we arrived at our rooms that overlooked the front entrance. How glad I was to take off my wet clothes and stretch out on the bed.

A simple meal was prepared for us later that evening in the refectory. There was bread, beer and a pottage - no meat, it being the rule that all the monks had 'to abstain from the flesh of four-footed beasts.' Before we went in (and again as we left) we had to wash our hands in little basins outside. Personally, I saw little need for the ritual, but thought it ill mannered not to follow suit as was the custom.

The meal was eaten in total silence, punctuated only by my own sneezes as my cold seemed to be getting worse. The abbot noticed it. 'You'd do well to have a course of leeches to cleanse your blood. And some violets would ease that cough.'

Not wanting to cause offence, I shrugged off the suggestion as politely as I could. 'Thank you, but it's just a chill.'

Yet in truth, my limbs really ached, my head was heavy, and I was glad to go to bed at the monk's early hour.

*   *   *

Late the next afternoon, as light was beginning to fade, we were holding council in my little room when suddenly one of my men came in to warn me that the King's forces had been sighted in the distance. He reckoned them to be some five hundred horsemen strong, fully trained and well disciplined under Lord Daubney's command. Already in low spirits because of my cold, I began to despair altogether at this news. 'Damn. We've had it now!' I cursed out loud.

'Not at all, sir,' replied Heron. 'You see, the King's made a grave error of judgement. He estimated that his forces would intercept us before we reached the sanctuary of the abbey; but he miscalculated. We arrived before him! And now we're here, we're safe.'

I was not convinced. 'Yes, but for how long?'

'Usually, sanctuary in a church would guarantee us immunity from arrest for about a week . . .'

'A week! What use is that?'

'Please sir, let me finish. This isn't the case for abbeys, especially one like Beaulieu that has special relics. We'll be safe here for a month at least. And by this time, the King will have lost his patience and will want to settle quickly.'

'But suppose he never gives up?' I persisted.

'Look! Do you see those stones, way over there in the distance? continued Heron. 'And those?' he said, taking me to another window. 'There are stones all round the abbey like that - all at a distance of a mile - special stones. As long as we stay inside those stones we're safe, safe from all pursuers.'

'And if they take no notice of those stones?'

'They wouldn't dare! If they did, they would be violating sanctuary. Their souls would rot in hell.'

In spite of my own fears of hell, I was not much comforted by reassurances of this kind; and, with these ever increasing worries and worsening cold, I scarcely slept at all.

★　　★　　★

I woke very early next morning to the sound of chanting from the abbey church. Evidently, the monks were used to rising half way through the night for Mass, and would return to the church for services seven or eight times during their day. Can you believe that men choose to spend their lives this way?

As it grew light, I could just make out the King's forces patrolling the distant outer wall. I was full of self-doubts. What could I do? There was no prospect of me escaping. For the moment, of course, I was safe. King Henry would surely not dare to violate the special privilege of sanctuary. But sanctuary was not going to last forever, even here at Beaulieu. After a few weeks had passed, I would become vulnerable once again. Would it be better, I wondered, to come to terms with Henry before that time?

Over the next few days, I turned over in my mind the merits of the few options I had left. To give in would be to admit defeat; but there again it might mean I would be treated more leniently at a later trial. To agree terms would be looked upon as an act of cowardice in the eyes of my men. To hold out might look brave and honourable, but would lead to humiliating terms if I was forced to surrender.

As it turned out, the decision was taken away from me; for less than a week after my arrival the King began to grow weary from waiting, and he sent out a herald, a young, friendly man with a broad smile.

Before the man was allowed to get too near the abbey he was searched for weapons, and at the entrance he was made to kneel, acknowledge that he was on holy ground and vouchsafe his good intent. Only then did my advisers lead him into the hall. He had been out in the rain all night judging from the state of his cloak which was wet through.

'What news?' I asked him.

He answered solemnly, rain dripping off the hem of his cloak. 'I have orders from the King to offer you a free pardon provided you submit to him at once . . .'

'A free pardon?' I stared back at him in disbelief. I could never have hoped for such terms.

'Yes sir. Provided you withdraw your claim to the throne of England. Provided you admit to your real origins as the son of a boatman from Tournai.'

Chapter 19

I knew that I could gain nothing, nothing at all, by holding out. The best thing I could do, the only thing, was to surrender with honour while I could do so. Assuming that the King would remain true to his word, I had nothing to fear: no proceedings would be taken against me, no court of law would try me; and I would be able to see my wife and my child again. Besides, after a few months, the King might grow less vigilant, become distracted by other, more pressing cares.

The herald returned to his superiors to give them my reply. After a while, three horsemen galloped up on their black war-horses and dismounted. One of them, the captain of the guard, a tall, muscular man in his thirties, stepped forward. 'I have orders from His Majesty, King Henry, to offer you a free pardon, provided you leave the Abbey and come with us this day to meet him.'

There was the briefest of pauses. 'Well? What do you say?' He stared at me intently, with the expression of one who seemed used to making bargains.

But no special bargaining was needed now, for I had already made my decision. I bowed my head, replying quietly 'I accept the free pardon and submit myself into your custody'.

'Very well. We shall escort you to Taunton, where you shall meet the King.'

They were ready to take me there and then; but I could not leave without first saying goodbye to my friend John Heron, who was to stay on as a guest of Abbot Humphrey. It was to be the last I saw of him. I had known him only a short while, but during that time he had been all that anyone could expect of a true friend - reliable, loyal, a good and sympathetic listener; but more than any of these things he had led me to safety. I thanked him and gave him my blessing.

The stable boys saddled horses for us. As we set off, the heavy rain of the last two days was beginning to abate, but the sky was still very dark.

With the King's men riding before and behind me, we left the grounds of the abbey and turned onto the Taunton road. On either side of us, meadows full of delicate wild flowers - yellow, pink and blue - fluttered in the breeze. Ladders lay perched against heavily laden trees in the orchards, where cheerful-looking farm hands were already taking advantage of the slight improvement in the weather to pick ripe red apples. I could hear their still unbroken voices calling out to one another in their attractive local accent.

However, as we continued on our journey, the sky became darker, more and more threatening. Grey clouds swirled over the Blackdown Hills, and it looked as though a fearful storm was brewing. Whole branches began to sway in the wind, gusts swept up clusters of stray leaves and blew them up into our faces, so that for a few moments we could not see the way ahead.

In view of the impending storm, the captain of the guard decided that we should stop overnight in the village of Wincanton at a newly built inn. The stop gave me an opportunity to get Astley to write down some notes so that I might be better prepared when called upon to give my confession before the King in Taunton the next day. Fortunately, the innkeeper, a jolly man with a blotchy red face, was able to provide us with parchment, a quill and some black ink.

Our host pointed to the storey above, from where we could hear laughter and stamping, and explained that he only had two rooms which were both full; but that we were very welcome to sleep in the serving room if we wished.

When he realised who we were, that we were on our way to meet the King, he began to apologise for the behaviour of those in the room above, and began frantically dabbing around at the dust on the table before us.

Amidst more apologies, he then prepared a simple meal for us of bread, cheese, some cold beef, apples and plenty of ale. A welcome spread indeed, which was spoilt not by the imagined dust, nor even by the noise from above, but by the sickening smell coming from the undercroft where the innkeeper kept pigs and sheep.

We sat around, talking freely under the influence of the ale, and belching with satisfaction while brimming tankards thudded onto tables, coins jingled in the innkeeper's hands, and the liquor warmed our insides. As the fire roared in the hearth, everyone was relaxed and contented. In such surroundings I did not feel as if I was a captive at all.

Becoming tired, we made ourselves as comfortable as we could around the remains of the fire. I wrapped my cloak around me to try and keep warm. The captain of the guard was slumped in the corner, and had started to snore.

I called Astley over and asked him to be ready to take down my confession. Slowly, I dictated it to him, from time to time pausing to think of the most suitable word, then going on, watching Astley make strokes in his characteristically clear and elegant hand, the hand that had written out so many account rolls and legal indentures. As we reached the last line most of the men around us were fast asleep, and only the dying embers remained of the fire.

*   *   *

The following morning the weather had cleared and we resumed our journey. My pulse quickened, I began to breathe more rapidly - for, later that day I would come face to face with the King himself and be made to explain my actions.

We had been travelling for several hours when, just as we were approaching a crossroads outside Taunton, I saw hanging from an oak tree a row of five or six men, their clothes in tatters.

'Thieves!' yelled my guards in unison.

'But thieves are usually branded, or they lose a hand, don't they?'

'They're not just petty thieves. They broke into a church, and stole plate and cups. They need to be made an example of. If they're not, what would prevent others from doing the same?'

Just as those men were being made to suffer, I too was being brought to account.

How would the King react when we met? Would he honour his promise of a free pardon? Or was it all just a trap? Perhaps he would not be able to control his anger? Evidently he was already in a foul mood as he had lost a great deal of money at cards some nights ago - as much as nine pounds, according to one guard. Would I end up being punished rather than pardoned?

We crossed a quietly flowing river and approached the gates of Taunton which were opened at once to let us through. The streets were very busy, making our progress through them extremely slow. Signs hung out from the shops, some almost close enough for us to touch. Sparks were flying in the blacksmith's shop as we passed by the sign of the three horseshoes swinging in the breeze.

On the ground outside one of the inns a brawl was going on between two men. Fists were flying but missing their target as both men seemed to be blind drunk. They were watched by a crowd of spectators, spurring them on, and a mangy black dog that danced around, barking wildly. A little further on we had to stop again to move on two boys who were standing legs astride, hands on hips, in the middle of the street, competing to see who could spit cherry stones the further.

It was market day, and the centre of the town was full of stalls and tradesmen of every description. In their rich accent they called out their wares - everything from butter and corn, to lace and velvet; for a moment, it brought back memories of my days in Antwerp, selling and modelling some of the finest silks in Europe.

The last time I had visited Taunton I had been thrilled by the reception I had received: its citizens had toasted my good health, and hundreds of its inhabitants had swelled the ranks of my army; but now I was being brought back through the town as a prisoner.

The mood of the inhabitants as they lined the main street to watch us go past was so very different now. Their cheers of welcome had been replaced by mocking jeers. Someone deep in the crowd threw an apple core, hitting me hard on my left cheek. Further along a couple of old women spat at me.

'Lying bastard!' yelled one young man, waving his fist.

'Down with the traitor! another man shouted .

Then his girlfriend joined in. 'Here here! Long live King Henry!'

On we went, past the pillory where James Shrubsole stood to await his punishment. He had sold a dozen pigeons, all bad. Now he would have them all burnt before his nose.

We entered the market. At the far end a platform had been constructed from beer barrels and planks of wood, and several very important officials in scarlet robes were flocking around it.

At first I could not see the King at all, as his stocky cup bearer was blocking my view. Then his servant moved aside and I caught a glimpse of him. He was a surprisingly slight man, weighed down by his heavy armour - a long glistening sword, a thick gorget that protected his throat. My eyes rested for a while on the shining helmet he carried in his right hand, with its great plume of green feathers.

Suddenly he looked up and fixed his dark, penetrating eyes directly on me. He beckoned to two stewards, and moments later I was brought before him and made to kneel. Here I was, face to face with the King at last. How insignificant I felt.

He began in a solemn tone. 'Sir, you have been brought here to account for your misdeeds and to repent. What you have done borders on treason. Many other princes would not hesitate to have you executed at once.' I felt a sudden twinge in my neck. 'But I am renowned for my mercy. I am willing to offer you terms. If you confess now and declare your true identity to me and all those who are gathered here, you will be granted the free pardon that I have promised you.'

There was a pause. 'I await your reply, sir.'

I reached for the roll of paper on which Astley had so dutifully recorded my confession at the inn the previous night. Before beginning I looked around. There was not a murmur from the platform, not a single word. I cleared my throat and then, in front of all the lords, began to read from it nervously: 'First, I want it to be known . . .'

My voice failed me. I had to start again: 'I want it to be known that I was not born in England . . .'

A cry of horror broke out from the crowd. When it had died down I did my best to continue. 'I was born in the town of Tournai in Flanders. My father was John Warbeck, a customs officer. My mother was born Katherine de Faro. When I was young she took me to Antwerp, and it was here that I learnt my native language which is Flemish. For about six months I stayed in the house of a cousin of mine, John Steinbeck. Then I had to go back to Tournai for safety, on account of the wars in Flanders. But within a year I had returned to Antwerp, this time in the company of a merchant called Berlo; but I was able to do little work, being ill with the influenza for several months . . .'

I was interrupted by jeers and mock sympathy.

' . . .When I was better, I went with Berlo to Middelburg where I was put into service with a merchant. There I stayed from Christmas until Easter, and greatly improved my Flemish. But I longed to see something of the world. And soon after this I had my opportunity, when Sir Edward Brampton and his wife agreed to take me to Portugal. As soon as I arrived in Lisbon, I was put into service with a knight - an unpleasant man with only one eye. I stayed with him for a full year but I grew restless. I wanted something more. I yearned for adventure.'

I paused and looked up. A ripple of interest had gone through the crowd. They must have wondered what I was going to reveal next. 'So, I put myself into service with a Breton merchant called Pregent Meno who took me to Ireland to model clothes. We first landed in the town of Cork. As I was so elaborately dressed in fine silks, a number of townsmen came up to me, mistaking me for the son of the Duke of Clarence who had been to Dublin some years before. I was surprised and denied it, but the mayor did not appear to believe me, and made me swear on the cross that I was not Clarence's son, nor any relation of his. After this, others came forward, being equally convinced that I was really King Richard's bastard son. Again, I swore I was not.'

The crowd listened, enthralled.

'By this time I was feeling confused and threatened. Why were they claiming I was one of these people? The mayor told me not to be afraid, that if I agreed to take on the role of the Duke of York, I could expect help from the leading earls to regain my throne. The pressure on me to concede to their demands was too great. I dared not go against their wishes for my own safety. So, much against my will, I agreed . . .'

There were gasps. I looked up. The King gave me a steely look. I tried to finish my story as quickly as I could. 'I was made to learn English, and taught what to do and say, so I could carry out my role convincingly. Soon after this, the French King invited me to come to Paris; and from there to Flanders; and from Flanders to Ireland; and from Ireland into Scotland where I was married to the King's own kin; and so into England, to Cornwall, where I have left my wife and child.'

The crowd had listened spellbound to what I had to say. Many already knew my true identity from Henry's spies; but they still needed to hear the awful truth from my own lips.

The King averted his gaze. His hand tightened on his sword. He looked at his men. The tone of his voice was severe. 'Now the truth is known at last to you all. There can be no more doubting the treachery of the men who put you up to these foul schemes.'

He turned to the captain of the guard: 'Ride to St Michael's Mount, seize the Lady Katherine Gordon, and bring her prisoner here.'

Chapter 20

It was hard enough that I was a captive: but now my wife was to join me. I had never thought that she would be touched. That same day I was to be taken to Exeter, not in style but as a prisoner of the King. What would happen there? Would my wife be treated with deference to her rank? If she were treated roughly I would never be able to forgive myself.

I felt guilty that I had been so absorbed in my own pursuits that I had not thought about her more. It was now the middle of October. Over a month had passed since we had said goodbye in Cornwall, since I had seen her silhouette at the top of the tower at St Michael's. And what about the health of our child? He seemed so fit and well when I had left him; I only prayed that he were still so now.

We passed through several villages and even a town or two between Taunton and Exeter; but what with the dreariness of the day and my troubled mind, I took little notice of them. At Tiverton we had a change of horses before following the course of the River Exe southwards through rolling countryside, draped in brown autumnal colours, towards Exeter itself. I remembered the city as a bustling trading place, so full of shops and houses that there was hardly an empty space within the walls - those walls that had so recently stood up to our assault.

As we neared the city we were overcome by a vile smell. 'Is that sewage, or is it coming from a tannery?' I asked, knowing the two smells to be similar.

'Sewage. It'll be Shitbrook,' said one of them, laughing. 'It's an open sewer. Look, you can see it, over there.' He pointed to a filthy ditch of water over to our left.

As we approached, the smell grew even more unbearable. Even the guards stopped making light of it and, like me, buried their faces in their cloaks.

We rode into Exeter through the East Gate, and were confronted with a different smell, this time from close by - the acrid stench of a heretic's burning flesh. I felt as though I was going to be sick.

We continued down the main street. Crowds of people standing on either side cheered heartily as they caught sight of the King. They had defended his cause with such determination, and doubtless expected to be thanked for their loyalty. In the daylight I saw clearly the damage we had inflicted to the gate, the battered walls, the missing battlements, and the torn up roadway where the terrible slaughter had occurred.

Any moment now I was to meet my wife again. When we had said goodbye to one another I had promised her that she would enter London by my side, as my queen. Now she was going to be confronted with the awful truth - that, in reality, I was an impostor, a mere pretender to the throne of England. How would she ever be able to trust me again?

We passed slowly by the fashionable houses of the wealthy cloth merchants, numerous little sandstone churches and many inns. I can remember their names to this day - the Bear Inn, the Blue Boar, the Eagle, and the grandest of them all, the New Inn where the wealthiest visitors lodged.

According to my guards, there had been a great deal of preparation for the King's visit. A suite of rooms at the New Inn had been especially decorated for him, with wonderful hangings and tapestries - even a new garderobe and water pipes had been installed in his honour.

A procession of men wearing brightly coloured robes was waiting to welcome the King when he arrived. They had set off from the Guildhall and were now filing solemnly through the main street.

A few steps ahead of the party came a young drummer-boy, perhaps only ten years old, beating out a battle step, together with four pages blasting out a shrill note on their brightly polished trumpets. After that - in strict order of seniority - came four sergeants carrying gleaming maces, followed by the sword-bearer, and then the Mayor of Exeter, John Atwell, splendidly dressed in a gown and cloak of scarlet, and followed by as many previous mayors as were then living, all similarly dressed. Behind the mayors came all the other officers: sheriffs and receivers dressed in their dignified crimson gowns of murrey, and finally the stewards and bailiffs in violet gowns.

All processed slowly along the high street, so close to me that if I reached out I could have touched them. They were on their way to meet the King, to hand over the keys to their city, especially polished for the occasion. The guards boasted that ever since William the Conqueror's time the keys had never passed through the hands of a single enemy. As they said this, their eyes rested on me, and I quickly averted my gaze.

I saw the mayor handing over the keys to the King who received them with gratitude, and went on to praise the citizens warmly for the loyalty they had shown to their country for so many years.

And so we entered the cathedral precincts and reached the Treasurer's House that had been made ready to receive the royal party. Here, four oxen, forty sheep and a great cask of wine from Bordeaux were given to the King. A gift of wine was also presented to Lord Brooke who had prevented me from escaping from Southampton by blockading the Solent. For Sir Edward Courtenay, the Earl of Devon, there was a sum of money. It was meant as a mark of appreciation from the citizens of Exeter; but when it was handed over a great hiss went up from the crowd, as many citizens hated the Courtenays who made it difficult for them to fish in the river.

Then it was the moment for Henry to come face to face with what remained of my army of Cornishmen, those who I had deserted so shamefully that night at Taunton when I had thought only of my own safety.

With halters still around their necks, they were dragged across the grass and the mud to the Treasurer's House, their cloaks ripped open, their backs bloody. Eight trees had been felled especially, so as to give the King an uninterrupted view as they were pulled across.

When they came within a few feet from where the King sat they were ordered to remain still, kneeling there pathetically. The guards stood back: there was an awesome silence.

Then Henry rose.

Another long pause. The King stood there, his legs astride, his chest puffed out, his face a terrifying shade of purple.

Then, coming forward a few more steps, he moistened his lips with his tongue, took in a deep breath and gave vent to the full extent of his wrath. 'Cornish traitors! You have hurt and injured me by your mean and malicious conduct. You were willing to do evil by helping this weak and most shallow of men. You deserve to be punished. The laws are there to be obeyed.'

He stared across at me. There was contempt in his eyes. Then he turned to face them again. 'Only those who took up this wretch's cause through ignorance shall have their lives spared. The rest of you must suffer the penalty you deserve, the only just penalty - death.'

All the Cornishmen fell forward on their knees in front of the King, clasping their hands, begging for clemency; but Henry would not listen to their feeble excuses, and ordered his guards to take them away.

Scores of my supporters were then marched off, wailing and protesting. Among them, sorry to say it, were my dearest friends and advisers Nicholas Astley and Edward Skelton, led away in their chains.

My turn was surely next; but nothing happened. My wife had not yet arrived from St Michael's Mount. I was told there would be a delay of several hours.

Not being allowed to wait here, I was led away to a dank cell in the depths of Exeter Castle. Over the last few days, I had been moved on rapidly from place to place, and this had stopped me from despair and self-pity; but now followed a period of enforced inactivity. Without my advisers, there was nothing I could do apart from brood.

At about noon, a jolly, buxom, redheaded girl came in, carrying bread and a pitcher of water. I was grateful for some company. 'Do you live in the city, or here in the castle?' I asked her gently.

She seemed unused to any interest being shown her, and blushed. 'I live 'ere,' she replied in a curious accent. 'With my father, who is the gaoler.'

'In this damp and gloom. How do you put up with it?'

'Haven't got to much longer,' she replied excitedly. 'I'm goin' a be married soon,' she beamed. 'To a fine, handsome man from Topsham.'

Wondering whether she had said too much, she changed the subject to me. 'Are you married yourself, sir?'

'Yes, I have been married for over two years now. Sadly, I've not seen my wife the last month but we're soon to be reunited - tomorrow, I hope.'

'Oh, that'll be lovely, sir.' Her red cheeks glowed: the girl was obviously very pleased for me; and, as she turned around to leave she beamed again.

Later that afternoon, while there was still light, I decided to write a letter to my mother. I always carried a small scrap of parchment and a tiny phial of black ink in a small leather pouch in the inside pocket of my cloak; and I still had the quill that poor Astley had used to write down my confession that evening at the inn.

Some good just might come of a letter home. I would tell my mother about my suffering and beg her to do what she could to influence others to rescue me. As far as I remember, the letter went something like this:

'*Dear Mother,*

I beg you to help me. Something has happened that I have to tell you about. Some Englishmen have made me say that I am the son of the late King Edward of England, his second son called the Duke of York. I am now in such a terrible situation that if you don't help me, I shall be in grave danger.

So that you have no doubt in your mind that this really is your son who is writing to you, let me remind you of some of the things that happened to me when I was little. Remember how I left with Berlo to go to Antwerp, and how you cried when you said goodbye. Remember the last letter that you wrote to me from Middelburg, telling me that you had given birth to a daughter; also when my poor brother and sister died of the plague. I understand that my father has died (God rest his soul). This news is hard to bear. God be with you.

I am in the hands of the King of England. But I am not his subject and do not see how he can try me. I have told him the truth and have begged him to forgive what I have done. I did what I did only to please some of his own subjects.

And so, dear Mother, I beg you to do what you can to help me.

Written in Exeter on the 13th October by your dear son.

        PERKIN ·

P.S.

Dear Mother, please send a little money to give to my guards, so they may be kind to me.'

I put my pen down. What was I to do with the letter now? How could I smuggle it out of the castle?

Then a thought struck me. What about the girl who had brought my meal? I had got on so well with her, after all. She would help me if anyone would.

So, when she brought me my supper, I seized the opportunity to talk with her again.

'You didn't mention your mother when we spoke before . . .'

Sadness came into her eyes. 'My mother's dead. She died more than two years ago. I just have my father now. What about you?'

'My father died a few years ago but my mother is still living.'

'In Exeter?'

I laughed. 'No, a long way away. Not even in England. She lives far from here in Flanders, in a town called Tournai, where I was born. She is ill, and I've been writing her this letter to help comfort her. But I have no way of sending it from here.'

'Don't worry your head about that. I can help you. For, the man I'm betrothed to serves on a merchant ship. He'll be able to get the letter to your mother.'

'That's very kind of you. Please let me do something for you in return. Please accept as a gift from me some silk to make your wedding dress.'

At first the girl said nothing, and I thought that she might be offended. Certainly, if I had offered money she might have seen it as no more than a cheap bribe; but far from being offended, my offer seemed actually to seal the agreement. She grinned and scurried away, clutching the letter to her breast.

The gaoler's daughter appeared to have every best intention, I know; but would the letter ever reach my mother? It had a long way to go. I never saw the girl again, so I have no way of knowing to this day whether my mother received it or not. Certainly I have never had a response to it. To think that my mother could have done anything to help rescue me from the King of England! It was naïve of me, I know; but I was so desperate by this time that I had to try every ploy.

Soon after she had departed, her father came to tell me that my wife had arrived in the city from St Michael's Mount, and that tomorrow I would be reunited with her. How would I be able to face Kate with my imposture? She had loved and trusted me all this while. Even when she had been afraid she had stayed by me so loyally. But would she stay by me still, now that I was just a commoner who had deceived her so?

Chapter 21

It was the following day. Although mid afternoon, a dismal mist still hung in the air as I was led from my castle cell to the Treasurer's House. Here I was to be re-united with my wife and child. My legs felt stiff as I had lain awkwardly that night, but I was forced to keep up with the guards to whom I was chained on either side.

As I went, I begged my captives to give me news of my family; but all they would say was that my wife was well, though very tired after her long journey all through the night from the very tip of Cornwall.

'And our child?' There was an awkward pause. 'What about our child?' I pressed.

'I know nothing of your child, sir,' replied the elder guard, cagily.

'My child, how is my child?'

Again, silence.

I was led down the main street, pushed when I did not keep pace. Again I asked about my child, but to no avail.

As we entered the cathedral precincts, the other guard stopped abruptly. Then, making the sign of the cross on his chest, he broke the news that I so dreaded to hear.

'I am sorry to say that the Lady Katherine lost her child about a week ago sir.'

My heart froze in my body as I heard those words. I could not believe it. I was devastated. It had to be a mistake. Our little boy had been so strong and healthy when I had left him only a few weeks ago. He had shown his strength by surviving a terrible ordeal at sea, cooped up in a barrel, only inches away from Henry's men. Surely he could survive anything after that.

My voice was faint, almost a whisper. 'How can this be? There must be some mistake.'

'Sir. The child has been buried at Marazion.'

'But he was a healthy little boy. Who is responsible for his death? The King?

I was angrier than I had ever been before. Then guilt took a hold of me. If it had not been for my schemes, we might still all have been in Scotland, and his little life spared. I clenched and unclenched my fists. Tears began to stream down my cheeks.

The guard's voice was sombre. 'He was taken by the smallpox, sir. Your wife begged the monks to let her return to Scotland - to the safety of her family - and was even on the point of boarding a ship, disguised as a servant, when his Majesty's men reached her.'

'And how is my wife now?' My voice was hoarse, barely audible through my tears.

The guard did his best to reassure me. 'She's calmer than she was. She has been given every consideration for her rank and . . .'

'I must see her! Straight away! Where is she?'

The guards led me inside the gloomy Treasurer's House and into the hallway. However, there were more delays, and I was made to sit and wait while three aldermen went in first.

At length they came out. Another delay, until eventually I was summoned in. I stepped into the room. It was even darker inside than in the hallway, and at first everything was indistinct.

After a while my eyes became used to the darkness and I began to make out the crimson and violet cloaks of some of the important people standing around the edges of the room.

I saw Kate. Her long flowing chestnut hair framed her pale face. I walked a few more steps towards her, then stopped. There were dark rings under her eyes: I knew she had been weeping.

She looked straight at me. I did not know how she would react. Would she smile? No, hardly that. Would her face show scorn and betrayal? More likely. Certainly, I expected some outward sign of emotion. But I was confronted only with a stony silence, and a cold and bitter stare. It occurred to me that she had already been told the awful truth about me; that she knew about my lies and deceits.

Suddenly the voices of the courtiers were stilled, and there was silence in the room. A steward had given the signal that the King was about to enter.

The doors were drawn slowly open, to reveal his cup-bearer and sergeant-at-arms. Behind them was the King himself, wearing a cloak of cloth of gold, edged with white ermine. Around his neck was a gold chain with a pendant bearing a Tudor rose. His face was pale and tired, apart from his dark eyes that he fixed on the company before him.

As soon as the King appeared, Kate sank to her knees and dissolved into tears; but Henry was touched with pity and received her kindly. His eyes softened, he bade her rise again and beckoned his servants to help her to a chair close to where he was sitting.

Then my guards were summoned to bring me across, until I stood directly in front of the King. Here, I was made to confess before my wife. If I were honest now, then Kate would surely be spared. It would, of course, be the end of my ambition; but my love for her was stronger than anything else.

And so I began my confession. 'Kate. Kate, I scarcely know how to say this . . . but I am not who I said I was . . . I am not King Edward's son. All my knowledge of the English court comes from my master, Sir Edward Brampton. He knew the court well . . .'

Kate looked up at me, her face still betraying no emotion. Tears began to well up in her eyes. When I had finished she drew a deep breath, loud enough for me to hear. She looked away, fixing her gaze on a distant corner of the high-ceilinged room, as though she wanted to shut out from her mind all that she had heard.

The King tried to comfort her. 'I am very sad it has come to this - a great lady such as you having been deceived by this contemptible fellow. You deserved a far better husband than this scoundrel. I shall make sure that your future is a happier one. You shall come with us to London at first light tomorrow, and I shall see to it that you are treated just as well as my own wife is. But your husband will stay with us here for a while, as I have a few more questions I want to ask him.'

It was a great relief to hear that my dear wife was not going to be treated cruelly. Perhaps Henry had softened towards her because of her noble birth. That must be it. Why else should he show such concern?

At last, the King gave Kate a chance to speak directly to me. In a weak voice that came from far back in her throat, she began nervously, clutching the folds of her badly creased blue velvet gown as she did so.

'You deceived me with your false stories . . . You lured me from my home, my parents, my friends. Look how wretched you've made me - and my parents too, when they hear about all this. The shame of it all. How I wish you'd never come to these shores! I have lost my baby and my child because of you . . .' Her voice failed and she broke down completely. Her hands went to her face. She clutched the folds of her gown even more tightly. ' . . . I should like to say more, much more, but it's too painful for me.'

With that, she turned away from me, and the King beckoned to his servants who led her away. I knew all her reproaches were justified. I could expect no more. Our life together was at an end, and I had no way of knowing whether I would ever see her again.

As darkness descended, the bell-man passed outside the window, his lamp casting an eerie shadow into the room. 'Look well to your locks,' he shouted, as he signalled an end to another day. Tomorrow would be the beginning of my long journey to London; and there was no knowing what would await me there.

Chapter 22

An hour or so after dawn the next day we began that long journey to London. Weak and watery sunlight seeped thro ugh a heavily overcast sky; and a stiff north-easterly breeze added a cold bite to the air. I rode near the front of the company, surrounded on all sides by the King's guard. Kate followed a good way behind, wearing a new black satin gown and black velvet hood that the King had given her especially for the journey. I prayed that he would be as good as his word, and continue to treat her well.

As we rode out of the city of Exeter, past the timber inns and tall merchants' houses, there were men and women of all ages swarming on either side of the street, shouting 'long live King Henry!' and 'down with the traitor!' Several times I had to duck to avoid being hit by rotten fruit; and at one point a chamber pot was thrown from an upstairs window and landed right in front of me, smashing into tiny pieces, and pouring its irksome, stinking contents onto the roadway.

Just outside Taunton, the landlord of the 'Ox and Plough' was fastening up a new sign on the roof bar: its shiny brass letters spelt out 'The King's Inn.' It was midday, and normally the inn would have been full to bursting with farmhands, munching great cottage loaves and cheese, and swilling back jugs of cider. Today, the innkeeper had chased them off, and had laid out his best jugs and tankards on the tables.

We had just emptied our tankards when the innkeeper appeared with a steaming game pie, quite as big as a wagon wheel. But alas, we never succeeded in devouring it as the grooms were quick to saddle our horses, and the King beckoned to his ministers to make ready.

★   ★   ★

In spite of our best efforts to make progress, by the end of the first day we had still only reached Glastonbury, where we were given hospitality for the night in the great abbey. Next day we set off in the direction of Warminster, then, by way of Salisbury Plain, we set a course for Andover.

At none of the places on our route was I allowed to speak to my wife who was always kept at a distance behind. I kept on asking how she was, and each time was assured that she was tired, though in good spirits.

Eventually, after riding for four days, we sighted in the distance the high grey walls of the city of London. As we drew near to the river embankment we passed a sturdy stone arena, and my guards explained that inside bears were chained to posts, and set upon by packs of wild dogs. I had heard of this going on in Paris and in Vienna. It sounded a cruel sport.

We crossed London Bridge - teeming with houses and little shops. From the back of one of these houses, a young apprentice boy wearing a long brown leather apron was hoisting up a pail of water; whether it was to cook with or to drink, who knows. Further along the bridge, an older man was emptying pans full of either slops or excrement from the back of his shop into the river.

The city was different to how I remembered it from the days of my youth, when I had stayed there with my mother and father. It now seemed smaller and much more compact. Scores of church spires, which I had not noticed before, filled the skyline. To the west was the massive cathedral church of St Paul, while to the east stood the grim outlines of the Tower of London, its high outer wall and fortified gatehouses shrouded in mist.

Instead of heading directly along the embankment past Billingsgate to the Tower, we continued up through Eastcheap and into Cornhill. Why had we taken such a circuitous route? There could only be one explanation: the King was keen to show me off to as many of the loyal citizens of London as possible. After all, I was his prize jewel who had eluded him now for many years.

Tradesmen flocked out of the taverns, and hung around in noisy droves, watching us go by, past the great hall of the fishmongers, the city's grain store and a cheese market. An abundance of tiny dark lanes led off to our left and right, some so narrow that a courting couple would have to walk in single file down them. But we kept all the while to the main road, and before long we were very close to the Tower.

Approaching from the direction of Tower Hill, we followed the course of the dry moat all the way round to the Middle Tower, where we rattled across a drawbridge. An iron-studded door was drawn back ahead of us, and we passed slowly under an arched gateway. Looking up, I noticed the sharp grid-work of a portcullis, and in the roof of the arch itself were gaping black holes through which stones and scalding oil could be poured on unsuspecting attackers.

The guards led me around the perimeter towards a tower in the south-east corner where I was to be kept prisoner. We heard the terrified cries of men being tortured in their cells, while in the distance rang out the determined rhythmical blows of a hammer. My guards told me that a scaffold was being prepared for an execution the following day.

'Julius Caesar's Tower!' exclaimed one of the guards. 'The Romans built a fortress around here. This tower marks an entrance along the fortress wall.'

He seemed to expect me to show some interest in how the tower got its name. If so, I must have disappointed him, as historical detail of this sort was the last thing on my mind. His words went unheeded. My mind was elsewhere - on my wife, who had been taken to the Palace of Westminster on the other side of the city. I recalled the King's words to her when we were at Exeter. 'I shall make sure your future is happier . . . I shall see to it that you are treated just like my own wife is.'

'Hey, York!' shouted the older guard. He coughed up some phlegm and spat it out in front of me. 'Wake up! Through here, and up these steps!'

He pushed me forward with such force that I almost lost my balance. As I climbed the spiral staircase I thought only of my wife. Thank God she was going to be treated well and not locked in one of these towers. She had been used to a life of finery in her native country: agreeable company, quality food, comfortable surroundings. Yet for many months now she had endured unspeakable hardship on my behalf - first at sea, then in solitude on a lonely isle in Cornwall.

I was put in a cell high up in the tower, where the dazzling rays of autumn sun pierced through an arrow slit and cast a shaft of light across the floor. Around me, the rough grey walls were festooned with scores of inscriptions that prisoners had made as they tried to while away the long days, awaiting their fate to be determined. Doubtless, others - those who the courts had already found guilty - had gone straight to their execution on scaffolds like the one that was being built on the green.

The cell was not locked and I was given what was called the 'liberty of the Tower,' which meant that I could move freely and see visitors. I was told I could have my own servants, and was allowed a chaplain and a doctor.

★　　★　　★

Early next day the older guard returned. He gave me a churlish grin. 'We've got orders to take you to the White Tower.'

'But I've made my confession. I made it for all to hear at Taunton, and again at Exeter. I've admitted who I really am.'

My heart began to race. A cold sweat broke out on my forehead. I expected the worst. I had heard rumours about the torture instruments in the Tower - hand presses, neck gouges, the rack. What more did they expect me to tell them which I had not told them already?

I was led down the stairs and out towards the White Tower. To my great relief, we passed by the torture chamber and went upstairs to the council chamber. Here, on a dais at the far end, sat three commissioners dressed in black cloaks edged with white ermine. Before them was a large polished oak table on which rested their notes and a flagon of wine. At a separate table by the wall, a harried looking scribe was poised, ready to take notes.

The inquisitor leading the proceedings blew his nose and then began. I was expecting a ruthless interrogation about my past; but he spoke softly, and there was no trace of malice in his voice. 'We have before us a copy of your confession. We have called you here to check some of the details and clear up a few points.'

Several minutes must have passed while he scanned the page. I looked about the chamber uneasily - the rafters overhead, the cold stone floor below, the streaks of light filtering in through the narrow windows.

'Please confirm your full name, where you were born and who your parents are,' he continued.

'My name is Perkin Warbeck. I was born in Tournai in Flanders in 1474. My parents - my father is now dead - were John Warbeck and Katherine de Faro.

They pressed me for details about my youth, especially the time I had spent in Malines with the Duchess of Burgundy. 'Who did you meet there?' asked the commissioner.

'Besides my aunt, only the Archduke Philip.'

'Whose idea was the imposture? Was it the Duchess's? Or were other exiles from the court of England also involved?'

'The idea came from none of them. It wasn't until I got to Ireland - when I was on business with my master Mr Meno - that the scheme was first suggested.'

'And when you were in Ireland, were the Earls of Kildare and Desmond the only men involved? Or were others involved too?'

'No, they were the only ones.'

'And the Mayor of Cork, John Waters?'

There was a pause.

'*John Waters*,' repeated the commissioner, emphasising every syllable, and giving the scribe ample time to make a very clear note of the name.

'Why, no. He gave me hospitality in his house, it's true; but he wasn't involved in any way.'

'Why didn't you resist these schemes? You must have known that to agree to what they were asking was to commit treason.'

'I didn't join in *willingly*. I had no choice. I dared not disobey their orders.'

The scribe rested his pen and looked across at the commissioners. But they had finished. They seemed satisfied that I had told them the truth. Little did they know how careful I had been to implicate as few of my companions as possible.

★　　★　　★

Two days later I was brought back to the commissioners, who dumbfounded me by putting to me many of the same questions all over again. Still, I told them once more everything they wanted to know, convincing myself it was necessary for them to check the consistency of my story.

At the end of this second meeting, the commissioners consulted with one another in hushed tones; then the presiding commissioner looked directly at me and smiled. 'We believe that you have told us the truth, Perkin. You will be taken from the Tower to the Palace of Westminster.'

I mouthed the words inwardly: the Palace of Westminster. There was a pinching sensation in my chest. That was where my wife was. I would soon be seeing her again.

'You will be given freedom to move at your will in the palace. And you shall be free to see your wife during the daytime hours.'

That afternoon, having gathered what few belongings I had - my cloak with its badly worn crest, and a little money - I was taken from the Tower. What a merciful relief to be free from these murky, depressing confines. The mist had almost cleared but a thin vapour still lay on the surface of the river.

I was escorted along Great Tower Street, then on to Cornhill and out of the limits of the city of London, into the western suburb of Westminster with its wealthy merchants' houses and numerous drinking taverns and inns. We passed the great inns-of-court around Holborn and Chancery Lane, the house of an important bishop and the town houses of members of parliament. And so we rode on in the direction of Westminster itself.

The Palace of Westminster extended from the Thames almost to the great abbey; but my guards only took me as far as the entrance, then returned to the Tower, while a fresh escort took me into the precincts.

I stood outside, looking up in awe at the grand building with its adjoining chapel, and wondered which room my wife was in. How would she react when we met again? In her last words to me she had chided me for having deceived her, for reducing her to such a wretched condition, without friends in a strange land . . . She was right, of course. I was to blame. But would time now have begun to mellow her feelings? Or would she never, ever, forgive me for what I had done?

As I was led to my own room, we passed through the Great Hall that was used as a banqueting room. Its impressive hammer beam roof, made from black oak, reminded me of the roof of the great hall at Stirling Castle, though this one was even more splendid. On the eastern side I was shown the royal council chamber - commonly known as the Star Chamber on account of the stars that adorned the ceiling. A court had been held there that very morning, a court that was renown for its terrible punishments - torture, whipping, horrible mutilation.

That evening my wife and I were to be reunited in the Queen's own presence chamber. It was hardly going to be the quiet private meeting between us that I had hoped for, what with servants forever coming and going, carrying gowns, lighting candles and closing shutters.

When I came into the room Kate had her back towards me. 'Oh Kate, thank God you're safe!' She did not reply. 'Are you well? How are they treating you?'

Slowly, she turned towards me. Her face looked tired and wan. Her long, flowing, chestnut-coloured hair lacked its usual lustre. The twinkle in her eyes that had so attracted me when first we met was no longer there.

She replied in a monotone, drained of all emotion. 'Do you really think you can woo me by asking after my health and my wellbeing. If you really cared for me you would not have treated me in the way you have done.'

I started to cross the room towards her.

'Don't you come near me!' she shouted. 'I've lost all respect for you!'

'But Kate, my love . . .'

'Don't try and get around me with words. They mean nothing to me at all. Do you hear me? Nothing! It's what you've done which matters; and you have betrayed me. Get out of my sight. I don't wish to see you ever again!'

I was stunned with shock. I could not believe she really meant what she said. But the expression on her face told me it was useless to remonstrate. I thought it best to leave, until she had a chance to calm herself. Surely, when she had time to reflect she would feel differently.

I bowed stiffly, said not one word more, and turned away from her.

Chapter 23

As the weeks slowly passed, I hoped beyond hope that Kate's attitude towards me would mellow. If she could not forgive me I would understand; but at least she might begin to see why I had done what I had. After all, I had been but a lad, impressionable, easily tempted, drawn into schemes devised by those who bore a grudge against the King of England, and who were plotting his downfall. I had not known what I was becoming involved in.

Alas, these were false hopes, and it was perhaps naïve of me to have entertained them in the first place. So far from Kate's attitude towards me softening, it visibly hardened. She became still colder, more and more resentful, deeply bitter. Feelings of betrayal showed behind her thin, tightly sealed lips; and as she spoke, she looked not at me but at a distant object in the room.

We were growing further and further apart; we began to see one another less and less often. I became more and more melancholy. I could not settle to anything during the day, and found it difficult to sleep at night.

There is no denying that I was treated very well by my captors all the while I was at the Palace of Westminster. I had a comfortable and well-lit room in part of the palace known as the King's Wardrobe; and provided I stayed within the confines of the Palace I was allowed considerable freedom. An elderly groom, a tailor and a forgetful butler tended to my every need. At table I had my own waiter, and was treated to the same fine food as was eaten by the King and Queen themselves. I was even given an allowance for clothing.

Yet what use were these comforts now that I risked losing the love and respect of my wife? The whole purpose of my life seemed to be ebbing away before my eyes; those beautiful white grains of sand that I had held so preciously in my palm as I came ashore in

Cornwall seemed to be sifting through my fingers, to be lost forever.

★   ★   ★

After some six months in my semi-captive state, I was becoming increasingly bored and restless with my surroundings. It was now early June, and although the evenings were long and light, there was nothing for me to do after dinner, other than play at chess or cards. Time was slipping away. I had never been one able to tolerate prolonged periods doing nothing; for my life until then had been one long adventure.

Somehow, I had to leave this place and return to my home in Flanders, forget the Duchess of Burgundy and her plans for me. I no longer sought excitement and adventure, merely the warmth and love which was so lacking here. I remember clearly the warmth and love that Rosita gave me all those years ago. Perhaps I could find her again, that it was not too late for us. My life with Kate was over - she had made that plain.

As I heard a church bell chime midnight somewhere in the distance, I resolved that I had had enough.

There was a warder on guard either side of my room, so I could do nothing for the moment; but when their chatter had stopped and I believed both men were fast asleep, I would prepare my escape, my return to Flanders.

Being more honoured guest than captive in the Palace, I had been provided with two fine linen sheets. These I now began knotting together to form a rope which I could lower from my unbarred window. When I was a boy, my mother had told me fabulous tales of escapes from castles like this. But this was real life. Would the sheets actually support my adult weight, the weight of a man in his twenty-fifth year?

Suddenly, a rumble, then a crash. I froze. I took off my cloak again and leapt back into bed. The noise seemed to come from right outside my room. For several moments there was silence. Then it came again. No, I had been mistaken. It was not outside but directly overhead, and was just something heavy, like a crate, being dragged across the floor.

I got out of bed again. Securing the end of the sheets to the bedpost nearest the window, I lowered the other end carefully outside. It did not reach the ground, or anywhere near it, but I thought I would be able to jump the rest of the distance. I only hoped that I had made the knot tight enough.

Taking with me a small pouch of silver coins which I placed in the inside pocket of my cloak, I gripped the twisted sheet and slowly eased my way down to where it ended, grazing my bare arms against the jagged stone wall. Then I jumped the rest of the distance, and fell without injury onto the ragged grass at the base of the wall.

I was free. Quickly I got up, and ran and ran into the dark of the night.

Through the little lanes and alleyways I dashed, rushing in the general direction of what I thought was the river embankment. In my haste I knocked against stalls and stabbed a toe on an empty beer barrel. A cat squealed as it shot out across my path. In places the lanes were slippery with horse shit and the remains of rotten fruit and vegetables.

I did not know the area at all; and all there was to guide me was the smell coming off the river - never a pleasant smell, but more putrid than ever on that warm summer's night. Yet, the river was also my lifeline to safety, and I hoped that the purse of silver coins in my pocket would induce a ship's captain to allow me to board his vessel and take me as far as the coast of Flanders.

However, this part of the river, unlike the stretch around Billingsgate that bordered on the Tower, was not busy. There were very few ships moored there, and it was impossible for me to obtain a berth.

So, my only option was to head for the nearest sanctuary. As far as I knew that was the House of Jesus of Bethlehem at Sheen, seven miles up river close to Richmond.

Fearing detection, I thought it safest not to walk along the embankment itself, but to keep a little inland. And so I set off on foot, plying my way through the narrow lanes at the water's edge, looking around me constantly, afraid all the while I might be caught. In a few hours time, these same streets would witness a hive of activity, as caterers and costermongers would set off in their carts to market; but now Londoners were sleeping, and all around me was still. Only the echo of my footsteps on the cobbles broke the silence.

All of a sudden there was a terrific screeching, right in front of me. Then a stamping. I almost jumped out of my skin. Before I knew it, a great shadow loomed up. I could only think that I was about to be attacked, but by whom or what I had not the faintest idea. In any event, the shock sent me reeling to the ground.

When I came to my senses, I realised that a horse, tethered to a post outside an inn had caused the commotion. The horse had been invisible to me (and me to it) until I was almost on top of the poor creature that even now continued to rear up on its hind legs, steam pouring through its nostrils. I did my best to avoid causing the horse any further fright; but as I walked away the poor thing was still neighing and stamping.

As soon as I had turned the corner I began to run all the way down to the river, without looking back once. From there, I followed its course until I reached Putney where I asked an old waterman to take me the rest of the way to Richmond in his lighter. As he was only used to ferrying people across the river, I could understand it when he hesitated, especially as he was being asked to make the journey at such an early hour. Only when I produced my small pouch of silver coins and promised to make it worth his while did he need no further persuading.

The old waterman rowed slowly, the oars cutting deep into the murky water; but with each moment that passed I sensed that I was that much nearer safety.

As we neared Richmond it was beginning to grow light, and a shimmer of sunlight glanced across the water. We moored at a spot the waterman knew well, and I paid him exactly half the coins I had in my pouch, saying that I needed the others for the return journey. It could hardly have been further from the truth. God forbid that I should ever return to Westminster the way things were. The truth was I dared not use up all my money. Besides, the waterman seemed more than pleased by the arrangement and touched his cap in gratitude. My handful of silver coins was probably more than he would earn that month altogether.

I scrambled ashore and made straight for the safety of the House of Sheen where I duly gave myself up to the Prior. Although he was not able to offer me anything like the length of safety I had been granted at Beaulieu (which had a privileged status), he promised I could spend a week or so there without harm.

Having been received into the priory by the monks, I was allowed that same afternoon, to watch an important ceremony in the chapel - the receiving of a lay brother into the Order. Until that day I would have despised a man who opted for such a life, so inward looking and useless, predictable and dull. But today I envied that man: he was entering a life of safety, freedom from worldly cares.

As for me, I would have to leave these protected confines in a very short while, and might well face the assault of my enemies, the wrath of the King, the understandable bitterness of my wife.

*   *   *

Within two or three days, the prior had managed to obtain for me another pardon from King Henry at Westminster; but this time the King had been very reluctant to yield. The prior did not mince his words: Henry was becoming very angry over the privileges sanctuary brought, and was determined to put an end to the arrangement altogether as soon as he could.

So, when I was led under armed escort from the Priory of Sheen, the King was not so forbearing as he had been when I had left the abbey at Beaulieu. This time I was taken to Westminster Hall and placed in stocks set up high on a scaffold made out of empty wine barrels. You will recall how my family had escaped from King Henry's men in barrels like these; and by an awful twist of fate I was now being imprisoned by them.

Crowds of people milled around me, taunting me, calling me a traitor, and low foreign-born scum. One of the aldermen made me repeat my confession and sign it; and as I did so, some of the crowd threw rotten fruit and vegetables at me.

That evening, I was brought back to the Tower of London and placed in a cell in the Wakefield Tower. The cell had no window, for the agreement was that I was to see neither sun nor moon. Inside it was damp and musty, and the walls were covered with dark green slime.

The following day I was taken to Cheapside, a district much busier than Westminster - full of all kinds of people, from country gentlemen to the humblest of street beggars. I was placed in the stocks outside the King's Head, next to a poor man who had been caught fighting in that same alehouse. Here I had to sit for five hours, and was again made to repeat my confession. In that confession I would like to have said more, much more - more about the support I had had from Henry's own advisors and from foreign princes. But the confession had been altered and shortened from that which Astley had helped me prepare the previous October in Taunton, and seemed to concentrate mainly on my humble origins in Tournai and on my parentage.

Afterwards, I was taken back to my cell in the Tower and kept in close captivity. Time passed extremely slowly, and only the twice daily entry of my gaoler, carrying the usual fare of stale bread and water, served to break up the awful monotony. Earlier hapless mortals who had occupied my cell had been reduced to scratching a tally of the days they had spent there, before being tortured or executed for their so-called 'crimes' - in reality, usually no more than a difference of opinion with the King.

I had to put an end to this line of thinking, as it served only to deflate my spirits even further. But there was nothing to look forward to, no hope, no company. I wondered whether my mother had received the letter that the gaoler's daughter in Exeter had promised to get delivered? I had no way of knowing. I did not even know for sure that my mother was still alive.

Yet all was not lost. For, by an extraordinary stroke of good fortune, I learnt from my guards that the cell directly above mine contained none other than the Earl of Warwick, the very man I had been mistaken for by the earls in Ireland. He knew full well that his claim to the throne was far better than that of King Henry's - indeed, second only to that of Prince Richard himself.

We began to knock on the wall and call out to one another, although it was his cell mate, Robert Cleymond, who did most of the talking. Cleymond's voice was rasping and coarse, but I could hear every word he spoke, as if he had been speaking right outside the door.

He said little the first time he spoke, it being late at night, so he was not able to disguise his voice by the busy daytime noises of the Tower. Even so, from the little he did say, it was clear that he was prepared to help me as much as he hoped to help his companion, the Earl of Warwick.

What a source of comfort I had found, for Cleymond seemed to understand our common misfortunes. Together we could plan for the future. Almost at once, my spirits began to rise, just as if I had imbibed a wonderful warm tonic. I began to have more energy, feel so much more optimistic.

Chapter 24

A month or so passed, and we were now, as far as I could make out, somewhere in the middle of August. The atmosphere was heavy, stifling. The foul air in my cell was leaving me drowsy, so that at times I could hardly breathe. It was only Robert Cleymond's words that gave me any hope at all.

One morning, several hours after daybreak when craftsmen, servants and laundresses were going about their daily work, I heard the heavy footsteps of two men, one close behind the other, descending the spiral staircase near to my cell.

Then there was a brief burst of conversation. One of the voices, gruff and curt, I recognised immediately as that of a guard. The other one seemed more refined but was indistinct, possibly not even English.

The two men paused at the foot of the stairs to finish what they were saying. It seemed strange that anyone should come down to the depths of the Tower at such an odd time, as there must have been an hour or two yet before a meal was due.

All the very worst thoughts started to race through my mind. Were they bringing news of my wife - bad news? Was she ill? Or perhaps they had come to question me further. Had they discovered something more about my past? Was my own life now in jeopardy?

A bunch of keys started to rattle outside.

Another pause, and a snatch of conversation. One of them really did seem to be foreign. How ever much longer?

Eventually, the door was pushed open, not brashly and violently as usual, but slowly and warily. Light began to trickle in from the passageway outside. The guard had already left with his burning torch, and the visitor stood alone on the threshold to my cell.

At first I did not recognise him, for, in spite of the heat of the day he wore a thick cape. Only when he spoke in his soft, gentle voice did I realise that it was the Bishop of Cambrai.

I had done business with the bishop many times in Flanders - he had even taught me how to play chess - but I had not seen him these last ten years. Had he come to get me out of here, to take me back to Flanders, to my home, to my family?

I went across to where he stood, and greeted him with a warm embrace. 'Your Grace. It's good to see you again.'

'You too, Perkin.'

Then he stepped back a few paces and gasped. 'Are you well? You've become so gaunt and bony.'

So shocked was the bishop by my appearance that for several moments he was unable to say anything more.

'When I last saw you, you were just a youth with streaming blonde hair. You held your head high, every bit as well as the noblest of men. But . . .'

He drew closer again, and ran a wisp of my hair through his fingers. 'What is this? You hair has become matted and seems to be almost grey. And you stoop so. What in God's name has happened to you?'

'You are right. I'm not well, Your Grace, as you can see. I have been worried sick, and my health's suffered.' I drew a deep breath. 'You see, since you last saw me in Antwerp, I have done something bad, very bad. I was persuaded by Earl Desmond and Earl Kildare to get involved with a scheme of theirs. I knew it was wrong, but I was tricked into it.'

'They tricked you? What have you done? What was this scheme?'

Surely he knew. The whole of London knew. 'They asked me to pretend I was the late King Edward's younger son. Oh, it was a game at first, flattering to have so much attention paid me; but as the years passed lies were piled onto lies, and things became more and more difficult. I have deceived my wife and ignored my children, who have now both perished. My health has deteriorated. Your Grace, you knew me when I was happy, selling velvet and silk. But all that has changed. I pace across the floor of my cell by day, and cannot get to sleep at night.'

'But why on earth did you agree to do as these earls asked? Why didn't you just say "no"?'

'I agreed because I dared not disobey them. When I arrived at

Cork they surrounded me, and I was unarmed. I had already made them angry by refusing to impersonate the Earl of Warwick. When I also refused to pretend I was one of King Richard's bastard sons, I annoyed them even more. But I knew I could not impersonate them convincingly. So, when they suggested I take on the role of Prince Richard, I dared not defy them any further.'

'Oh Perkin! You are too easily led . . .'

What he said was true, but if I dwelt on his remarks it would only make me despair even more. I had to keep my hopes up. 'Bishop,' I interrupted. 'Please, help me. Please use your authority to get the Constable to release me from this miserable place. Look at this gloomy and airless hole. It's taking away my will to live.'

I seized his hand. 'I beg you, for the sake of my wife, my mother alone in Tournai . . .'

Before he had a chance to reply, the gaoler returned, and was making it abundantly clear by fumbling with his keys that the bishop had been there long enough and was now expected to leave.

'Perkin, if only I had the power to help you, to intervene on your behalf. Alas I do not. I have no influence over Constable Digby. It is merely my duties, my duties to the church that have brought me to London. When I heard that you were here, I naturally wanted to see you again.'

He held me against him, made the sign of the cross on my forehead. 'God bless you and have mercy on you!' he said softly.

The gaoler motioned him out of the room, to the other world above. I imagined him surfacing in the blistering glare of the late morning sun, crossing the drawbridge where I had entered, going off to pursue his wretched church business.

*   *   *

I had just begun to brood again when suddenly there was a knock, not on the door but on the ceiling of my cell. Then came Cleymond's voice, even clearer and more penetrating than usual.

I looked up, trying to work out how it was that the voice sounded so close. As I did so I saw a stick being poked through a small hole in the corner of the ceiling, a hole which had perhaps been scraped away by prisoners held here many years ago.

The voice came again, now so clear and loud that it was as

though Cleymond was standing right beside me. 'Perkin, cheer up!'

'Cheer up? I've nothing to be cheerful about, nothing . . .'

'You have a great deal to look forward to, mark my words.'

There was a pause, and when he spoke again his voice was much softer. 'I have just received a letter from a man called James. He's a clerk living in Flanders. He'll help you. He'll raise an army against Welsh Harry. He'll help you become king!'

'Let me see this letter!'

'Tomorrow. First we must plan your escape from here. I've thought up a plan which will easily outwit that fool Digby, and give us possession of the Tower!'

'Go on. How are we going to do it?'

The voice was now almost a whisper, eerie, seductive. 'More of that tomorrow, Perkin, more of that tomorrow. Be patient. You shall soon be King of England.'

The remainder of that day passed all too slowly. Eventually it grew dark. In the distance, I could hear the familiar daily sound of the Chief Yeoman delivering up the keys to a sentry. It must be ten o'clock then. I caught a few words:

'Whose keys?'

'The keys of King Henry.'

'Pass King Henry's keys. All is well.'

I smiled. Soon those keys would be mine.

* * *

Early next morning, as I was still drowsy, a voice came from above - not Cleymond's irritating whine but the mellower, educated tone of the Earl of Warwick himself.

'Perkin!' he whispered. 'How are you this morning? Have you slept well?'

'Any more news of this plan? I asked anxiously.

'It's already begun. Cleymond knows a fellow by the name of Thomas Ward, a clerk, here in the Tower . . .'

'Can he fix up some disguise for us; or get us smuggled out?'

'No, that kind of stuff is for cowards. (Goodness, those were my own words to my men at Exeter). Act *boldly* Perkin.'

'What then?' I was growing impatient. Earl or no earl, I wanted to seize him by the scruff of his neck and force the plan out of him. 'What?' I repeated.

'This last half hour he has sent Thomas Ward a special token made from wood. When Ward receives it, he will know it is time to set our plans in motion . . .'

'Yes, yes? Well, what are these plans?' I persisted.

'Four guards are involved. Tomorrow night after the great supper, when all the officers have retired to their chambers - drunk - the guards will go to the Constable's chamber and create a great commotion outside. When he opens the door and steps out, they will crack open his skull with their cudgels. Then they will release all the prisoners. Yourself, your friend John Waters . . .'

I gasped. 'John Waters? Is he here?' I had no idea that he had been brought to London.

'Why yes - awaiting trial. But he will never be tried because we shall act before then. We shall seize the gunpowder in the Tower, and set it alight. Then, with torches held high, we shall head for Westminster Palace. We'll murder the usurper and crown you Richard IV, King of England.' His pace slowed, his tone changed. He was serious again. 'Perkin. Do you agree to it?'

Could it be that all was not lost after all? This was my last chance for freedom. But why me? The Earl of Warwick had a genuine claim to the throne. I had publicly confessed to being an impostor. Could it be a trick of some sort? But what could they hope to gain by it? Warwick, too, would be in desperate trouble if we were caught. It *must* be true. I told myself that I had to seize this last throw of the dice fate had given me.

'Perkin. Do you agree to it?' came the voice again, breaking into my thoughts.

'Yes! Yes!' I shouted. I would risk everything rather than rot here in this dank cell.

Suddenly, there was a terrific crash, then a lot of shouting. It came from upstairs, from the Earl of Warwick's cell.

A few heartbeats later - without any warning, no footsteps on the stairs, nor in the passageway outside - my cell door was flung open with great force.

I looked up, absolutely petrified. Standing there in the doorway were four armed guards. One of them stepped forward. His thick moustache made him look fierce.

His little pig eyes shone out as he moistened his lips ready to speak.

My knees felt weak, almost as though they were going to give way completely.

'Perkin Warbeck. I arrest you on a charge of high treason!'

Chapter 25

Oh how easily I had been duped into taking Cleymond at his word! He had really been working for the King, that much was now horribly clear. How naïve I had been to fall into their trap. Everything had happened so quickly. Now, the fate I had escaped time after time could be put off no longer. There would be no more pardons, no more chances.

Next morning, Constable Digby came to my cell in person, and announced brusquely:

'Your trial will be held at Westminster Hall at noon the day after tomorrow.'

So, a date had been fixed. I begged him for more information.

'Who will be trying me?'

'Why? The lord justices, of course,' he replied with a shrug.

'What chance will I have to defend myself, to call my own witnesses?'

Digby did not answer. He just shrugged his shoulders again vaguely, and left.

*   *   *

The day came. As I was led from my cell, I drew my cloak right up to my neck, as there was a distinct chill in the November air. Was it a ghastly premonition of what was to come?

As we approached Westminster Hall, I could hear the murmur of many voices outside. We passed some little houses that nestled under the solid grey turrets at the entrance. The turrets looked forbidding, they seemed to be pressing in on me, cutting out the light.

The crowds were shouting out. I could not hear what they were saying but I knew it was something hostile as they shook their fists as they shouted.

I was kept waiting below the hall in a cold and musty prison cell. 'Go to hell!' my guards shouted in unison, as they threw me inside.

'What do you mean go to hell?' I asked.

'That's what we call this cell, Hell!'

'And you'll never get out of there alive!' laughed the other guard.

I knelt and prayed for God's protection. He had protected and saved me all this while - from the hands of King Henry's men when they had searched my ship as I sailed to these shores from Ireland. He had saved me from the enemy at Exeter. More recently, when I thought all was lost, he had even given me sanctuary at Beaulieu and again at Sheen. I now asked for his saving hand once again - only this time I was more desperate than ever before.

The dark oak-wood door was ajar. I looked up and caught a glimpse of the great mass of people sitting in ranks, one above the other. The noise began to increase: the galleries were becoming full. As the sound of their muffled voices filtered down to me I became more and more worried. I wondered whether I was going to keep my composure at all.

Suddenly there was silence. The guard pushed the door open and beckoned me forward. Heads turned but at first I could see nothing.

As my eyes grew accustomed to the light, I saw a procession come into the hall. The clerks entered first, then the officers of court in their robes, followed by a number of lawyers and judges. I wondered which of the lawyers would be leading the case against me.

All of a sudden, one of the guards called out 'Pray silence for His Majesty's justices, Sir John Sygly and Sir John Trobilfield!'

The two justices came into view, first Trobilfield, plump and balding, then Sygly, a tall stooping figure. Sygly held a scroll in his hand and kept a few paces behind Trobilfield all the while, as if to emphasise his own seniority.

People had started to talk again. Someone shouted out 'Silence in court!' But there was still a lot of noise.

'Silence in court on pain of imprisonment!' This went some way to bring about the desired response, but there was still a lot of muttering.

Then another voice called out 'Bring forth the prisoner. Perkin Warbeck, come forth and answer the charges brought against you!'

As I passed through the low doorway of the cell, I was forced to bow my head. The usher led me up into the hall. A vast expanse of stone floor stretched out in every direction. I felt overawed by it all.

I looked up. It was not after all the grand decorated building I had expected. The interior was plain, just walls, painted black and red, staring at me. There was some light in the hall, coming in from arched windows in the recesses and a great window at the far end; but it was still very shadowy and miserable, made worse by the greyness of the day.

On either side were galleries, full of people, with the best seats in front being occupied by the more important citizens. I now stood before them. Finally they stopped murmuring, and there was silence.

The usher brought me forward until I was about half way down the hall, where I made a low bow in the direction of the lord justices who were sitting at the far end on a high dais. As I drew closer to them, I fell to my knees and bowed my head, overcome by the sheer number of people around me.

The senior judge impatiently told me to rise.

I stood up and bowed again before the court. When I raised my head, the great beams above seemed to be pressing on me, working against me. The guardian angels carved into the beams looked down at me. But would they guard my fate now? I felt so insignificant, peering around at the company, at the justices who were there to try me. No longer was I in the company of the monarchs of Europe, treated as their equal. Now, I was reduced to this, on trial for my life.

I was told to approach the judges. Lord Justice Sygly, robed in scarlet and ermine, leant forward and spoke to the crier. 'Have you the charge?'

'It is here, my lord.'

'Then please read it.'

'Perkin Warbeck is here on trial for high treason. All persons who have aught against him are now to stand forth.'

His voice reverberated around the hall. Would anyone speak? The crowds leant forward on their elbows to get a better view. But there was no response.

Sygly looked across at the lawyer for the prosecution and nodded - a signal that the case against me was about to start.

Taking a great breath and looking sternly at the assembled crowd, he began to speak in a solemn tone. 'Perkin Warbeck, you are brought into this court to answer the charges brought against you by the knights, esquires, burgesses and commons of this land.'

This led to a great deal of muttering in the galleries.

When the whispers had died down, the lawyer continued. 'I charge you, Peter Warbeck of Tournai, being an enemy to the King, that you did conspire with many other traitors and rebels to falsely claim to be Richard, the second son of the late King Edward the Fourth, and you did treacherously plan to bring about the death and destruction of our master, the King himself . . .'

'Not so!' I shouted. 'I was forced into the scheme . . .'

'Silence!' roared Sygly. 'Wait your proper turn to reply to these charges!'

Then, turning to the lawyer, he said calmly 'Please go on.'

' . . . that you did treacherously plan to bring about the death and destruction of our master, the King himself, with the intention of making yourself king. So that, on the third day of July in the tenth year of the reign of our said lord the King, at Deal in the county of Kent, you did draw up forces against our lord King.'

There were more murmurs and a few gasps, as many people heard the full details of what had happened for the first time. 'Then, on the seventh of September in the thirteenth year of the reign of our gracious sovereign King Henry the Seventh, at Penzance in the county of Cornwall, you did raise war against the King. Soon after this, you and other rebels were conquered and dispersed, and were taken to the Tower of London to be kept there as prisoner. Until Edward Earl of Warwick and other false traitors, on the second of August the following year did conspire to bring about the death and destruction of the King. You agreed, did you not, that they would set you free, and create you, Peter Warbeck, King of England.'

During the whole speech there had been almost total silence. Sygly then turned to me and asked 'How then do you answer the charge?'

'Not guilty your honour. I had no choice other than to agree with what Earl Kildare and Earl Desmond asked me to do. If I am guilty of any crime at all, it is of being too naïve. For I now realise that they used me. They *used* me as a pawn.'

Sygly frowned. 'Please will you repeat that last remark.'

'The Earls used me as a *pawn*, your honour. I was not acting of my own free will. Therefore I cannot be held responsible for my actions.'

'Not responsible for your own deeds? Does that mean you are a madman, then?'

I heard some muffled laughter from the company.

The prosecuting lawyer continued. 'If what you say is true, why didn't you inform the King of these earls' treason, and throw yourself on his mercy?'

It was clear that he did not believe me; that he thought I was just making up a feeble excuse - as no time was allowed for me to answer the question.

Sygly looked across at me. His expression was now grave. 'Perkin Warbeck. Do you have anything to add to your testimony, or do you wish to alter it in any way?'

Again, he gave me no time to speak. They did not seem to be interested in anything I might have to say in my defence. I was going to be ignored. The result had been decided already.

The judge gave a signal to the usher that the proceedings should move on, and announced that witnesses would now be called to give evidence against me.

I was led off in despair, past statues of the kings of England, to the side gallery where I was motioned to a seat. I sat down, thankful not to be the centre of attention, but worried about the witnesses. What would they say?

Sygly leant across once again to the lawyer and nodded.

'Call forth the witnesses!' the lawyer shouted.

The figure of a man arose from somewhere at the back, but I could not see who it was.

The murmurs began again.

'Silence in court!'

When silence resumed, the lawyer prosecuting continued. 'I now call on Robert Cleymond.'

'Robert Cleymond. Come into court!'

'Robert Cleymond!' The name echoed all around the hall.

I felt numb and sick. I had taken this man to be a friend: it was he who had suggested the plan in the Tower of London.

Cleymond, a skinny, nervous looking man with a long face, came forward and bowed awkwardly before the court. It was the first time I had ever seen him.

Then he went over to the usher, kissed the Bible and repeated the oath after him. 'I do solemnly swear that the evidence I shall give before the court be the truth, the whole truth and nothing but the truth: so help me God.'

He walked over to face the bench of justices and the lawyer.

'Robert Cleymond. You were kept captive in the same tower as the prisoner. Is that correct?'

'Yes, your honour.'

'While you were there, were you at any time witness to any plot or scheme perpetrated by the prisoner?'

'Indeed I was. The prisoner did frequently communicate with the Earl of Warwick who shared my cell.'

'And what were the nature of these [he cleared his throat] . . . communications?'

'They were scheming to free the prisoners, set fire to the gunpowder and kill the constable.'

A gasp went up from the company. I jumped to my feet and started forward. Guards restrained me, pulled me back.

'You lie! It was *your* idea. *Your* suggestion!' I shouted.

'Hold your tongue!' roared Sygly. 'How dare you behave like that! If we have any further outbursts from you, Warbeck, you shall be put in chains!'

Turning to Cleymond again, the lawyer asked him to continue.

'They spoke to one another all the time through a hole in the floor of our cell.' He turned towards me, staring at me defiantly. 'They were plotting treason against the King.'

Abruptly, the prosecuting lawyer turned to the judges and declared 'My lords, I have done! It is only too clear from the testimony of this witness that the accused is guilty of treason.'

He looked self-satisfied. There were a few nods and whispers from some of the company opposite. Sygly turned to the judges. 'You have now heard evidence of the treachery of this man from the lips of an eyewitness. My lords. Please retire to consider your verdict.'

The judges filed out of the room.

What chance did I have? I was in black despair. The words of the judge lay imprinted on my mind: 'the treachery of this man.' It seemed almost certain that the verdict would be guilty.

The wait seemed like an eternity. Eventually they returned and I was called forward to stand before them.

'Is the prisoner, Perkin Warbeck, guilty or not guilty of the charges laid against him?'

Sygly looked across at the judges. 'Guilty, my lord!'

There was absolute silence in the room. I went cold with shock. My hands were clammy.

Sygly quickly went on. 'The prisoner has been found guilty of high treason. Before passing sentence, do you, Perkin Warbeck, have anything to say in your defence?'

I took another step nearer to the judges, then threw back my head. 'Yes my lord, I do.'

The judges were clearly annoyed to hear that the proceedings were to be extended.

I took a deep breath. 'I am an innocent man who was led astray by others. These men are subjects of King Henry; yet where are they? They are not here at court today. I admit that I am not English, that I was born in Tournai. But the idea was not mine. Others tricked me into it. As a foreigner, I claim immunity from the proceedings of this court. The courts of England cannot try a foreign subject!' I had saved this remark to the last: it was my final try for freedom.

My claim for immunity caused a stir among the assembled throng. The usher cried out for silence. Sygly stood. 'We are astonished that you dare to excuse your conduct in this manner. You have conspired against King Henry, like any common spy. As such, you are subject to the jurisdiction of this, his court.'

I felt as though my heart had stopped beating. I dug my nails hard into my hands. Almost in the same breath, he went on to pronounce the sentence. 'You have been found guilty of high treason. The sentence of this court . . . is that you shall be taken from here to the Tower of London and kept there until a time and a place be appointed for your execution.'

I stumbled, and put a hand out as if to save myself; but there was nothing to save me now.

Sygly spoke again. 'You shall suffer the same fate as your partner, Mayor Waters of Cork . . .'

My eyes widened. So my friend had already been tried and found guilty.

' . . .You shall be drawn on hurdles from the Tower through the streets of London to Tyburn where you shall be hanged, and cut down alive. Your bowels shall be taken out and burned, your head struck off. Your body shall be quartered, and your head and quarters disposed of at the King's pleasure.'

I felt only the grip of hands on my wrists as they drew me away. Otherwise, just a feeling of emptiness: I seemed totally alone now.

Chapter 26

As I left the hall, the cold easterly wind ate away at my lungs. I wrapped my cloak around me more tightly, as I did not want people to think I was trembling with fear. Two guards bundled me roughly into a cart: around my wrists they secured iron chains, and about my ankles they clamped tight fetters. Then they took their places either side of me, so close to me that I could hardly breathe.

The cart trundled away slowly while a crowd of onlookers jeered loudly and shouted insults. Their voices filled the air, full of venom and spite. Some yelled out 'traitor' and 'long live King Henry.' Several raised clenched fists. One threw a stone that grazed my forehead. Another spat at me, the saliva running down my face; but as my wrists were in manacles, all I could do was to rub my cheek against my sleeve.

The horse dragged the cart wearily up Whitehall, along the Strand and Fleet Street and into the busy part of the city. Here, little pockets of people were gathered among the busy market stalls to watch me go by. Some of them were jumping up and down on the spot, breathing on their hands in order to keep warm in the bitter chill.

As soon as they saw me, more jeers and cries of abuse went up from them. One man came right up to the cart and threatened me with a cudgel. My guards yelled at him and pushed him away just in time. A moment longer and he would have struck out at me.

And so on, through Aldgate, to the Tower of London. Weak sunlight was by this time trying to penetrate the mist, but to little effect; and the severe grey outer wall of the Tower looked bleaker than ever.

As we neared the drawbridge, the portcullis was lifted high above my head. I shuddered as I passed beneath it and looked up to see its stark outline inside the gateway. The clanging sound it made as it was lowered behind me has haunted me ever since, every minute of the day and night.

I was taken to the cell where I am writing this, a prisoner in the cold and dark, my feet chained to a rusty iron ring in the wall. There is so little air, and what there is foul and putrid. A streak of light filters through the narrow slit of a window, barred by an iron grill.

Before me is a rough trestle table on which I am resting these pages, recording the history of my life and adventures, so that people may know the truth about what happened to me, and not the lies that my enemies have put about. It is now late afternoon and growing dark. I shall cease my writing very soon, and implore my confessor to accept and make public this, my life story.

Suddenly, I stopped. I had heard the thud of an outer door being closed. Hushed voices, indistinct, impatient, footsteps on the spiral staircase. Voices again, but now much clearer. I recognised both of them at once. One was the rough tone of Jonas, my guard. As for the other! A tremor went through me when I heard that second voice - that unmistakably soft, lilting voice that could belong only to Kate, my wife.

Our last meeting had been so bitter, so full of reproaches and recriminations. I did not expect to see her again. Was she coming to see me of her own free will, or was she here out of a sense of duty? When she heard of my sentence, perhaps she felt that it was no more than what I deserved for deceiving her? But surely I could hope for some reconciliation now, as we faced our final farewell.

A key was inserted into the lock, my cell door swung open. Standing there in the shadows was indeed Jonas.

'Your wife's come to see yerr!' he announced brusquely.

Jonas stepped aside, and there stood Kate. Her face seemed drawn, her complexion even paler than usual. Her hair, normally like a shining stream of silk, was covered by a dark cloak.

'Perkin!' I could tell from her voice that she had been crying.

I went over to her and held out my hand, hoping that she might take it. But would she take it?

She came forward.

I took her in my arms and held her close. I could feel her tears against my face.

We stood there in each other's arms, in silence. What was there to say? She knew my fate, that this was to be our last farewell.

Finally, I broke the silence. 'Forgive me for all the pain that I have caused you. Try to remember the happy times, when we were together, what we suffered together through the loss of our children.'

I began to choke. I could not go on.

Kate slipped to her knees beside me, clinging to me.

I tried to continue, though my voice was barely audible. 'Try to be brave, as I will. Forgive me.'

'Forgive *me*,' she cried, 'for what I said to you when we last met. I cannot bear the thought of what awaits you. I feel *my* life will be at an end too. What is there for me in the future? Our children both dead, and now I am losing you.'

'Try to be brave. We must *both* be brave. My life will soon be at an end but you must go on. You are a young woman, you have many years ahead of you. You will love again. You will marry and have children. Try to forget me.'

'No!' she cried. 'How can I.'

'You will find happiness again, I'm sure of it. I pray that you do.'

She raised her head, and gazed at me. Her eyes were red from weeping.

'I will remember what you have said but I can never forget you. You are my husband.'

She pressed into my palm a gold chain to which was attached a small crucifix.

'Take this, my dearest, and carry it with you tomorrow.'

I recognised it immediately. It was her chain that she always wore around her neck.

'I have worn this since I was a girl. I give it to you with my love and forgiveness. Know that I shall be praying for you, that you will always be in my thoughts.'

I lifted the chain to my lips and kissed it. As I twisted it around my fingers, I realised that I had only one thing of value left that I could give her in return - the wedding ring she had given me on that happy day at Stirling that now seemed so long ago. I removed it from my finger and pressed it into her hands.

'Take this, my love, and remember me.'

Suddenly, there was the sound of footsteps outside. Jonas had returned. At this we drew apart.

'Come on, now. Enough!' he growled.

I stood there motionless.

Kate moved forward again, and for a brief moment held my hand in hers. She bent her head and raised my hand to her lips and kissed it - just the once.

Then she quickly turned away and reached the door.

She looked back one more time. In a voice choked with emotion she murmured 'Goodbye my love.'

Then she disappeared from view. I stared at the spot where she had been only a moment before, as if transfixed.

The door clanged shut and I was alone.

Postscript

I am writing this account at the request of Perkin Warbeck, a young man - scarcely twenty-five years of age - who, on departing this world, wished the circumstances surrounding his cruel fate to be known more widely.

At eleven o'clock in the morning on 23rd November 1499, it being St Clement's Day, Perkin Warbeck, together with his companion John Waters, mayor of Cork, were drawn from the Tower and taken to Tyburn, the place of execution. The journey, which ran through the very heart of the city, took almost an hour. It was a bitterly cold day, and a thick frost hung on the shutters of the shops we passed. Our horses shivered, and their steamy breath rose up before us, at times completely obscuring the way ahead.

As we went, Perkin bowed his head in prayer. I heard him praying for his wife, that she should be looked after, come to no harm. I knew she would not be present to see him breathe his last, thank God.

Beside him, his friend John Waters sat calm and resigned, ready to accept his ordeal, even asking me for details about the execution itself - whether the noose would be secured so, or so [he demonstrated]; who the hangman was; how long it would be before he breathed his last?

Perkin, on the other hand, was unwilling to take his fate as sealed while there were a few stones still left unturned. He was ever the optimistic one, even when on the verge of the scaffold itself. As his story proves, there had been many times during his life when he had overcome all manner of setbacks. The fellow had a fighting spirit and a determination to carry on.

Clutching now to the faintest of hopes, he asked if it was true that some men had managed to survive the hangman, who had strangled them without breaking their neck? I had heard much the same tales myself but thought it ill advised to encourage any false hopes. Instead I put my hand on his forehead, blessed him, and tried to calm him with soothing words.

As we approached Tyburn, we could see in the distance a huge crowd of people. Drawing nearer, we could see gentlemen in their jackets, prosperous tradesmen, shopkeepers, the poor. The noise was deafening, the crowd almost out of control. Men imbued with ale and with their fists raised lent forward over the barriers that had been erected quickly from wooden staves and ships' rope. As soon as we came into sight they hurled abuse, threw stones and spat on us.

The magistrates tried to patrol up and down as best they could, but their horses reared up on their hind legs as they were provoked by the great mass of onlookers. I certainly did not envy their position as they tried to hold the crowd back, and restore law and order as best they could.

Londoners are used to seeing thieves hung. They are also used to seeing traitors hung, drawn and quartered; heretics burned at the stake. But they showed special interest in Perkin - they had heard about his adventures, and there was an air of the extraordinary surrounding his daring imposture.

Even at this late hour, Perkin believed that there was a possibility of him being granted a pardon. He *had* to believe it for his own peace of mind. Even at the very foot of the gallows, he was still hopeful that a writ would arrive from the King, reprieving him - a man foreign-born who had no right to be tried in this country, and who in any case had been led astray by the King's own wanton subjects.

He looked expectantly across at me, as I stood there with the other clergy and friars. It was St Clement's Day. But would clemency be shown? I knew what thoughts were passing through his head. Could they not plead for him and grant him a reprieve? And what of the crowd itself? Did he not have sufficient supporters within it who might help him escape, get him to a ship and smuggle him back to Flanders?

We both looked up at the same time. A beam had been placed across the branches of two trees to make a small scaffold. Against the beam was set a ladder, draped with a black cloth. Although for much of his life Perkin had been treated as a prince, he was, after all, to suffer the death penalty of a mere commoner.

With a black mask covering his face, the executioner stood ready

– ready to do his job. No man covets such work, and it had been very difficult that morning to find a hangman prepared to carry out the deed.

Before the execution took place, Perkin was made to read his confession one final time - a confession that was to be printed and circulated throughout London on the orders of the King. He said how sorry he was for the imposture, how foolish he had been, and he begged the King for forgiveness.

Both Perkin and Waters accepted death, when it came, with dignity and composure. Their necks were tied with halters that were fastened to the branches above their heads. Here they hung for several minutes while a great cheer went up from the crowd.

Then, without warning, the beam was pulled away to leave them swinging by their necks, like carcasses in a butcher's shop, in the cold winter air - a terrible spectacle for all to see.

By this time the crowd was in frenzy; and there was surely more to follow. The court's instructions had been explicit: both men should be struck down while alive and disembowelled. But thank God the executioner was merciful, waiting until they had breathed their last before he severed the rope, cut off their heads and disembowelled their bodies.

After that, their bodies were brought to the Augustinian Friary and buried in an unmarked grave. Their heads were taken in a basket to London Bridge where they were put on long spikes, as a dreadful warning to other pretenders and those who might in any ways consider taking part in their schemes.

And so I have done my duty. I have completed the final chapter, and recorded the events of Perkin's last hours. My task is over. But I have yet to decide what to do with this manuscript, whether to show it to His Majesty King Henry, or not. It might be more prudent to destroy it. I shall pray to God for guidance, and for the soul of the unfortunate Perkin Warbeck.

FRIAR MATTHEW